BRIDE OF A HUSTLA 2

Destiny Skai

Ca$h Presents
Bride of a Hustla 2
A Novel by *Destiny Skai*

Destiny Skai

Lock Down Publications/Ca$h Presents
P.O. Box 1482
Pine Lake, Ga 30072-1482

Visit our website at **www.lockdownpublications.com**

Cover design and layout by: Dynasty's Cover Me
Book interior design by: Shawn Walker
Edited by: Lauren Burton

Stay Connected with Us!

Text **LOCKDOWN** to 22828 to stay up-to-date with new releases, sneak peaks, contests and more…

Submission Guideline.

Submit the first three chapters of your completed manuscript to ldpsubmissions@gmail.com, subject line: Your book's title. The manuscript must be in a .doc file and sent as an attachment. Document should be in Times New Roman, double spaced and in size 12 font. Also, provide your synopsis and full contact information. If sending multiple submissions, they must each be in a separate email.

Have a story but no way to send it electronically? You can still submit to LDP/Ca$h Presents. Send in the first three chapters, written or typed, of your completed manuscript to:

LDP: Submissions Dept
Po Box 1482
Pine Lake, Ga 30072

DO NOT send original manuscript. Must be a duplicate.

Provide your synopsis and a cover letter containing your full contact information.

Thanks for considering LDP and Ca$h Presents.

Acknowledgements

First, all thanks are given to the man upstairs for blessing me with my pen game. All things are done through Christ, so he comes before anything. As always my kids, Torrence and Ethan, are my reasons for going so hard. I do this for them and this time around I had to put Torrence's name first because he had a fit about Ethan's name going first, just because he is the oldest.....LOL!!! What can I say?

A big shot out goes to my LDP family and fans, you guys and gals are awesome! Ca$h, thanks for believing in my dreams and guiding me down the right path. Coffee, thanks for schooling me and making me reach my full potential, when I was discouraged. Your words were heard LOUD & CLEAR, along with your actions and I am forever grateful.

Last and certainly not least, thank you to my family. No matter what dream I chase, they are always in my corner backing me up 100%. And no I am not naming all of y'all again. All of you received recognition in the first book...LOL!! We not doing this every book.

Before I close, I want to give myself a pat on the back for going so hard and pulling all night flights to get my book complete, along with my book and movie trailer. My movie, Bride of a Hustla, will be released in the spring of 2017, follow me on Facebook, Instagram and Twitter for updates. I am now signing off and for the record my name is Aneesah McNeal, but my pseudonym is Destiny Skai. I received so much static about my real name not being in the book...LOL!! For the ones that said it, you know who you are and this is for you (SMOOCHES) I LOVE YOU ALL!!!

Preface

Sasha was frightened, but she still snatched away from him. She knew she had crossed the line for the last time, and no words could save her from what was about to happen. Her only chance of survival was to try to get out of that house before it turned into a crime scene.

Sasha walked away slowly. She could hear his footsteps behind her, but she didn't bother to turn around.

Pow!

A sudden gunshot whizzed past her head and struck the door, leaving a small bullet hole. She stopped dead in her tracks and her heart began to pound. Shaking badly, she turned to face Quamae. "I'm leaving," she said on a quivered breath.

"Oh yeah? Walk out that door and I'll put a hole in the back of your head! I promise I won't miss this time." His grip was tight on the handle of his gun. Of course Quamae knew the answer, but he wanted her to say it.

Sasha just couldn't bring herself to admit what the video confirmed. "It's not what it looked like," she muttered.

"If you confess with your mouth all of your sins, then you may be forgiven," he quoted a piece of Romans from the Bible and adlibbed the rest.

Sasha's face was blank, emotionless as fear took control of her body, as the moment of truth settled in on her conscience. She nodded yes to indicate she did what he accused her of.

"Nah, I can't hear you. What was that?"

Tears were pouring from her eyes like a running faucet. "I'm sorry, Quamae, I didn't mean for any of this to happen."

All he could see was red, and before she could finish her sentence, the butt of his Glock was crushing the left side of her skull. Her scream was horrific, but so was her betrayal.

"Ho, you fucked the nigga in my house, where I sleep!"

Sasha was dizzy from the blow. "I didn't mean to. He came in the room on his own," she pleaded. She held her head and stumbled toward the door, but he delivered another painful blow, causing her to hit the floor.

"But you didn't stop him!" he spat. "I'ma kill your ass!"

"Quamae, please!" she begged. "I don't want to die."

Her maternal instincts kicked in, and all she thought about was her baby. She managed to pull herself into the fetal position and cover her head with her arms.

He struck her again. The blood from the laceration splattered onto his face. Quamae had a crazed look in his eyes, as if he was having an out-of-body experience.

"You should've thought about that before you betrayed me!" He struck her across the face two more times, and she lost all consciousness. He lifted his foot to stomp on her head, but then something stopped him, and he realized what he had done.

He sat the gun on the floor and, as he wiped the blood from his face with his hand, he stared down at her motionless body. Instantly his eyes watered and a few tears ran down his face.

Quamae dropped to his knees and choked up. He cradled her bloody head in his hands and wept. "Sasha, why did you make me do this to you? Huh? Why couldn't you just keep it real?" His tears dripped onto her soiled shirt.

He held her like that until his tears dried and his survival instincts kicked in. Thinking quickly, he gently laid her head back on the floor, and then he ran upstairs and changed clothes. After that, he emptied out his safe, removed the security tapes, and fled the scene, leaving Sasha to die all alone.

Chapter 1

Carmen had been calling Sasha's cell phone for the past half hour. Growing worried, she called Quamae's phone, but when he didn't answer she called India. They met up and went to find her.

Upon arrival at Quamae's house, the truck wasn't there, but Sasha's car was in the driveway. They walked up and knocked on the door, but there was no answer, so they knocked again.

The heat from the sun was burning their skin. India wiped the sweat from her face and swiveled her head in Carmen's direction. "It's hot as hell. Don't you have a key?"

Carmen suddenly had an epiphany and walked away from the door. "Damn, I forgot about that. I just remembered where she keeps a spare key for emergencies." Not even a minute later she returned with the key and unlocked the door.

India walked in first, but stopped in her tracks and let out a deafening scream from her gut.

The sound ping-ponged off the walls and sent chills down Carmen's spine. She jumped with her hand on her chest while clutching her shirt. "Girl, what the hell you screaming for? Dumbass girl."

India pointed to Sasha's motionless body on the floor.

Carmen ran to her friend's side, dropped to the floor, and cradled her head in her lap. "Call the police," she screamed.

India was stuck. She couldn't move or speak.

"India!" she screamed again. "Call the police, now."

She pulled out her cell phone and dialed the number with shaky fingers.

911, what's your emergency?

India provided the operator with all the information requested and joined Carmen on the floor to wait for help. Five minutes passed and the sound of sirens from the ambulance could be heard. India jumped up to meet them in the driveway. There were a few nosey neighbors standing on their porches, but she ignored their presence.

She waved her hands in the air. "Please hurry," she screamed. "My sister is dying."

The paramedics rushed up the driveway and into the house. One of the medics grabbed Carmen by the shoulders and lifted her body from the floor, but she resisted. "No! Stop! She needs me."

"Come on, ma'am, let us try to save her." He remained calm and continued to pull her away from her best friend's limp body. "Please calm down, ma'am, and let us do our job."

India rushed over and grabbed Carmen. "I got her." She held her by the waist and the medic let her go. "You have to let them help her." India put her arms around Carmen as she sobbed loudly on her shoulder. "Everything is going to be okay."

"No, it's not. He killed her. He finally did it, India."

India's eyes grew wide as she looked to see if anyone heard what she said. "Carmen, be quiet. We don't know that." There was no proof he did it, and based on the lifestyle they lived, it could've been anybody. She didn't want to make that assumption until she had the facts in front of her.

After they checked her vitals, her body was placed on a gurney and wheeled out. India suggested Carmen ride with the paramedics and she would follow them, since she was the only one in her right mind.

As soon as she got in the car she tried calling Quamae. He didn't pick up, so she left him a message.

When they arrived, they took her straight through the emergency room doors and into surgery. Carmen and India were instructed to have a seat in the waiting room. Several minutes later the police and detectives were swarming the emergency room like bees. They had a thousand and one questions about the events that occurred earlier — questions that no one had answers to. They didn't have a clue what the injuries were, either.

Once they documented everything Carmen told them, they left and the room was quiet, so she went outside for some fresh air.

Moments later India walked outside to find Carmen crying. "Are you okay?" she asked.

Carmen shook her head.

"The doctor wants to speak to us. Come on."

She sniffled. "What of she doesn't make it?"

India hugged her neck. "We have to pray for the best."

They let go of each other so Carmen could follow her through the sliding doors.

India spoke first. "Dr. Turner, this is my sister, Carmen."

"Nice to meet you both." He extended his hand. "I'm sorry it's under these circumstances, of course. Now, your sister is in the Intensive Care Unit. She suffered from blunt force trauma to the head. Her injuries include a fractured skull, a broken cheek and jawbone. She's not conscious and she's unresponsive."

Carmen started to cry hysterically. "Is she going to make it?"

He took a deep breath. "I can't say right now because anything could happen throughout the night. I'm sorry."

"What about the baby?" India asked.

"We're trying to see if she will take a turn for the worst before we conduct an emergency C-section."

"Why is that?"

"Miraculously, the baby doesn't seem to be in distress, and we don't want to put her in any danger. I'm assuming the first blow to her head took her by surprise, so she didn't have time to panic or stress because she never saw it coming."

Carmen was skeptical about what happened. "Exactly what was she beaten with?"

"Judging by the bruise on her face, it looks like the butt of a gun."

India jumped in, clearly missing the point of what was just said. "Hold up. Did you say a girl?"

"Um." He thumbed through his chart. "Yes, it is a girl."

India and Carmen were happy to hear a little good news.

The doctor continued to explain. "She required a lot of stitches in her head — thirty-five — and we also had to put a plate in her cheek."

"Damn," they replied.

Carmen was furious. All she wanted to do was find Quamae, and get some answers. She couldn't believe he would go this far and put his very own baby in danger.

"Can we see her?" India asked.

"We usually don't allow it, but I will make an exception in case she doesn't make it. We are going to monitor her all night just in case we decide to do a C-section." The doctor turned on his heels to lead the way. "Follow me."

They walked behind the doctor closely, not knowing what to expect when they saw her. Dr. Turner had them cover up in white gowns and masks.

As soon as India laid eyes on her, she broke out in tears. Carmen attempted to comfort her, but she broke down herself. Sasha's head was covered in bandages. She had tubes running from here to there and an I.V. The sight was horrific. Her face was swollen and her eyes were completely shut due to the swelling. She was beaten literally beyond recognition. Just seeing her like this brought tears to their eyes. The pain they were feeling was indescribable.

"Can we stay with her?" Carmen asked.

"Not up here. If she makes it through the night I can move her to a private room and monitor her from there. Then you could spend all of your time with her."

"Thank you."

"I'll tell you what, can you come back tomorrow morning?"

"Yes, we can," she replied.

"Okay, you may arrive anytime after eight."

"I really appreciate that, doc."

"Just doing my job."

***

Quamae drove around with no destination in mind, trying to digest his actions. He saw an unknown number trying to reach him, but didn't bother answering. The voicemail icon popped up shortly after. He listened to the message:

Quamae, this is India. There's been an accident and Sasha is on her way to the hospital. Please call me when you get this message.

Her voice was frantic, so he knew it wasn't good. He contemplated calling her back, but changed his mind. After riding through the city, he made his way by the trap house to holla at Dirty. When he pulled up, he saw Chauncey's car and anger filled his heart. Jumping out of the truck, he slammed the door and took long strides to the front door and snatched it open.

Dirty jumped and looked back to see who just busted in without knocking. "Damn, my G, what's up with you?"

He ignored his question. "Where is Chauncey?"

Chauncey came from the back room. "I'm right here. What's up, bruh?" He peeped the cold stare in his eyes and knew something happened. "What's wrong, bruh?"

"That's fucked up, nigga, how you gon' do some shit like that to me."

Chauncey was lost, because he had no idea what he was barking about. "What the hell you talking about?"

"You know what the fuck I'm talking 'bout! You been fucking Sasha."

Dirty's eyes stretched as he glanced back and forth between the two in silence.

"Nah, man, not me."

"Nigga, don't fucking lie to me. The bitch told me y'all was fucking while I was in the hospital."

"She lied."

Quamae pulled his phone from his pocket and retrieved the video to show him the proof. He held the phone up and pressed play. "What's this, then?"

Chauncey was dumbfounded as he watched the video of him and Sasha. "Q, that's not what it looks like." He shook his head because there was no way he could explain it. "Shit wasn't even supposed to go down like that."

Quamae walked up on Chauncey calmly, and Dirty stood up in case he needed to intervene. "Nigga, I trusted you, and you stabbed me in the back like that?"

Chauncey was about to answer him, but as soon as he opened his mouth Quamae hit him in it, causing him to stumble. Blood leaked from the split in his lip as he stared into the eyes of the man he saw as a brother.

"Square up, nigga. I'ma give you a fair fight."

"Come on, Q, don't do this." Dirty walked up and stood between them with one hand on Quamae's chest. "Y'all 'posed to be brothers, man."

Quamae pushed him out of the way and swung on Chauncey again, but this time he shook it off and took a swing at Quamae. He ducked and Chauncey grazed his chin. They squared off, looking each other eye-to-eye. The hate Quamae felt was real, and he wanted the traitor in front of him to feel his pain.

He rushed the enemy, delivering fast blows to his body and face. Chauncey was able to dodge a few punches and catch him in his ribs, awakening the pain. Quamae took a step back when he felt it, then Chauncey rushed him, grabbing his waist. Quamae caught him with a three-piece combo to the head, sending him crashing down to the floor.

Dirty finally jumped back in and grabbed Quamae, pushing him backward toward the door.

"Pussy nigga, you can hang up getting this money, 'cause I ain't giving you shit. Get it in blood, fuck-ass nigga."

"Man, come on, you done Kimbo Sliced that man."

"Fuck that nigga, he deserved that shit." He grabbed the handle on the door and snatched it open. "That nigga should've never crossed me, him or that bitch. He lucky I ain't off his ass." Quamae got back into his truck and burned rubber on the way out.

Chauncey's connection to the supply was over, and he would never see the profit from what they sold together.

Fuck that nigga. He ain't getting his money. He can get it in blood!
And he meant every word.

Quamae drove in silence to Gigi's place. The betrayal, hurt and lies were just too much to handle. His mind was racing back to all the times he sat with Chauncey, pouring his soul out to him about his marriage, and he would turn around and fuck his wife? The love he had for Chauncey was real, but fucking his bitch was unforgiveable. He had to be dealt with, and that was on God.

He pulled up into a guest parking spot, grabbed his duffle bags from the backseat, and tucked his burner into his waistband. He checked out the parking lot before heading up the stairs to her apartment door. When he stepped in he could hear the shower running, so he walked into the bedroom and sat the bags in the closet. Then he stretched out across the bed. His body was aching, and he was in need of his painkillers, but he was afraid of becoming dependent on them. Therefore, he wasn't taking them. He closed his eyes and tried to relax in an effort to make the pain subside.

Moments later he heard the water shut off and then footsteps. Gigi screeched upon seeing him. "You scared the shit out of me."

"My bad, bae. I didn't mean to."

"That's okay, my love," she whispered sweetly before crawling into bed with him, wearing her bathrobe. She kissed his neck and earlobe.

"Not right now, please."

She snapped out of nowhere. "What the hell you mean not right now?" She pushed his head. "Oh, I can't touch you all of a sudden?"

"Gianni, stop. I'm serious."

"Oh, I'm Gianni now? Don't come over here with no attitude, because you could've stayed wherever you were with the bullshit."

"Man, you trippin' for nothing. Just chill out. I'm not in the mood."

She sat on the edge of the bed. "So you just finished fucking and now you not in the mood?"

He pushed himself up off of the bed and stood up to leave. "You got that. I'm not about to argue with you right now." The one place he thought would bring him peace was bringing him drama. He would've rented a room had he known she was in her feelings about nothing.

Gigi rose as well, sizing him up and down as if she was ready to take off on him. "I know I got that, 'cause it's the fucking truth. Where the fuck are you going?"

"I guess you know, then," he mumbled as he walked away to avoid confrontation. All he wanted to do was lay down, and she was making that mission impossible.

"So, you bragging?" she pushed him hard in the back.

He spun around quickly, ready to snap. She was oblivious to the Quamae who whooped ass, but she was about to find out. "Stop putting your hands on me. I'm not gon' say it no mo'."

Gigi slapped him across the face, but he didn't budge. She was really testing his patience while he tried to remain calm.

"What you gon' do?" She raised her hand to slap him again. "You—" Before she could form another word, Quamae mashed his hand in her face and she stumbled backward onto the bed.

"I told you to stop putting yo' fuckin' hands on me, but you don't listen."

"Fuck you." She stood and adjusted her robe.

"Gianni, watch your mouth when you talkin' to me." He pointed his finger in her face. "I told you I'm not in the mood. Just let that shit be." He tried leaving the room once again. "I'm not in the mood to fight nobody else. I'm tired, okay?"

"Who were you fighting?" She brought the volume in her voice down a notch after realizing the situation was not a joking matter.

He paused at the door with his head hanging low. "Sasha and Chauncey." He was nonchalant with the response because at that point he didn't care to keep any secrets from her.

"Fighting them for what?" she asked, forgetting the fact she was mad about the push.

"They was fucking in my house while I was in the hospital." He turned around, walked back to the bed, and sat with his head buried in his hands. He figured he could be open with her and she would understand how he was feeling and eventually calm down.

"And you mad about that?"

He looked up at her with a cold stare. "What the fuck is that supposed to mean?"

"Just what it sounds like." She rolled her neck with her hands on her hips. "Why the fuck are you mad if you don't want her? I'm confused."

"Do you know how stupid you sound right now?" It was true he didn't want her, but she hurt him by sleeping with the man closest to him. Out of all the men in Broward, she chose that nigga.

She folded her arms across his chest. "No, enlighten me."

"I'm telling you my best friend and wife was fucking in my house and you coming at me sideways and shit."

"Ex-wife!" she rolled her eyes.

"Can you stop being childish for a few minutes and understand where I'm coming from?" he exhaled deeply, making an effort to calm himself down since she was only adding fuel to the fire. "You missing the point. I don't give a fuck who she giving her pussy to, but she crossed the line with him. It could've been anybody but him."

"You sure about that?"

"Yes," he sighed. "I don't want her." He reached for her hand and she held it out for him to hold. "I'm where I want to be. You just have to be a little more understanding with me."

Quamae's phone alerted that he received a text message. He let her hand go, grabbed his phone from the dresser, and unlocked the screen. It was Emani.

Sis: *What's up pops?* ☺
Pops: *Nuthin' much cum down tomorrow*
Sis: *Is everything okay*
Pops: *Yeah we just need to talk*
Sis: *Okay I'll be there. Love you*
Pops: *Love you too*

When he looked up at Gianni, the anger in her eyes had been replaced with sadness. She glanced slightly to the left to avoid eye contact. She knew she was wrong for blowing up for no apparent reason. "I'm sorry. I overreacted."

He pulled her close to him and stared into her beautiful hazel eyes. "If we are going to be together, you have to trust me. And if you can't, we can end this right now and co-parent." His voice was soft, but stern. He needed her to understand he was serious. "I just got out of one bad relationship, and I'm not looking to do a repeat of the last one. It's all or nothing, faults and all. You know what I am and what I'm capable of doing. So you rockin' wit' a nigga or nah? 'Cause I can be single."

She smiled. "I'm rockin' with you, baby."

"Good, that's what a nigga need to hear right now."

Gigi put her jealousy on the back burner for now. She worked too hard to get her man back, and she wasn't about to lose him. No way, no how. She cradled his head close to her stomach and rubbed his back. "I'll never let you go."

Destiny Skai

Chapter 2

Blue was getting angrier by the millisecond. He had been calling Sasha's phone for the past few hours and it had been going straight to voicemail. Of course he thought the worst, so he grabbed his pistol and headed out the door to look for her. It wasn't in her behavior to have her phone off, so it was odd to him. On the interstate he stuck to the speed limit. Granted he was in a rush to get there, but he couldn't risk being pulled over by a trooper with his heat in his lap. It was already dark outside, and that was a risk he wasn't willing to take with all of the police shootings going on.

The first place that came to mind was her old house. He knew she didn't live there anymore, but he didn't have many options to go on, especially since he didn't know where Carmen lived.

When he pulled up in front of Quamae's house, his blood began to bubble like hot lava. Her car was in the driveway like it belonged there, and he was ready to show his natural black-ass.

He put his truck in park and stepped out with his heat visible in his hand. "This why the bitch got her phone off," he said out loud. Blue was strapped and ready for whatever would transpire from his pop-up visit. He owed Quamae for all the times he sent her back to him rocking a black eye, broken ribs, or a busted lip. He was gon' pay today.

Blue stood on the porch and banged on the door as if he lived there, but forgot his key. It was disrespectful, but he didn't give a fuck. *I wish she would be in here fucking this nigga.* He continued to beat on the door until his hand was sore. Realizing that was going nowhere, he pulled out his phone and called her again. This time it rang, but she didn't pick up.

He finally decided to walk away and clear it. She made her decision, and he was done with her. "Fuck this bitch!" He got into the truck and revved up the engine. He was 38 hot.

As he drove out of the community, his cell phone rang. When he looked down it displayed a picture of Sasha. He hit the Bluetooth in the car. "What the fuck you calling me for? I just left the nigga house and you didn't come to the door. I guess y'all was in there fucking. I'm good on you, ma," then he hung up.

The phone continued to ring constantly, but he wouldn't pick it up. He had made his decision, and he wasn't fucking with her anymore. What they had was over before it could fully develop. He turned the volume up on the stereo and allowed the subwoofers to drown out the sound of the ringing.

"Well, everybody know the truth hurt, everybody get played, everybody fuck around. Hate to say it, but you know I had to do it first, baby girl. I'm tryna give you the universe. Don't you really love the feeling when you feeling her? When shit got bad you start giving up, start acting like it was never us."

He rapped along in his feelings. "Speak that shit, Lucci. These bitches don't recognize a real nigga when they got one."

Blue had been home a little over an hour. He lay across the bed, flipping through photos of them together when his phone started to vibrate off the hook. He shook his head because he had no words for her, but the way his heart was set up he had to answer. He needed to hear what her excuse would be for running back to the man who caused her so much mental and physical pain.

Right before the voicemail picked up, he answered. "What?"

"Is this Blue?" Carmen asked.

"Who is this?" Blue frowned.

"It's Carmen. I need to tell you about Sasha."

"Listen, man, I don't know what type of games y'all playin', but I ain't on that shit."

Carmen rolled her eyes at the phone and sucked her teeth. "Ain't nobody playing games with you. Sasha is in the hospital, and it's bad."

He was on high alert when he sat up at attention to listen to the bad news. "How bad? What happened to her?"

"We don't know, but she's in a coma and she might not make it."

"I told her to stay from around that nigga."

Carmen automatically knew he was referring to Quamae. "We don't know if he had anything to do with it."

Blue wasn't buying that shit at all. He knew better, and he knew Quamae was behind it. Nobody was about to tell him anything different. "What hospital she in?"

"Memorial West."

"A'ight, thanks."

"No problem, but you have to visit her tomorrow. They won't let you in tonight."

"A'ight."

After he hung up, he felt numb. The woman who stole his heart in a short period of time was in the hospital unconscious. Then his thoughts went to the baby, possibly his baby, and it ripped his heart apart. It hurt because he could've seen her had he not ignored every call from her phone.

He tried to sleep, but every time he closed his eyes he saw her face. Never in a million years did he think he would feel that way about a woman. Looking up at the ceiling in deep thought, Blue's phone alerted him he had a message. When he looked at the screen, he saw it was a text from one of his old flames.

Unknown number: *You busy?*

Blue: *Laying down*

Unknown number: *Come lay with me* ☺

Blue: *Nah*

Unknown number: *Why not? Yo' girl got you on lock?*

Blue: *Tired*

Unknown number: *So you just gone one word me to death?*

Blue: *I have a lot on my mind right now*

Unknown number: *You wanna talk about it?*

Blue: *Nah I'm good thnx ne-way*

Unknown number: *Just come over. We don't have to talk. We can do other things to take your mind off of it. Besides it's been a while since you slid up on me and in me for that matter*

Blue: *Lol... man u crazy take yo horny ass to bed*

Unknown number: *OMG!!!!! I HATE THAT U GOTTA GF WITH YO' WANNA BE FAITHFUL ASS. BYE.*

Blue sat his phone face down beside him. The last thing on his mind was cheating on his girl while she fought for life. He laughed because all of his old chicks were mad he was off the market. No more late night booty calls for them. He was okay with that, and they would have to respect his decision.

***

There was a full moon, and 11:30 p.m. had approached quickly. Chauncey stretched out in Monica's queen size bed while he watched ESPN. She still hadn't made it home yet. *She is really trying a real nigga!* He thought about calling her, but hounding a female wasn't his style. He decided to just sit back and wait on her to arrive.

12:30 a.m. had come, and there was still no sign of Monica. All of a sudden a sense of concern hit him. He knew he needed to check on her, so he dialed her number. Before the phone could ring completely he heard the door unlock. He lay back with his back facing her side of the bed. She crept into the room quietly, assuming he was asleep. She took off her clothes and lay down quickly and quietly.

Waiting until she thought she got away with sneaking in after the curfew he gave her, Chauncey surprised her. "What the fuck you sneaking in here for?" He sat up in the bed and looked at her with sleepy eyes.

"I wasn't sneaking. I thought you were asleep, and I didn't want to wake you up."

"Tell me anything. And why are you just getting in? What did I tell you earlier?" He tried to make eye contact with her, but she looked away, staring at nothing in particular.

"I know, and I'm sorry. I didn't mean to come in so late."

He stood up and put his shoes on.

"Where are you going?" she asked.

"I'm out."

"For what?" He could be so stubborn, and it was ridiculous. Everything had to be his way or no way, but a bitch couldn't put him on lock.

"Because you hardheaded. I told you what time to get home and you still came in late."

"Man, stop tripping." She didn't want to argue. She wanted to be intimate with her man. They hadn't made it official yet, but they were working on it, and she was a few steps closer to being in a monogamous relationship with him.

"I'm going home. I'll holla at you later."

She walked out behind him, begging him to stay. "Chauncey, don't leave. I said I was sorry. What else do you want me to say?"

"Nothing." He stopped in front of the door because she was blocking him. "Move so I can go."

She begged and pleaded, but he wasn't giving in. Then she leaned her head to the side when she noticed a knot on his cheekbone. She grabbed him by his jaw to get a closer look. "What happened to your face?"

"This nigga I been beefing with caught me off guard." He pushed her hand out of the way. "It ain't shit."

"Well, let me make you feel better."

"Nah, I'm good. I'm goin' to the house."

She knew he was a sucker for head, so that was one advantage she had over him. Monica reached for his belt buckle, loosened it, and dropped to her knees. Getting ready for what was about to happen, Chauncey put his back against the wall. She was willing to do anything to make him stay. She reached inside his boxers and pulled out a semi-hard Ramrod, referring to his penis with the name she gave it. She stroked it three times before putting it in her mouth and sucking on it.

"Shit," he moaned, grabbing a handful of her hair. She used her tongue like a paintbrush on his shaft, then sucked him off wildly, using two hands to twist and apply pleasurable pressure.

With one hand on her head and one hand against the wall, Chauncey held his weight up to keep his knees from buckling. He grunted.

She knew she was doing her thing because she had his ass on his tippy toes.

"Damn, bae, you sucking this dick good." He was ready to catch his nut and go home. He closed his eyes and focused on what was in front of him. Seconds later he busting down her throat.

He pulled his pants up and fastened them.

"What the fuck are you doing?" She stood up.

"Going home. I told you I was tired. You thought that was gon' change my mind, but you gon' learn today."

"No," she whined.

"See, if you would've come home like I told you, then we wouldn't be having this problem." He unlocked the door. "Use this time to think about what you did and I'll see you tomorrow."

"Oh, so this is payback?" He remained silent. "Chauncey, don't do this."

"Why not?"

"'Cause I need it right now."

He was enjoying every minute of this. He kept her tamed with good sex and head, but listening to her beg was a nut within itself. She was persistent, though. She tried everything in her power to make him stay, but he walked out the door without looking back.

She slammed the door behind him, leaned against the door, and wiped her mouth. "Son of a bitch!"

When Chauncey made it to his car, he called Sasha. He wanted to call her earlier, but decided against it. The phone rang a few times before she picked up.

"Hello."

"What happened earlier?" he asked, not paying attention to the voice on the phone. "That nigga came to the trap on one today."

"This is Carmen." She exhaled.

"Oh, my bad, where is Sasha?"

"In the hospital."

He frowned. "For what?"

"She's in a coma." Carmen was halfway asleep.

His gut told him Quamae beat the brakes off of her ass when he found out about the affair. "What happened?"

"I don't know."

"Thanks, Carmen."

"Yeah."

Chauncey's mind was all over the place. He could only imagine what he did to her, and apparently it was much more severe than what he received.

After riding around for an hour, he ended up in Lauderdale, getting off on the Broward Blvd exit. There was a strip club up the street, Club 54, and that was his destination. When he pulled up the parking lot wasn't full, but he got out anyway.

On the inside there was probably a total of twenty people. At the bar he ordered himself a drink and posted up. Not even five minutes later a redbone approached him.

"You want a dance? Your friend told me to give you a few dances." Lil' mama was fine with long inches that stopped at her ass.

"What friend?"

She pointed in the opposite direction. "That guy over there."

Chauncey looked, but no one was there. "I don't see anybody."

"He was just sitting over there in the corner."

"It don't matter. Do ya thang." He leaned up against the bar and let her work her magic. Redbone pressed her ass against his crotch and ground on him.

One song turned into several, and he was ready to go. All that dry fucking had him ready for the real thing. The only thing left to do was find out if baby girl was 'bout that life. Fucking Monica was always an option, but she disobeyed his order and had to be punished. Therefore, new pussy was on the menu for the night.

Chauncey placed his hand on her waist and made his way down the bikini bottoms that gripped her ass just right.

"What time is your shift over?" he whispered in her ear. He purposely let his lips touch her earlobe.

She threw her head back and glanced up at him. "Whenever you want it to be," she teased. Baby girl's voice was so seductive when she said that shit.

"Well, shit, let's hit it then."

"I have to pay my tip out first."

Chauncey pulled out some cash and gave her two hundred dollars. "Hurry back."

She winked. "Okay."

Chauncey took baby girl to the Comfort Suites located on Commercial Blvd. They walked into the room and she tossed one of her bags on the floor. "I need to shower first," she claimed, then sashayed to the bathroom.

"Go 'head." Moments passed before he decided to join her in the shower. Butt naked, he walked into the bathroom and stepped in with her.

She turned around to face him and smiled. "I see somebody couldn't wait for me to get out." Her eyes then drifted down to the package she had been grinding on all night.

"I figured I would join you and make things a little more interesting."

She bent over and grabbed the Dove body wash she carried with her and squeezed some on his dick. Using her hands to lather it up, she stroked him up and down until it was covered in bubbles. Placing a hand on his chest, she ushered him in front of the shower head so he could rinse off.

Chauncey turned back to face her and she dropped to her knees. His dick looked bigger when she wrapped her small hands around it before putting her mouth on it. Her head game wasn't the best he ever had, but for tonight it would do.

Once they made it to the bed, he was ready to go full-throttle. Baby girl was horny as hell, and she could feel her juices starting to flow. The alcohol she consumed that night, made her want him badly.

He lay back on the bed. "Come get this dick."

Crawling on top of him she leaned forward, kissing and sucking all over his chest. Her moans in his ear were turning him on in the worst way, but he didn't want none of that foreplay shit. He waited until she tried to ease herself on top of him before he reached for a condom off the nightstand and flipped her on her back.

He rammed heavy inches inside of her with one strong stroke and pushed it all the way in. She moaned, gripping his waist. "Mm." The fullness of his length filled her hole completely and her muscles gripped him tight. His strokes were long and deep, as he pushed in and out of her tight wet young pussy.

"Ow. Um. Um." She squeezed her eyes tight and held her breath. This was some pressure she never felt before. She had only been with one boy, and she was only nineteen.

He grabbed her ankles and pinned them behind her head. "Ah," she hollered, feeling all that meat in her guts. "Ooh."

The wetness from the sex made loud smacking noises that echoed throughout the room. Chauncey stood up tall in it and applied monster pressure, causing the sweat beads from his forehead to drip onto her face.

The penetration gave her clitoris stimulation and her body started to shiver. "I'm about to cum," she cried.

"Cum hard on this dick," he moaned.

"Ooh, I'm coming," she cried out.

He put his thumb on her clit and rubbed it in a quick circular motion, thrusting harder and harder until she came all over him. Once her body relaxed, he went balls-deep in the pussy again.

"Put my legs down." She held her breath, thinking that would ease the pain.

"Unh, unh, be quiet."

Her moans started to get louder and louder and he still wouldn't ease up on her. She could feel his balls slapping against her ass. This was torture for her. She dug her nails into his back, but he didn't seem to feel it. He continued to pound on her pelvis like he was trying to break something.

He spoke in between breaths. "Damn, you got some good-ass pussy."

He watched her squirm like a worm under his muscular frame. Then he pinned her all the way down so she couldn't move at all. Long stroking her until he came, Chauncey pulled out of her and snatched the rubber off.

Her legs were so numb she felt paralyzed. Her breathing was so heavy she thought she would pass out at any moment now.

Destiny Skai

Chapter 3

The next morning

The sound of the iPhone ringtone caused Blue to jump up out of a horrible dream. His heart was racing fast and he was covered in sweat. He took a deep breath to slow down the pace. The picture in his head was clear as day: the doctor from the hospital had just called and gave him the horrible news that Sasha passed away. He wiped the wetness from his eyes when he realized it was just a dream.

His phone continued to sound off, so he searched in between the sheets to find it. When he finally located it. He saw he had a missed call from one of his homies. He hit his boy back and put it on speaker.

"What's up, bruh?"

Blue yawned. "Shit, just getting up."

"Aye, I got the word from the streets that the hit on Unc wasn't random."

"G-shit?" Blue planted his feet on the floor. "What's the word, then?"

"Come holla at me later on so we can chop it up. You wanna hear this shit, bruh. I'm telling you."

"A'ight, I'ma slide in a few hours."

"Yeah, do that."

Blue got up to handle his morning hygiene so he could head up to the hospital to check on his baby. When he was finished he left the house in a hurry. He had been waiting on the streets to deliver the news about his peeps, and that day just so happened to come when his heart was already aching.

When he reached the hospital and walked through Sasha's room door, there was a brown-skinned chick sitting next to her.

She looked him up and down and smiled. "Damn, she ain't say he looked that good," she mumbled under her breath.

As he approached the woman, he extended his hand. "I'm Blue, you must be Carmen?"

"That is correct. How are you?"

"I'm good, for the most part." He turned his attention to Sasha, taking small steps toward the bed. Her head was covered in bandages. There were tubes running from here to there and an I.V. hooked to her arm. That beautiful face he had grown to love wasn't so pretty anymore, but he still loved her. It was swollen, and her eyes were completely shut. She was beaten beyond recognition. Blue grabbed her hand and squeezed it. Just seeing her like that made him cry. "I can't believe you in here like this. I failed you. I promised to protect you, and I failed." The presence of a stranger didn't bother him one bit as he confessed his love for her. "I promise I will never let anything else like this happen to you. When you get through this, I will keep you and our baby close to me. I promise that no harm will come your way. I put that on everything, bae."

Carmen couldn't believe what she was hearing, but apparently he cared for her more than she thought he did. Watching him cry at her bedside in front of someone he didn't know broke her heart all over again. "You love her, don't you?"

He glanced at her with red, wet eyes. "More than she knows." He placed his hand on her belly and rubbed it. "Damn, baby, I'm so sorry. I swear I am."

"I hope so, 'cause she needs someone that does, besides me." She paused for a second. "Do you believe that's your baby?"

"I hope so."

"And what if it's not?" she probed, trying to see where his head was at and if it was really with Sasha, or if he was just another fly by night.

"It doesn't matter. I'm gon' be there regardless. She's been through enough, and she don't need that pressure."

"I hope I'm not overstepping my boundaries."

"Nah, ma, you good. You just looking out for your girl. No harm, no foul."

Carmen felt obligated to give him some alone time with Sasha while she stepped out for some fresh air. "I'm going to step out for a few and give you some alone time with her."

He watched Carmen walk out the door, then turned back to his baby. "Damn, bae, he fucked you up bad this time. I should've killed that nigga myself when I had the chance." He kissed the open space on her forehead. "But don't worry, 'cause I won't rest until that nigga gets his. I promise you that." He rubbed her stomach, leaned over the rail, and planted a soft kiss on it. "I'm doing it for both of y'all. I'll be back when I handle that, baby." A stream of tears rolled down his cheek. "Please don't die on a nigga, bae. I love you. I never felt this way about a woman before." He shook his head in disappointment. "Why did you go over there by yourself? You gotta fight, Sasha. Fight for us, fight for our family. Don't leave a nigga like this."

Blue was torn up on the inside and out. The pain showed in his face and the guilt was heavy on his heart. He wiped his face with his hand and walked away from the bed toward the door to go meet up with his boy. The only thing on his mind was revenge, so tonight was gon' be an all-night fight. He wasn't going home until he sent Quamae to his final resting place.

Blue left the hospital en route to the East in Lauderdale to link up with his boy. Dred was like a father figure to him, the reason he was a hustler in the first place. After Blue's father was killed when he was 13, his uncle, his dad's brother, stepped up to the plate to help his mom. He owed it to Dred to seek revenge on his killer or killers. Just the thought of the murder brought tears to his eyes. He used the back of his hand to wipe the tears away.

The phone call he received was clear as day as it replayed in his head. *"Aye, bruh, I got some bad news for you. Dred was killed in his bed last night. Him and his lady was executed."*

There was too much going on in his life — first his uncle and now his lady. If it wasn't for bad luck, Blue doubted he would have any luck at all.

During his ride there his thoughts drifted back to Sasha, and he felt bad for the way he treated her the day before. Going forward, if she came out of her coma, he was prepared to make her the happiest woman in the world. And that was a promise!

When Blue pulled up to the corner/liquor store on 13th street, his peeps were posted up in the parking lot. He greeted them all with a fist bump, but he greeted Zoe, the one who made the call, with their special handshake.

"What up, Zoe?"

"I can't call it. You hangin' in there?"

"Yeah, bruh, I'm maintaining." He stood there with his hands in his pockets. "So, what's the word on the street?"

Zoe placed his hand on Blue's shoulder. "Walk with me." They took short strides toward the road so everyone was out of earshot. "The nigga Keith slid by my crib this morning, all paranoid and shit. I don't know of that nigga was on fleek or what, but he went to rambling on about Dred and shit."

Blue nodded his head to acknowledge he was listening. "Is that right?"

"Yeah." Zoe tapped Blue's chest with the back of his hand. "But peep this, the nigga said it was him and Dred idea to take the nigga Quamae bricks."

Blue scrunched up his face in confusion. "What?"

"Yeah. He said they was coppin' work from the nigga and it was Dred idea to take the shit." Zoe adjusted the hat on his head. "I don't know why he did the shit without a solid plan in place, 'cause he know them niggas 'bout that gunplay."

"I'm 'bout that gunplay, too, and I don't see none of them niggas."

"I know that, bruh, but if the nigga ain't lying, we already know they pulled the trigger."

"You don't believe the nigga?"

"Nah, I believe the nigga. That's the only thing that makes sense to me. When the blue devils searched the house they didn't find drugs or money, and we know for a fact Dred was loaded with that cake."

"Blue devils?" Blue asked.

Zoe laughed. "Them punk-ass pigs, nigga."

"You shot out, my nigga."

Zoe looked behind him to make sure everyone else was still at a distance. "So, what you wanna do? We retaliating or what?"

Blue was unsure if he wanted to include his boy in his plan, although he was a solid nigga. However, if push came to shove, he could probably use his help. "I don't know yet. Ain't you cool with them niggas?"

"I know the niggas, but I ain't on that friendly shit. You already know that you and Dred like family, so don't ever doubt me on that, bruh."

"I know that, bruh, but shit crazy outchere. Nowadays you can't trust yo' own homies, you know."

"You got me, bruh, and I put that on my kids. I'm down for whatever, just give me the word."

"That's real. Nah, I'ma hit you when I figure out how I wanna hit them niggas." They did their handshake once again and Blue cleared it.

Darkness lurked in the clouds, and the sun was slowly fading away. Blue was ready to send Quamae to his final resting place for taking away the only father he had in his life. He sat in front of his enemy's house in a rental car, awaiting his return. The limo tints kept the nosey neighbors away.

The info Zoe dropped on him earlier was enough to make him stalk his prey solo, without a plan. He pulled his strap and attached the extended clip. It was time to light this bitch up like bombs over Baghdad, but in the suburbs. Ready for war in his army fatigue pants and black tee, he pulled his dreadlocks into a ponytail and covered his head with a baseball cap.

Three hours later, Blue was still sitting in the same place and Quamae still hadn't shown up. Frustration settled in and he was itching to finger fuck the trigger. All he needed was for his victim to pull up so he could blast at his ass with no hesitation or words. The pleasure of Quamae seeing his face before he died was good enough. He looked around for any type of movement.

"Damn, where the fuck this nigga at?" he mumbled under his breath. Blue told himself he would wait a little while longer before he moved on to the next one.

Another hour had passed, and this time he was sitting in front of the Crystal Lakes Apartment Complex in Hollywood. Blue leaned back in the seat when he saw headlights from a car, indicating they were about to park. Exiting from the car was a female carrying a baby. Waiting for her to walk up the sidewalk, he crept quickly and quietly behind her. In the midst of her closing the door, he stuck his size nine, all-black timbs into the doorway.

"What the fuck you doing?" she snapped. Blue raised his shirt to reveal his heat. She backed up with her hand slightly covering her mouth. "Take what you want, just don't hurt me or my baby, please," she pleaded.

He stepped in and closed the door, locking it behind him. "Call your baby daddy."

Kenisha was afraid. She had no idea who the handsome stranger was or what he wanted as he stood in her living room. "Okay, I'll call him now."

"Tell that nigga it's an emergency."

She dialed his number and waited on him to pick up. Saying a silent prayer in her head, she hoped he would answer, because sometimes he didn't if he was busy. The phone rang several times before he finally answered. "Please come home now, bae. It's an emergency, and I need you."

Blue could hear him asking questions, so he walked up to her and snatched the phone, then hung it up. "Good job. Where this nigga at?"

Kenisha held her baby tightly in her arms. "If you came to kill him, please don't kill me and my baby. I promise I don't know what you look like. All I know is a masked man came in and I never saw his face."

He pulled the gun from his waist and waved it at her. "Go sit over there." The baby started to cry. "Give him to me," he demanded.

"Please don't hurt my baby," she cried.

"Just give him to me."

Kenisha handed the baby over, not knowing what to expect. Blue's fatherly instincts kicked in and were in full effect. He had no intention of killing her or the baby, but she didn't know that. He smiled. "What's up, uncle man? Stop all that crying like a girl." The baby suddenly became quiet as his little hands reahed for the gun. "Oh no, you can't play with that."

Blue heard the door unlock, so he backed up a little to hide himself. Once the door closed, Blue smile again. "Showtime," he whispered to the baby boy.

Kenisha was sitting on the couch crying when her babydaddy walked in. "What's wrong?" he asked. She didn't utter one word, but she pointed in the direction of the stranger. His eyes followed her hand to where she was pointing, and he nearly had a heart attack once he saw who was holding his son with his left arm and the heat in the right hand.

"Blue, what the fuck you doing, man?"

"I'm asking the questions, nigga. Sit 'cho ass down," he barked.

"Blue, don't hurt my son, please," Dirty begged.

Blue's laugh was so wicked and scary it sent chills down Kenisha's spine and pumped fear into Dirty's heart. "We vibin', ain't it, young soldier?" He bounced the baby in his arms and waited on Dirty to take a seat next to his bitch.

"Yeah, nigga, this shit ain't no fun when it's yo' family that's in danger, nigga. This what y'all did to my uncle?"

Dirty's facial expression was a dead giveaway. He couldn't pretend to not know what was going on if he tried, but it was worth a try anyway. "What you talkin' 'bout, bruh?" He attempted to play it cool.

He waved his gun back and forth. "Don't disrespect me by calling me *bruh* when you had a hand in killin' my muthafuckin' uncle."

"I didn't do shit, man. I swear."

"Nigga, don't sit here and lie in my face." He aimed his gun in his direction. "Y'all niggas murdered my uncle Dred and his lady in cold blood," he snarled at him. "I'll bust yo' head to the white meat in front of yo' lady and baby if you lie to me again." He paused for a second. "Did you think I wasn't gon' find out? But now you gon' help me, believe that."

"How am I supposed to do that?" Dirty felt like a real bitch in front of his babymama and shit. There was no way out. Blue had Dirty by the balls, and the bait he held over his head was his babymama and son. He was curious about how he knew where she lived, but then it dawned on him that Blue had given him a ride to her house before.

Blue glanced in Kenisha's direction. "Come get the baby."

She got up quickly to grab her son. Like any caring mother would do, she clutched him tight in her arms and kissed his face. "It's okay, Mommy's here." Kenisha went back to her spot next to Dirty. The frightening, yet disgusted look on her face was worth a million words. All she could think was how could he let another man come into her home and not protect her or their child. At the moment he was less than a man in her eyes. He would have to redeem himself if he ever wanted respect from her again.

"What did you do?" she asked, just above a whisper.

"Nothing." He didn't lie to her, but he didn't tell the truth, either. "I don't know what's going on."

"So he just holding us hostage for no apparent reason?" she probed, not believing a word he said.

"Bae, just chill."

Blue was waiting for his chance to chime in. "Why you lying to your lady, man?"

"Bruh, can you put the gun away in front of my git?" he pleaded.

"Get 'cho ass up, we leaving anyway."

Dirty got up and walked to the door to wait on Blue's next set of instructions.

"Where is he going?" Kenisha cried. "Please don't kill him."

"As long as you don't call the police, he'll be back in time to fuck you before you go to bed."

"I won't, I promise."

"Bae, please don't call them. Everything gon' be okay. I promise."

"You shouldn't make promises you can't keep," Blue added.

When he was close enough, he opened the door and pushed him out. "Walk to the parking lot."

"Where we going?" Dirty asked.

"Just do what I said." He then pulled out his phone and placed it against his ear, as if he was talking to somebody. "Aye, bruh, we on the move. If you don't hear from me in 30 minutes, run up in that nigga crib and let loose."

Dirty didn't need a college degree to know Blue was referring to his family. "Come on, man, you ain't gotta do all that. Call them boys off."

"I will after we finish." They got into the car and rode off. "As of right now, I don't trust you 'cause your loyalty ain't with me."

"I'm telling you I ain't have shit to do with that." Blue cut his eyes over at him as if to say *nigga, please*. He certainly didn't believe him and Dirty could feel it. "Yeah, they robbed me, but I had nothing to do with your uncle getting killed.

"Who you trying to convince, me or yourself?"

"I don't know what else to say."

***

The Next Day

"I can't believe them niggas killed Unc, man."

Blue and Quint sat out back on the patio by the swimming pool, rolling a blunt. Seeing Blue in such a delicate state was detrimental, and he would do anything to help his brother from another mother cope with his loss.

"Money is the root of all evil, and we knew this. Dred knew this, too." Had the shoes been on the other foot, they would've done the same thing.

"They fucked up when they pulled them triggers." He nodded his head up and down. "Them niggas gon' pay severely."

"Fo' sho, we gon' make them niggas feel it. I'm down for whateva." They did their handshake. "They ain't gon' know what hit 'em."

Blue's smile was treacherous. He contemplated the revenge, and he couldn't wait to put his plan into motion. "Oh yeah, I ran down on that fuck-nigga Dirty at his baby mama house."

Quint knew his boy was straight savage and wouldn't blink on a chance to kill the beef solo, but that wasn't the best move at the moment. Slip-ups were not an option. "Solo, dolo?"

"Yep."

"Come on, bruh, stop doin' that. Why you ain't call me?"

"After I left the East from choppin' it up with Zoe, I was on ten and ready to murk something." He put the blunt to his lips and took a hard pull, then released it slowly. "I ain't have time to make no calls."

"Shit too hot to be slidin' solo. I'll kill a nigga whole family if they touch you — mamas, daddies and babies. Shit, they all can get it." He took the blunt and took a hit.

"I already know how you rockin', but you know how I'm rockin' when I'm heated."

"So what happened when you slid up on him?"

Blue sat up in the chair and leaned in closer to Quint, to explain every single detail about that night. All he could do was laugh at the fact Blue was certified crazy.

"So you mean to tell me you was rockin' the nigga baby when he came in and he ain't do shit?"

"What the fuck he was gon' do? Besides get rocked in front of his bitch and his git. That nigga would've been rockin' a wet, red shirt."

"Damn, that's crazy."

"Tell me 'bout it. Then I told his fuck-ass he gon' help set them niggas up."

"What he said?"

"Exactly what he 'posed to say."

"You think he gon' do it?"

"Whether he do it or not is on him. He got two options, his life or theirs. He gotta figure out which one is more important."

"We gotta be careful with that nigga, 'cause he might try and set us up."

"I got the upper hand on that bitch. I know where he eat, sleep, shit, lay, and fuck. He ain't got shit on me. I always kept that nigga in the dark."

Chapter 4

Emani sat diagonal from Quamae at the kitchen table, trying to wrap her head around everything he confessed to her. She was an emotional mess, and she needed an explanation. "How could you keep something like that away from me? I could've lost you forever."

He felt bad for keeping her in the dark, but he did what he thought was best for her. "E, I wanted to tell you, believe me I did, but I thought it was best you didn't know."

"You did what was best for you."

He leaned back in his chair. "I couldn't let you see me in the hospital all defenseless and shit. That would have only made matters worse."

"Worse for who? Certainly not me. I thought our bond was better than that." Emani was hurt, and she made that known. "But I see I was wrong."

"This has nothing to do with our bond, but there's more to the story than what you know."

She folded her arms across her chest. "So, are you going to tell me or do I have to wait for another near-death experience to find out?"

"I'm divorcing Sasha."

"Why?" Emani didn't seem surprised at all. "Is it because you have a new girlfriend?"

"Because that baby she carrying ain't mine."

Her face squinted up as if there was a foul smell in the air. "What?" She heard him the first time, but she needed him to say it once more for clarity. She just knew her ears were deceiving her. "Say that again."

He locked eyes with his sister and suddenly the room became silent. Time felt like it was at a standstill, but the ticking of the clock brought back reality. There was no simple way to break the news, and there was no point in beating around the bush. "She cheated, and now she doesn't know who the father is, and there is no way I'm staying with her."

"Damn," she sighed. "I'm sorry to hear that. Are you okay?"

"Yeah, I'm good."

"How long have you known about this? Did she tell you?"

"I found out before you moved."

"But you two seemed happy back then. What happened from then to now?"

Quamae shook his head. "E, we wasn't happy. That shit was a front in your presence to keep you out of it. She wanted to make it work, but I can't do it. We're over for good."

Disappointment was plastered on her face. She wanted to talk to Sasha about hurting her brother the way she did. "Just when I thought I was finally getting a niece or nephew, I get hit with the bullshit."

"You still getting a niece or nephew." That was the first time he smiled since their conversation began.

"You just said that's not your baby, and I'm not talking to her after what she did to you. I'm straight."

"I have a baby on the way, too."

"From who?"

"Gigi."

"You're ex?" She rocked her head side-to-side, grinning.

"Yeah."

Emani stood up and walked to the fridge. "So, y'all was cheating on each other?" She giggled as she opened the door to grab a soda from the box, closing it behind her. "That's crazy, and that's the reason why I'm never getting married." She twisted the top off and took a swig of it.

"You right about that," he agreed. In his eyes no man would be good enough for his baby sister unless he was a book-smart nigga instead of a street nigga.

"Well, I'm about to meet up with some friends at the mall and go shopping." She walked over to the spot where she had been sitting and gathered up her things. "We're going to LIV tonight."

"That's all you wanna do: shop and party." He didn't mind as long as her GPA stayed above a 3.0. There were no worries on his end about her grades because she had always been an exceptional student, which is why he spoiled her so much.

"Duh!" She slapped him playfully on the shoulder, exposing her full set of pearly white teeth. "I'm a college student. What do you expect from me?"

He stood up to walk her outside. "Good grades and no babies is what I expect from you. The world is yours as long as you stay focused."

"Got it, pops." Emani led the way to the front door, then opened it. She stopped and looked back at him. "Oh yeah, congrats on the baby, and tell Gigi I said the same." Then it hit her. "So that's who was in your background that day I called you?"

"Yeah, that was her." He opened the car door so she could get in.

"Tell her she could've spoken to her old sister-in-law." She fired up the engine and turned on the air. "I knew it wasn't over between y'all. She was a good fit for you anyway, but I guess you wanted a popular chick that doesn't work."

The sarcasm was hilarious, their laughter was contagious. It was everything he needed from her since she was no longer upset with him about keeping secrets from her. "E, drive safe and be careful tonight up there. Those niggas in Dade are ruthless."

"I'm always careful."

"Next weekend I'm taking you to a weapons class so you can learn how to shoot and get your permit to carry a concealed weapon."

"Great!" she exclaimed. "I can't wait. See you later."

"I love you."

"I love you, too." She backed out of the driveway thinking about Sasha. Emani wanted to talk to her, but she was too upset to call her.

***

Quamae had just made it back inside when he received a phone call from Officer Freeman. "Yeah."

"Aye, boss, I need you to meet me somewhere right now. It's important." A sense of urgency was present, and he knew something was about to go down.

"Meet me at the diner on State Road 84 and I'll be there in 20 minutes. Are you in plain clothes?" Quamae asked because he couldn't risk being seen fraternizing with the law. State Road 84 was a private strip with lots of hotels and motels. It was known to be the cheating strip, so if a person wanted to catch their significant other in the act, nine times out of ten they could catch them at any one of the hotels.

"Yeah, and I'm on my way," Freeman replied as he took off in his car. Quamae dialed Gigi immediately to let her know he was going to be late, but she didn't answer. He unlocked the door to his truck and sat down in the driver's seat. He dialed her again.

"Hello," she answered.

"What you doing? I just called you." He pulled out of the driveway and headed in the direction of I-95N.

"Oh, sorry, I was in the bathroom and I didn't hear the phone ring."

"I was calling to let you know I won't be there for another hour. I have an impromptu meeting I need to attend, but when I'm done I'll be there."

"I'll be waiting," she purred into the phone, causing him to laugh.

"Yeah, I know what you waiting on."

She played it off innocently. "I don't know what you're talking about."

"Yeah, I bet you don't, but I'll see you soon."

"Okay, daddy."

When Quamae arrived at the diner there were only a few patrons in the establishment. He spotted Officer Freeman in the corner, so he walked over and took a seat and got straight to the point. "What's going on?"

Freeman talked just above a whisper. "I got a promotion today, so now I'm a detective."

The waitress walked up in the middle of their meeting to take their orders. "What can I get for you gentlemen?"

Quamae placed his order. "Let me get two orders of the country fried steak breakfast with grits and two western omelettes to go."

She wrote down his order. "Would you like a drink with that?"

"Orange juice for both."

She then turned her attention to Officer Freeman. "And what can I get you, sir?"

"Um, let me have the steak and egg breakfast with coffee."

"Okay, coming right up."

Quamae couldn't wait for her to walk off to address what he stated. "That's what you called me here for, to tell me you got a promotion?"

Freeman folded his hands together. "Yeah, but that's not it. I've also been selected to be the lead detective and investigator in the case that involved the incident with your wife."

He showed no emotion when he heard the good news. With Freeman on the case there was no way any evidence would surface, let alone prosecution. "Is that right?"

Freeman knew he was over-stepping his boundaries with the next question, but he needed to ask. "Did you have something to do with that?"

That caught Quamae off guard. It was bad enough he didn't trust the muthafucka, but he had the nerve to question him?

"Stand up!" Freeman did as he was told. "Where is your cell phone?"

"Right here." Freeman pulled it out of his pocket and handed it over before sitting back down.

"Didn't I tell you to leave your cell in the car whenever we meet up? I don't trust you, nigga," he spat angrily.

"I turned it off."

Quamae checked to make sure it was indeed off and sat it face-down on the table.

"You know I wouldn't do no shit like that. Man, I'm loyal to you, and you should know that. We've been doing this for years. You know me."

He was really trying to convince him he didn't have to worry about nothing. He feared Quamae because he knew he wouldn't hesitate to kill him or his family at any moment, and he would get away with it. That's how savvy he was.

"Nah, I don't trust nobody. Niggas bite the hand that feeds them every day." He was referring mainly to Chauncey. "Niggas will betray you even if y'all grew up from the dirt, so no, I still don't trust you."

He stood up, and what he did next shook Freeman to the core. He hovered over him and reached down in his shirt to see if he was wearing a wire.

"Quamae, what you doing, man? I'm not wired." He looked around to see if anyone was watching. Luckily they weren't.

When he didn't find anything, he sat back down and carried on with the meeting. "Safety measures," he replied. "Now you know better than that, to ask me if I did it!" There was no way he would admit to shit. "Did O.J. kill Nicole?" he asked.

He blinked twice. "Urgh. Um." He was stumped on what to say.

"My point exactly. So, what's going on with her? Because I don't know, we're separated." He trained his eyes on him.

Not once did he blink, and that intimidated him. Freeman fumbled around with the silverware on the table, unable to look Quamae in the eyes. "You are aware that it happened at your house?"

He grinned slightly. "I am now." He leaned forward and interlocked his fingers. "What I need to know is how will you make this investigation disappear?"

At that moment Freeman knew he did it, but it didn't mean shit since he didn't admit to it. "Do you have surveillance cameras in your home?"

"Yeah," he answered comfortably, knowing he wasn't being recorded.

"I guess I don't need to ask if you removed the footage."

"No. Just tell me what you're going to do and stop with the questions." His patience was wearing thin with all of the questioning.

"Well, first I need to go over what little evidence they think they have. There's no need for me to go back to the house, but I will tell them I did a full sweep and I was unable to find anything useful."

He paused when he saw the waitress return with his order. "Here you go." She placed Freeman's plate down in front of him, along with his coffee. "I'll be right back with your to-go orders."

Freeman picked up where he left off. "You should know you're a suspect in the case, but don't worry about that. I'll handle everything and close the case."

Quamae nodded. "I expect you to do that."

The waitress returned with his orders in a plastic bag and his orange juice in two Styrofoam cups. "Here are your to-go orders and bill."

Quamae handed her two twenty-dollar bills. "Keep the change."

She smiled graciously. "Thank you, sir, and you have a nice day."

He smiled back. "You do the same."

She walked away, happy with her tip.

Quamae's smile disappeared quickly when he turned his attention back to Freeman. "Make this go away, and call me when you do." He stood up and grabbed his orders. "I'm out."

"Wait, there's more."

Grabbing his attention, he sat back down with great anticipation. "What's that?"

"I got the names and address of the suspects who shot you in the bar." He pulled a piece of paper from his pocket and slid it across the table.

His eyes grew wide. That was the moment he had been waiting on. Street justice. There was no need to let a jury decide their fate when he was gonna do it. He would be the judge and jury in this case. He picked up the paper and scanned over the names to see if they were familiar. He frowned. "These some Opa-locka niggas, I see."

"Yeah, so be safe and watch how you go in on they asses. They roll deep. Plus this is out of my jurisdiction, but I have my way of getting things done."

"Good looking out. I'll hit you up with some cash later for the tip." He was on his feet once again, letting him know their meeting was adjourned. "Oh, and keep me posted on the investigation."

"Got it, boss," he replied. He was happy when Quamae finally left because he was starving and he hadn't taken one bite of his food since he received it. The last time he tried eating during the meeting Quamae took his plate, slung his food on the floor and hit him over the head with the glass plate. He was still rocking that scar, which was a constant reminder to never disrespect him again.

He munched down on his food hungrily as his boss left the diner.

***

On the way to Gigi's house, Quamae felt relieved knowing Freeman had been assigned to the case and he didn't have to abandon his home. The first thing he was going to do was hire somebody to go and clean up the mess Sasha left behind. He vibed to Yo Gotti during his ride because he was speaking some real-life shit and talking about what he was going through.

I can't fuck wit' you no mo', ho, and I'm sorry (I'm sorry)
You a disloyal-ass bitch, ho, you sorry (You sorry)
You probably ain't pregnant, ho, you flaugin' (You sorry)
That probably ain't my baby, I need Maury (I'm sorry)
A ho gon' be a ho, they ain't a hunnit (They ain't a hunnit)

And when a nigga broke them hoes act funny
When he made it in the apartment complex, he sent her a quick text.
Quamae: *Open the door*
Gigi: *K*
He could see her standing in the doorway, rubbing her full and perfectly round stomach as he approached her. She stared at him with dreamy eyes. "Hey, sexy. Where is your key?"

"Hey, you." He bent down to greet her with a kiss before stepping inside. "My hands are full."

"What's in the bag?" She closed the door and followed him into the kitchen.

"I picked up some breakfast for us."

"Good, 'cause I'm starving." She sat down at the table with her hands folded on top of her stomach and waited patiently for him to open the bag and set her food in front of her. "It smells good, too."

"You always starving," he joked.

She stuck her tongue out. "We be hungry over here."

They sat down and ate breakfast together. Gigi didn't leave anything on her plate. "Damn, you was hungry for real, huh?"

She washed down the food with her orange juice and a burp soon followed.

"You are so nasty," he teased.

She threw a napkin at him. "Don't judge me."

"You get a pass 'cause you pregnant," he said in reference to the burp.

Once breakfast was over, they went to lie down and watch a movie. "She's excited, Feel my stomach." She reached for his hand and placed it on her belly so he could feel the baby kicking and moving. "I think the orange juice made her happy."

"He kicking hard as hell. Maybe he ready to come out."

"Baby, it's a girl, and she better relax because she has a few more months to live in here, and after that she has to vacate the premises."

He rubbed and kissed her belly. "Yo' mama ain't no good. She trying to evict you already. Kick her harder." When he spoke to his unborn child the kicks became harder, as if he or she was following his directions.

"Damn, she listening to you."

Gigi just lay there while Quamae communicated with his baby. She was happy he was happy with their bundle of joy on the way.

He grabbed Gigi's hand and held it. "I was thinking you should move out of here and come live with me." He figured she would be happy with the news, but when she frowned he knew she was anything but pleased with his proposition.

"You mean the house you shared with your wife?" She sucked her teeth. "Nah, I don't think so."

"I paid for it and it's mine, so quit tripping."

She rolled her eyes because the last place she wanted to be was in the home they shared. She wanted a new place for new memories. Those old memories were bad rubbish.

"You want me here every night with you, and I have to stay home sometimes."

"Not every night, because I do work, in case you forgot," she rebutted in her defense.

"Oh, yeah, about that, when you leaving your job?"

"Right before I have the baby. I still have to work, you know," she rubbed the side of his face.

"No, you don't, because I pay your bills." He was gonna make her stop working whether she wanted to or not. "I don't want you working while you're pregnant. You should be at home relaxing and getting prepared to be a mother."

"No, I need to have my own money, and you know how I feel about that. Who's to say y'all won't reconcile and then you leave me?" She was determined to get her point across.

"Reconcile? Are you fucking crazy? I told you what she did. I'm not fucking with her, period."

"But what if that's your baby?"

"I wouldn't give a flying fuck. I'm not going back to her, but I will take care of my child, though. And if you worried about the money, I can wire you twenty grand right now into your account to make you feel secure with your decision. Our baby needs a two-parent home. And besides, there ain't enough room in this apartment for the both of y'all. My baby needs his own room."

"No, she don't. We can sleep in the same room."

Quamae laughed because she was so adamant about keeping her one-bedroom apartment and being independent. The place was fine when it was just her, but she would have a permanent roommate in less than four months. "I'll be happy when we find out the sex so we can stop with this he/she shit. But I'm going to let you have that. If it's a girl, that's cool. As long as it's a healthy baby, it doesn't matter to me. Besides, I don't want her to see or hear how I put this dick on her mama."

"Whatever!"

He put his hand underneath her maxi dress and rubbed her clit. "You know I bring the noise, baby," he said, making her moan.

"Ah," her eyes rolled to the back of her head. "I guess so."

"Why you not wearing panties?"

"Easy access."

Quamae took that as his cue to handle business. He helped her out of her dress and crawled between her legs, staring face-to-face with her kitty. He licked her clit slowly and dove his tongue in and out of her hole. She became wet on contact. He slurped the juices, then sucked on her clit once again.

She rubbed the back of his head while he feasted on her goodies. "Sss," she moaned.

Quamae came up for air and licked his lips. "Turn on your side." With her belly in the way, missionary was out of the question. She turned on her side and lifted one of her legs to allow him entrance. The wetness allowed him to slither in like a snake with no resistance as he took a few strokes. Her cave was warm, and her pussy muscles gripped his throbbing pole tight, causing him to thrust deeper.

Suddenly, images of Chauncey fucking Sasha popped into his head, and that made him fume. He plunged deeper, and the sound of skin slapping filled the room. He was out of it as he punished Gigi inadvertently. She hollered out for him to slow down, but her screams fell on deaf ears. "It hurts," she cried. "Slow down."

She held the bottom of her stomach while he beat up her box. The pain was too much to bear. He was holding her ankle and grunting loudly through clenched teeth. "Grr, shit. Damn." Gigi bit down on a pillow to muffle her screams. At any moment she just knew he was going to send her into labor early.

Seconds later he emptied his sac and pulled out.
"That's the noise I don't want her to hear." She punched him in the chest. "I know you heard me telling you to stop."
His contagious laughter caused her to laugh, too.
"I know, but I had to prove my point. So, do you understand what I'm saying now?"
"I'll think about it," she said, although her mind was already made up.

Chapter 5
South Bay Correctional Facility
One week later

Nate was lying on the bench, pressing three hundred pounds when he was approached by one of the officers on the compound.

"Black." He addressed him by his last name. He stood there with his right hand on his baton. "Your counselor just called for you."

Nate stopped, placed the bar back in its place and sat up. "Thanks, Dean."

"Anytime, my brother. It's about that time, huh?" he smiled.

"Finally," he sighed. Fifteen years was a long time to be locked up, and even worst when you were alone. His boys were there from time to time, but he wanted his woman to be there for him. He took that bid to keep her safe because he knew she wouldn't survive one day in prison, and she had the nerve to turn her back on him during the first year of his sentence.

Officer Dean had been in corrections for 22 years, and he watched Nate transform from a boy to a man. When he first came in he was a rebel, but then Dean got hold of him and became his mentor. His transformation was lethal. When he first came in he was a buck sixty soaking wet, but now he was 220 pounds of straight muscle and well-educated. He stood up and pulled his shirt over his 5'11" frame.

"Listen to me. Remember everything I taught you and don't come back here. I'll give you my cell number, and I want you to keep in touch. That transition is going to be hard, so you call me if you need anything."

It was a sentimental moment. Dean was there when he wanted to commit suicide on more than one occasion. "I will, and that's my word. I appreciate everything you did for me since I been here."

They shook hands and Nate made his way off the yard and into the building. His time had finally come, and he was about to grace Sasha with his presence. She had a lot of explaining to do.

One of his boys had reached out to him claiming she had his baby and gave it up for adoption. He also claimed he knew where his son was living and would show him when he touched down. That wasn't the first time he heard she was pregnant after he left. Over the years he learned to be slow to anger and quick to forgive, but he wasn't sure if he could forgive her for not telling him about his child.

Nate walked up to the counselor's door and tapped it lightly with his knuckle. She waved for him to enter. He walked in and closed the door behind him.

"Hey, Mr. Black. You ready for that change?" she smiled.

He took a seat and folded his hands in his lap. "How you doing, Ms. Wright? And I must say I am. I spent a lot of years behind these walls."

She shuffled through the papers on her cluttered desk. "Oh, yes, you were a rowdy li'l fella when you got here," she laughed, reminiscing on the way he used to be. "I need you to sign your release papers for me, and in the morning you are free to go."

"In the morning?" He had to make sure he heard her correctly.

"Yes. I know I said next month, but because of the limited space and the newcomers they decided to let you go early."

A heavy wave of emotions took over Nate's soul. He never thought he would see the streets again, and he was certain his dying days would be in a cell. "I can't believe it's finally over."

"Believe it so you won't come back." Just like Officer Dean, she took a liking to him and felt the need to go that extra mile to help him.

"I promise I'm not coming back." Nate signed his name and pushed the papers across the desk.

"Good. You've come too far and you have really transformed into that strong, educated man we discussed." She choked up a bit. "If you need me, you know how to reach me. Please don't come back here."

She stood up, walked around the desk and stood face-to-face with her protégé. "I know I shouldn't do this, but to hell with the rules. Give me a hug, because I'm going to miss you."

Nate heard her sniffle. "Don't cry, Ms. Wright. I won't forget anything you taught me, you or Officer Dean."

She let him go. "I'm such a big baby."

"It's okay. I'll cry later on in the shower." He joked. "Thanks for everything, and I'll be in touch."

Nate walked away feeling like a new and improved man. When he touched down he was causing hell, but not enough to get himself in trouble, and he definitely couldn't wait to see the look on Sasha's face when she saw him.

He stood face-to-face with the payphone, thinking of Slim's number. The exciting news made him draw a blank, and then it finally hit him. Dialing the number quickly, he waited on the recording and then for an answer.

"What's crackin', fam?" Slim was excited to hear from his homie.

"Nothin' much, just calling to give you some good news."

"What, they letting you out right now? You need a ride?" he rambled, not giving him a chance to respond.

"Not right now, but in the morning I will."

"My nigga coming home!" Slim shouted. He'd been there since day one, awaiting his return to the streets and it was finally happening.

"Hell yeah. I can't wait to see the look on these bitch-ass niggas' faces when I step to 'em."

"Fuck them niggas. We hittin' the mall and get you fresh so you can get some pussy. I know you tired of jacking off," he chuckled.

"Hell yeah."

"Nigga forearm stronger than a bitch."

"Strong enough to knock a nigga out with one punch," Nate replied.

"Strong enough to strong-arm some pussy, too." Slim was on a roll with his jokes. "What time I need to be there?"

"Be here at six in the morning. I'm running when I hit the gate."

Slim laughed. "Shit I don' blame you. And when you running, do not look back."

They joked around on the phone for the remainder of the call until the recording let them know the call would be disconnected in fifteen seconds.

"Well, the phone about to hang up, so I'll see you in the morning."

"In the morning," he repeated, then disconnected the line.

Nate walked to his room and sat on his bunk to gather up all of his belongings. It was finally happening. In less than 24 hours, he would be a free man. Being behind those walls taught him a lot, such as there were no such thing as friends or girlfriends when he was caged like an animal. That famous line, *out of sight, out of mind*, was a classic and proved it was an accurate statement.

"What's up, celly? Where you going?" That was Nate's roommate, Joe.

"I'm out this bitch in the morning."

"You getting transferred?"

"I'm going home."

Joe's eyes lit up. "You serious?"

"As a heart attack."

"Damn, that's good to hear. Congrats to you, man."

"Thanks."

Joe had been down for two years and had three more to go. When he got there they immediately connected and had been rocking together ever since. Joe was also from Lauderdale, but he was younger than Nate, so they didn't run in the same circles. They did know some of the same people.

Joe flopped down on the bunk next to him. "I hope my next celly ain't no funky-ass nigga. You know how these nasty niggas get down."

Nate thought back to his own experiences with funky cellmates and laughed about it. "I can relate to that. I've had enough cellmates to last me a lifetime, and shared more showers than I care to remember."

"I'ma miss you, homie."

"Hit me up on my boy phone. I can't guarantee you no letters and shit, but I can drop a few dollars on your books and accept your calls."

"Shit, that's good enough for me."

"You can have all this shit, too," Nate said, referring to all of his items he collected over the years.

"The MP3 player, too?"

"Everythang."

They chopped it up until it was lights out. Nate tossed and turned all night, anticipating his departure in the next few hours.

***

As promised, Quamae took Emani to the weapons class so she could get her license to carry. While she was learning about the rules and regulations and taking her test, he was in the range letting off a few rounds. *Pow! Pow! Pow!*

"All headshots," he said to himself, satisfied with his aim. "That's how I'm aiming at you niggas."

Quamae pulled off his target practice photo and threw it on the floor beside him. Setting his gun down, he reached inside his pocket and pulled out his next target. Unfolding the paper, he hung up the photo of Chauncey and smiled.

"This for you, you disloyal muthafucka."

For the next twenty minutes or so, he shot multiple rounds at Chauncey's headshot.

Emani approached him when his time was just about up. He had just taken down the photo and balled it up in his hand. The last thing he needed was for her to see what he was up to and start asking questions. With every fiber in his body, he made sure she stayed out of harms way. Behind his sister, he was willing to catch a life sentence.

"You missing all the targets?" she laughed.

"I'ma vet. I don't need practice, but you do."

"I just passed my class and my test. I am ready for the festivities. I wish a nigga would try me!" She used her index finger and thumb, and pretended to pull the trigger.

"Just think before you shoot."

"I got this, pops." She slapped her hand across his shoulder. "I can out-shoot you."

"What you wanna bet, then?"

Emani tooted her lip up. "You mean money?"

"What else I'm talking about?"

She scratched her head. "Oh, I was thinking like a chore or something ridiculous. Money is too easy."

"You know what? You are so right. Why would I bet you when I would only be winning my money back?" He shook his head. "You are so right."

For the next hour Quamae taught his baby sister how to hold, aim, shoot, remove the safety, and take the gun apart. Those were key factors she needed to know if she was going to carry a concealed weapon.

From the day Emani was born, he vowed to take care of his sister until she could take care of herself. That's why he hustled when he was younger, so he could send her to the best schools. During middle school and high school, he made sure her tuition was sitting off to the side. Now, as an adult, she was on her way to being independent.

Their time had come to an end, so Quamae drove her back to her apartment and saw her through the front door. No matter how grown up she was, she was still his baby in his eyes.

Emani hugged him. "Thanks for the day out. I love you."

"I love you, too. See you later, and lock up."

"I am, don't worry." Emani smiled and closed the door.

On the way home, Quamae thought back to his plan and wondered if the sentence was too harsh, or was it just right? Loyalty meant so much to him, and once it was broken, there was no coming back. He rubbed his hands together, grinning deviously. The plan he mapped out was done with perfection and executed with percission. The only thing left to do was sit back and watch it spread like a wildfire. He had to pat himself on the back for that one. The man was an *evil genius!*

Chapter 6
One month later

Several days after Sasha finally opened her eyes. After her close call with death, she was alert, but had no memory how she ended up there. Her speech was slowly progressing compared to the first day, and Blue was still by her side, along with Carmen. Confusion was present the same way it was the days before, and it showed. She looked around the room and saw an abundance of flowers and balloons all over the place.

"What? What am I doing here?" She sat up in the bed and placed her hand on her stomach. "Is my baby okay?"

Blue looked at her in amazement. After sitting with her on a daily basis, he was happy she could finally talk. He grabbed her hand. "You were in a coma." She looked at Carmen for approval. "And yes, our baby is fine."

Carmen nodded and smiled, relieved her girl pulled through. "It's true."

"Why?"

Carmen answered before Blue could get a word out. "We'll talk about that later. Let's focus on getting you better in the meantime."

She looked up at the handsome face gazing at her appearance. "I heard you talking to me. You said you failed me, you were sorry and you loved me?" Her eyes squinted, searching for the truth. "Did you do this to me?"

"I would never put my hands on you. I love you too much for that. I failed you because I didn't protect you." The sincerity in his voice was real, but his actions spoke louder than words.

"Protect me from who?"

He didn't want to discuss this in front of Carmen, so his response was short and sweet. "From anybody who wants to harm you."

"Somebody pushed me, and I was falling from the sky, and there was no one at the bottom to catch me. I could hear voices, but no one bothered to rescue me." She glanced around the room once more. "Where did all these flowers and balloons come from?"

Blue responded. "I brought these here for you."

"Is India okay? Is she going to make it?"

"What do you mean?" Carmen was curious as to what she was talking about.

"She was in a car accident. I saw her and there was blood everywhere."

"She wasn't in a car accident. That had to be a dream. India was up here earlier, but she had to go to work. I will call her and let her know you are awake." She leaned over and hugged her. "Girl, you had us worried sick up here." She nodded her head toward Blue. "And he has been up here every day to see you."

Sasha scratched the top her head, but paused quickly when she felt lumps on her skin. She was frantic. "What is this?"

He grabbed her hand. "You had stitches."

She felt all over her face. The bandages had been removed and the scars were plain to see. Her hands were shaking rapidly. "What happened to my face?" She pulled the blankets off of her and slung them off to the side. "I need a mirror." She tried getting out of bed

Carmen grabbed her. "Sasha, you have to relax."

She snatched away from her. "No, I need to see what's wrong with me. Let me go."

Blue signaled for Carmen to let her go. "Bae, relax and I will walk you to the bathroom." Helping her from the bed, he held her around the waist and escorted her to the bathroom. Before he switched on the light, he gave her a pep talk. "I don't want you freaking out when I turn this light on. You are beautiful to me, and time will heal all wounds."

Sasha stood in front of the mirror, waiting on him to turn it on. She closed her eyes and took a deep breath. Her body language and sweaty palms showed how anxious she was. The sound of the fan coming on let her know the light was on. She opened her eyes slowly, afraid of what she looked like.

Staring back at her in the mirror was a creature that belonged in the movie *The Hills Have Eyes*. She didn't recognize herself with the scars on her face and head.

"I look horrendous," she cried. "What happened to me?" she screamed. She touched her cheek. There was a small incision under her lower eyelash.

"Baby, calm down. It's okay. They had to put a metal plate there to shift your cheekbone back into place."

"No, it's not. I look like something from a scary movie."

He grabbed her and hugged her tight. "I love you, and that's all that matters. You're alive, and I'll take you like this over death any day."

"Yeah, right. You gon' leave me because of how I look."

"Sasha, stop talking crazy. I'm not going anywhere. If I wanted to leave you, I would've left you before you woke up. So please stop beating yourself up over this." His voice wasn't loud, but he needed her to understand he wasn't with her for her looks. "All of this will heal one day."

"Why? Looks like somebody already beat me up."

"Come on, that's enough. You need to go and lay down." He turned off the light and walked her back to the bed.

Carmen felt bad about the situation at hand, but all of that could've been avoided if she would've pressed charges like she told her. "Is she okay?"

"She will be." He tucked her in bed and made sure she was comfortable.

"Can you lay with me and sing me a song, please?" His voice could calm any storm, and right now she needed to feel loved.

His job was to fulfill her every want and need, so he climbed into bed with her and put his arms around her, then cleared his throat.

"When you need me, I will be right by your side. When you need me, I will be there before you can call me. When you need me, you don't have to worry or cry, 'cause when you need me, I will be there."

Tears from her eyes wet the pillow, but not because she was hurting. The lyrics he sang matched his actions because she needed him more than he knew.

Carmen was surprised he could sing. She rocked in her seat to his perfect melody and smiled at the man in front of her. "I didn't know you could sing. I guess you have a sensitive side to you."

"Only when it comes to her," he smiled. "I'll do whatever it takes to make her happy, and that includes singing in front of you."

She laughed. "Why me?"

"Because I don't sing in front of people, but I had to make an exception for her."

"That's what's up."

Over the past month Blue had been faithful to Sasha, so it wasn't a surprise when he rocked up hard and fast from spooning with her. He would've stayed in that spot until it went down, but he had to pee so badly. If they were alone he wouldn't care, but there were an extra set of eyes in the room. Ten more minutes passed and he couldn't hold it any longer, so he tried getting up discreetly to keep Carmen from seeing his dick standing straight in the air. The basketball shorts did no justice because all of his business was out. He moved quickly to the bathroom and closed the door.

Carmen shook her head and laughed. Now she knew why Sasha couldn't leave that young nigga alone.

When Blue stepped from the bathroom, there was a knock on the door. He and Carmen looked at each other strangely, not knowing who to expect. The door creaked open slowly and in came a black man displaying a gold bitch badge on his belt. Clearly he was a detective. He walked over to where Blue was standing and extended his hand.

"I'm detective Freeman, and you are?" His demeanor screamed cocky and arrogant, but Blue wasn't moved by the nigga's presence. He could get it just like the rest of the niggas on the streets if it came to that.

He shook his hand and shot him an alias quick. His name was clean, but he didn't fuck with nobody in law enforcement. "DJ." In his eyes he looked like a dirty muthafucka. That dirty cop smell lingered in the air like some cheap-ass cologne when he came in. Growing up around drug dealers all his life gave him a nose like a K9 to sniff that crooked bullshit.

"I need to ask Sasha a few questions about the incident that took place."

"I'll wake her up, but she doesn't remember anything."

He walked up to Carmen and extended his hand to her as well. "And you are?"

"Carmen."

"Nice to meet you, Carmen."

"Likewise." Her smile was as fake as a three-dollar bill.

Freeman pulled out a notepad, headed over to the bed, and waited on her to open her eyes.

Blue shook her lightly until she opened them. "Baby, get up. This detective needs to ask you some questions."

She blinked a few times and scratched her ear. "Huh?"

Freeman took the initiative to introduce himself. "I'm detective Freeman, and I have a few questions for you. We are conducting an investigation to see what happened and who did this to you."

"Oh." Clearly she was out of it, but he didn't care because he had a job to do and his boss was awaiting the results.

"Can you state your full name for me?"

"Um. Yeah. It's Sasha Banks."

He scribbled in his notepad. "And do you recall the incident that happened about a month ago?"

She rubbed her head. "No, I don't remember."

His eyes hovered over the notepad like he didn't believe her. "So you have no idea who did this to you?"

"No."

He continued to question her for the next twenty minutes. They were the same questions, but he asked her in different ways like he was trying to coach her into the right answer. "So maybe somebody was trying to rob you and they forced you into the house."

She looked at Blue with sad, teary eyes, begging for help. "I don't know."

Blue stood up and stepped in between him and Sasha, blocking his view of her because now he was aggravated and pissed off at the way he was interrogating her. "Listen, man, that's enough. My lady said she don't remember, so take your fuckin' notepad and haul ass. We'll call you if she remembers anything."

Freeman looked him up and down, staring into his eyes, trying to intimidate him. "I say when it's over. So boy, go and sit down until I'm done."

He had the face of a boy, but he was a grown-ass man standing in the flesh, and no one could get away with disrespecting him. He didn't give a fuck about Freeman's authority. "Check me out, you Uncle Tom-ass nigga, don't fuckin' try me. I don' give a fuck about your pussy-ass badge. You just a fuck-nigga in blue." His bass voice echoed through the room like thunder.

"Boy, you betta sit yo' ass down before this shit gets ugly."

"I got yo' muthafuckin' boy." He pointed his finger in Freeman's face. "Take off that muthafuckin' badge and show me. You think you tough 'cause you got that shit on. I don' give a fuck about none of that shit. I'll beat yo' ass in this bitch about mine," he barked.

Sasha and Carmen looked at Blue as if he was crazy. However, it made her feel good he would check authority for her. The way he defended her was a turn on, and he looked sexy doing so.

The door flung open hard, crashing against the wall and causing the girls to jump. Some nigga looking like Robocop in a tight-ass uniform stepped in.

He addressed Freeman. "You straight?"

"Yeah, I'm good." He took a step back and Blue took a step forward, looking like he was about to swing on him. "This lil' nigga just acting up, that's all."

A sudden feeling of panic rushed over Carmen, so she tried to diffuse the situation. "Blue, calm down, so do what he needs you to do and leave."

"I ain't calming down. Fuck this nigga and his sidekick," he spat.

"Nah, fuck you, nigga."

Blue's fist connected with Freeman's jaw quickly. He grabbed his mouth and his security rushed Blue and pinned him up against the wall.

His arm was under his chin and they were face-to-face. Any closer he could've kissed him. "You don't wanna do this, 'cause I'll haul your ass down to the county faster than you can say Black Lives Matter."

"Let the li'l nigga go. Let him go outside and calm down for a few. Ain't no pressure." There was no need to arrest him because he would have Quamae on his ass soon.

Robocop let him go and stepped to the side so Blue could walk away.

"I ain't going no-muthafuckin'-where."

Freeman snarled at him. "You have two choices: you can leave or I can book you on assault charges on an officer."

Sasha finally spoke up, not wanting him to go to jail. "Bae, just go outside, please. I need you here with me. Please."

He hesitated. Robocop put his hand on his weapon secured in his holster. "Take a walk, now."

Blue's eyes followed his hand. "Oh, that's a threat? You wanna shoot me now?"

"I would, right here, right now," he replied with his hand still in place.

Sasha cried out, "Carmen, get him, please!"

She stood up and grabbed his arm, pulling him toward the door. "Come on, because you know they don't have a problem shooting an unarmed black man." He snatched away from her and stormed out of the door with Carmen on his tail.

The duo took the elevator down to the first floor and went outside to the parking lot. Blue was heated and he needed to calm down before he ended up dead or in jail. He made a beeline to his truck with Carmen still in tow. Clicking the remote, the engine fired up on its own and the doors unlocked, giving access to enter. Once inside he pulled out of the parking lot and onto South Flamingo Road.

Five minutes into the ride she broke their awkward silence. "Where are we headed?"

"Liquor store." The response was short. His mood was sour and he didn't feel like talking. There was no bad blood or ill feelings about his passenger since he didn't really know her to begin with. If it wasn't for Sasha, she wouldn't be in the truck, period.

He powered on the stereo to kill the silence and to keep her quiet. He drove around Pembroke Pines until he reached the ABC liquor store.

Inside he walked down the cognac aisle and grabbed a fifth of Remy. Blue looked over at Carmen. "You can get what you want."

"Thanks." She walked away and picked up a bottle of Apple Crown Royal, a pack of cups, and an apple juice to go with it before meeting him at the counter for checkout.

Back inside the truck, she fixed herself a cup. Blue broke the seal on his bottle and turned it up to his lips. She cut her eyes at him. "I guess you don't need a cup."

"Nah, I'm good. I prefer mine hot and from the bottle."

She snickered. "Oh, okay."

The drive back to the hospital was more relaxing thanks to the alcohol. They bopped to the music and flowed through every traffic light.

His mind was on Sasha, wondering if the stupid-ass cops left her room yet.

In the parking lot they sat in the truck and vibed to Jay Z and Beyonce's *On the Run* song since they were only gone for approximately an hour.

Cross the line, speak about mine
I'm a wave this tech, I'm a geek about mine
Touch a nigga where his rib at, I click clack
Push your motherfucking wig back, I did that
I been wilding since a juve
She was a good girl 'til she knew me
Now she is in the drop bussin' Uey's
Screaming.

Blue pulled out some wrap and weed to roll up. "You smoke?"

"Hell yeah."

After rolling up he took a few puffs and passed it to her. "Them niggas had me heated in that bitch."

"Yeah I saw that." She took a pull. "Yo' ass is crazy."

"Fuck them niggas. They ain't wanna do shit. They just rapping 'bout nothing. I'll email Jesus 'bout that girl."

"That's what's up."

Another hour had passed and they were still in the truck. He glanced over at Carmen, who appeared to be on a different planet. Turning the music down, he chuckled. "Ma, you good over there?"

She blushed. "Yeah, I'm good. This liquor and weed done kicked in and got me feeling lov-a-lee." They both laughed.

"Good, let's head up and check on my baby."

"Alright, let me finish my last cup for the day."

"Don't get too fucked up, now. You have to drive home."

"I'm a big girl. I can handle it."

"A'ight."

He leaned back in the seat and shut his eyes, thinking about his girl. Unbeknownst to him, he fell asleep. All he wanted to do was get her out of that hospital and take her home. Sex would be nice too, since it had been a month. In his mind he drifted back to the first time she gave him head and it was amazing. That shit was golden compared to half-ass blowjobs he received from the younger bitches he used to fuck with.

The dream felt so real he actually moaned out loud. "Shit."

When he opened his eyes, Carmen had his dick in her hand, jacking his shit.

He pushed her off of him quickly. "Man, what the fuck you doing?" he zipped his pants.

That wasn't the reaction she was hoping for, and it startled her. "Sorry. I guess I just got caught up in the moment. I thought." The hesitation was like a thick lump in her throat.

"You thought what? That I wanna fuck you? I don' know what you got going on, but I don' rock like that." He tilted his head to the side, mugging her hard 'cause she had him fucked all the way up, especially if she thought he was gon' cross his girl like that.

"I thought the feeling was mutual."

"Nah, you ain't think that. I was only vibin' with you off the strength of my girl," he pointed at her. "Yo' homegirl." He cut the truck off and got out.

As he walked away, he clicked the alarm without taking a second look at her, but he could hear footsteps behind him. "Are you gonna tell her?"

He turned around quickly and put his hand up towards her, stopping Carmen in her tracks. "I don' think you should come up. That's some foul shit you just tried. I'll tell her you had to leave or some shit."

He left Carmen standing there and went back inside, never answering her question.

Chapter 7

Baby girl was cuddled up under Chauncey, sleeping like a newborn baby. His cell phone was ringing and ringing and ringing. He finally rolled over and picked it up. His voice was groggy.

"Hello."

"Where the fuck you at?" Monica yelled angrily through the phone, exercising all of her throat muscles.

"Home," he replied, never opening his eyes.

"You a muthafuckin' lie."

"Man, how you gon' tell me where I'm at? I'm home in the bed."

"You might be in the bed, but you damn sure not home." Monica was at his apartment.

"Whatever, man."

"I'm at your apartment right now, and you are not here."

That woke him up immediately. The stripper chick was lying right next to him, fast asleep. She had a very light snore, so he knew she couldn't hear him. He walked into the bathroom and took a piss.

"Man, you tripping. Where you at?"

"I just told you where I'm at. Now, where the fuck are you?"

"It's too early for this shit, and why you over there anyway? You stalking a nigga now?"

"I'm looking for your lying ass."

"Listen, I'll be over there today." She didn't say anything. "Are you listening to me? When I leave my mama house I will be there," he lied.

She was pissed off with him and his lies. She knew damn well he wasn't at his mama's house. "You know what, Chauncey? Fuck you. And don't bring your ass over here. I'm so sick of going through this bullshit with you. Me and my baby don't need you, so fuck you and the bitch you with." She hung up without warning.

It took a minute to conceive the words she just spit at him, but he was certain he heard her say *her baby*, or in other words *their* baby. He called her back right away.

She picked the phone up and snapped. "Why the fuck are you calling me?"

"You pregnant?"

"Isn't that what you heard?"

He paced the floor, rubbing his head. "So why didn't you tell me?"

"I just did."

"Damn," he sighed. He was definitely not ready for no damn kids.

"*Damn?* Is that all you have to say? You don't have to be here for my baby if you don't want to, and I'm not gon' force you to, either."

He took a deep breath. "Man, chill. I'll be there in a couple of hours." Chauncey walked back into the room and sat on the edge of the bed. That news fucked him up big time.

"Are you okay?" li'l mama asked, interrupting his thoughts. He hadn't even been aware she was awake.

He looked over his shoulder. "Yeah, I'm cool."

"You sure about that?"

"Yeah. I have a few things to do so, come on so I can take you home. Put your number in my phone so I can call you later." He handed his phone to her.

"Okay." She programmed her number up under her government name, Ayesha.

They got up and put their clothes on to leave so he could check on Monica. She had given him an earful, and he needed to talk to her face-to-face with no interruptions.

Chauncey drove her to some apartments down the street from the hotel called Hidden Harbour. "Is this where you live?" he asked.

"Yeah."

"Who you live with?"

"Myself. Why, you wanna come in?" She knew he had to leave, but she asked anyway. After that good dick he put on her he could spend the night and get his own drawer.

"Not right now. I have a few errands to run, but I can check you out later if you not busy."

"Okay, just call me."

Chauncey watched her walk away and go inside her apartment before he pulled off. Although she gave up the goodies with little effort, he decided not to give her curbside ho service and pull off before she was safe indoors.

Two hours later he was walking through Monica's front door after going home to wash up and change clothes. She was sitting on the couch talking on the phone. She glanced at him and turned her head. "I have to go."

Before she could finish what she was saying, he snatched up the phone. "Who is this?" he roared into the phone, but the caller hung up. "Who were you on the phone with?"

She rolled her eyes. "Why did you do that?"

"Girl, don't play with me, and who the fuck was you on the phone with?"

"Don't come in here questioning me after the way you left here last night." She was pissed, and she wasn't about to back down from the argument.

"That better not had been a nigga."

"And if it was?"

"I'll beat your ass."

"So you can fuck who you want to and I can't? You got me fucked up."

Before he knew it his hand was wrapped around her throat.

She was surprised. He had never touched her before. "Chauncey let me go," she begged.

"Nah, talk that shit you was talking earlier."

"You're hurting me. Stop," she pleaded.

Chauncey had never put his hands on her, and for the first time he saw how easy it was for Quamae to snap on Sasha when provoked. "Talk that shit now."

"Is that all I had to say to get you here?"

"Don't try that reverse psychology shit on me, save that shit for school." Her eyes began to turn red and fill with water. He didn't know what had come over him. This was so unlike him, so he let her go. "So what's this shit talkin' 'bout you pregnant?"

"I am."

"Nah, you playing with me?" He was hoping she was just saying that shit to make him mad.

"I am not playing. You think I'm making this up?"

"I hope so."

Her face balled up in a frown. "You hope so? Are you fuckin' serious? What did you think would happen, having unprotected sex?"

"Aren't you on birth control or some shit?"

"Yes, I am, but I missed a few doses."

He was hot with her, and now he felt like she did that shit intentionally. "Yeah, you did that shit on purpose."

"I didn't do shit on purpose." By this time she was hurt and on crybaby mode. "So you don't want this baby?"

"No, I don't." He didn't want to hurt her feelings, but she wasn't having this baby. "You have to get an abortion. I'm not ready for this yet, and you not either. We're not keeping this baby."

Those were the last words she thought he would say to her. Just when she thought a baby would bring them together, it did the complete opposite. She didn't know what she was going to do, but she would find out soon enough.

***

"So, this is where they got my boy staying at, huh?" Nate asked his homeboy Slim as he freaked a Black 'n' Mild. He stared at the home that was in need of some major renovations and some fresh paint.

"Yeah dawg, shit crazy, man. She ain't even come back and look for ya son after she got married. She gotcha boy out here hustling and struggling while she living the high life with her husband." He looked at Nate and shook his head. "That's a cold bitch, nigga, even after you took that charge for her." Slim was the one who kidnapped Frank back in the day so they could murk him. "What you plan on doing when you catch her?"

Nate lit the cigar and took a pull before he responded. "I don't know, man. I'm still thinking about that shit. I did 15 years for that bitch, and she left a nigga for dead in that shit." He looked over at Slim with his eyebrows slanted. "You say she married?"

"Yeah, to a nigga name Quamae. They got married a few years back. I'll show you the bitch on Facebook." Slim scrolled through his phone until he found Sasha's page and handed the phone over to Nate. "I followed the bitch a few weeks back. I almost took the bumper off that bitch's car. She live in this nice-ass neighborhood in the Pines."

He was in awe over her beauty and the way she transformed over the years, but the picture of her round stomach made his blood boil like hot lava. "Damn, that's fucked up. She gave my son away and let the streets raise him." He sacrificed his life and freedom for her. The least she could've done was keep his junior. "She didn't even have the decency to let me know she was pregnant. I know y'all boys would've looked out for my git and my baby mama while I was gone."

"You already know," Slim replied.

Nate took another drag from the black and cracked the window. The sun wasn't too bad after the rain stopped, leaving tiny specks of water on the windshield. In fact, it was actually breezy. He sat in the passenger seat of an old Cutlass and waited for his son to hit the block. Slim had already told him NJ was out there hustling, and it broke his heart to know he was following in his very own footsteps. The dope game was all he knew back then, but due to his long stint in prison, he was a changed a man. And he hoped he stayed that way.

As he looked out the window, he could see a bunch of kids walking toward them. He checked out every person in the group, but his son wasn't among the crowd. So he sat back and waited. As soon as the crowd cleared, he noticed a slim figure headed his way with a young girl in tow. Nate stared at a younger version of himself and became overwhelmed with guilt. He wished he could've been in his son's life, but Sasha ruined that for him. He could tell he was eating just fine by the way he was dressed. He was rocking a True Religion fit with some Royal Blue Timberland boots.

The chick he was with was wearing the smallest shorts she could find, a fitted polo shirt, and some long-ass hair. She rocked the same Timbs as NJ. Right then and there he knew she was his chick. She was appealing to the eyes, but a hoochie nonetheless.

Nate and Slim got out of the car and stood on the sidewalk to catch NJ before he walked into the house. NJ stopped in his tracks to acknowledge Slim. "Whadap, fam?" They fist bumped.

"Nothing much, just maintaining." Hoochie mama stood close by with her hands on her hips, popping her gum, waiting impatiently to go in the house.

"What brought you to the block?" He eyed Nate hard, wondering who the hell the dude was.

"I have someone I want to introduce you to." He was curious, but he continued to stare at Nate as he listened. "This ya daddy, Nate Sr."

He turned to look at his girl and then handed over the house key. "Go in the house. I'll be in there in a minute." She walked away without saying a word. He focused his attention back to Nate. "My daddy?" he questioned.

"Yeah," Slim responded.

Hearing those words brought back some painful memories. He always wondered who his parents were and why they gave him away, but he never got the answers he was looking for. Every foster home he resided in didn't last long because he was a problem child with lots of issues. The only reason he was at his current address was because Ms. Walker had an undercover drug addiction, so she let him hustle as long as he supplied her needs. She didn't care what he did or how many girls he brought over as long as she got her fix.

"Nah, I don't have one of those. 'Cause if I did, I wouldn't be in the predicament I'm in right now."

It hurt Nate to hear him say that, but what could he possibly expect after their first time meeting one another? Nate spoke up to defend himself: "If I knew about you, none of this would've happened like this in the first place. I just wanna talk to you. Can you give me a chance, please?"

"No disrespect, bruh, but nah, I'm good on the daddy tip. I haven't had a daddy or a mother for 15 years, and I ain't interested in getting to know you."

Slim intervened because the youngster had no idea what went down between his parents. He placed a hand on his shoulder. "I know you upset, but if you hear him out, I'm sure you would find a new-earned respect for the man who gave you life."

"Slim, I respect you as a man, so I'm gon' say this with the utmost respect. I ain't got shit to say to this nigga, and next time you come by my crib, come solo." NJ walked away and headed to the front porch.

Nate looked on with pain in his heart and sadness in his eyes as his only child rejected him. The old Nate would've snatched him up by his collar and kicked his ass, but the new self-righteous Nate decided to keep his cool and be patient. Giving up wasn't an option, so he would come back another day.

Slim looked at him and immediately felt bad about the way their encounter went down.

"I'm sorry, dawg. I ain't think the li'l nigga would act like that."

Nate shrugged it off as if it was no big deal. "It's cool, fam. I'ma give him a little time before I come back around." They got back into Slim's car and drove off.

Inside the house, NJ walked into his bedroom and slammed the door behind him, causing Jazz to jump. "What's wrong with you?" she asked.

"Nothing," he lied.

Jazz rolled her eyes and sucked her teeth. "Why you be lying all the time?" He walked over and sat on the bed quietly. "NJ!" she yelled.

"What?" he yelled back.

"Was that yo' daddy?"

"Nah, I ain't got no muthafuckin' daddy, and don't ask me that shit no mo'." He was beyond heated, and every word out of her mouth was pissing him off.

"Don't fuckin' curse at me 'cause you mad at yo' daddy. I ain't do shit to yo' dumb ass."

NJ stood up in front of her. "Who the fuck you calling dumb?" He was breathing heavily with his hands balled up at his sides.

She rolled her eyes again and folded her arms across her chest. "You, dumb-ass boy, and get out my face."

NJ reached back and slapped her in the face. *Whap!* It sent an echoing sound through the room. Jazz was stunned. She placed her hand over her cheek and cried. He looked down at her without an ounce of sympathy. "You must think you talking to one of them lame-ass niggas you used to fuck. I'll beat your ass in here. Now try me again, pussy-ass ho," he spat.

"Fuck you. Real men don't hit women," she mumbled under her breath, thinking he didn't hear her.

NJ snickered because she had lost her rabbit-ass mind. He decided to let her slide with her slick comment. "Start acting like one instead of a little-ass girl and I would treat you like one."

Jazz was livid. In her mind she felt like she was a woman because she was shaped like one, but mentally she was still a child and had a hard time expressing her feelings. His comment bruised her mentally.

"Fuck you, pussy-ass nigga. Maybe if you had a daddy you would know how to treat me."

Jazz had officially crossed the line, and she knew it when he asked her to repeat herself. "What the fuck did you just say?"

If she had any street knowledge she would've known there was one thing you never call a man, and that was it. She should've spit in his face for that matter, because that was exactly what it felt like.

"You heard me." She wasn't about to repeat herself. She could see the veins pop in his forehead and neck. She knew she went way beyond her boundaries and it was about to get ugly. He walked up to her and grabbed her by her hair.

"Repeat what you just said."

"NJ, let go of my hair, I'm not playing with you," she demanded.

"What the fuck you gon' do? I bought this muthafuckin' hair, and I'll snatch yo' ass bald in this bitch."

She stood motionless, not thinking things would turn out this way. Jazz was used to throwing tantrums and getting her way, but that wasn't working today.

"I knew you wanted a nigga who was gon' beat yo' ass."

Jazz began to shed tears in hopes he would release the hold he had on her.

"Bitch, fuck your tears. You wasn't crying when you was talking that shit."

He snatched her head back and squeezed her jaw. "Now, try me again and I'll break your face. I'll have you in this bitch eating from a straw."

He let her go, but he hit her in the eye in the process, causing her to scream and cover her face. Jazz walked away broken and confused. She had officially created a monster with her little girl ways.

NJ had mommy abandonment issues, and that caused him to be disrespectful to women. His foster mothers weren't motherly at all, and he was only used for the sake of getting a check. So, at a young age he decided women weren't shit. He had multiple chicks on his dick, and they all knew their roles. There was no main chick on the roster, but Jazz was the one he spent most of his time with.

Jazz was a submissive bitch who got out of line every now and again with her flip lip. He let her slide one too many times, but today she wasn't so lucky. He watched as she looked into the mirror, checking for a bruise. He giggled on the inside. *That will teach you about getting slick, dumb-ass bitch! You got a real nigga fucked up!*

He lay back on the bed and started messaging a chick in his DM on Instagram. "It goes down in the DM," he sang.

Between the pop-up visit from his estranged father and the bullshit with Jazz, he didn't want to fuck her no more. So he hit up another chick he was smashing to take his mind off the drama unfolding.

Chapter 8

Quamae was just leaving his attorney's office to make sure Sasha received the divorce papers before she left the hospital and went MIA. He wanted to end the marriage as soon as possible. There was no need to keep pussy-footing around because there would be no counseling sessions to repair something that was permanently ruined. He walked through the glass doors and out onto the street, en route to the parking garage. His mind was elsewhere when someone grabbed his arm. He turned around with his hand on his gun, ready to blast. When he saw the woman in front of him posed no threat, he moved his hand. It was hot as hell outside and she was dressed in layers of clothing with a bandana on her head. She looked every bit of 100 years old.

"I didn't mean to startle you, son, but the Lord wants me to tell you to be careful." Her voice was old and shaky.

"What?"

She could tell he was confused by the expression on his face. "Someone close to you is trying to kill you." Quamae just stood there in a daze. "You need to pray and cover yourself in the blood of Jesus if you want to live and raise those babies."

The message sent chills all over his body. He snatched his hand away from her and backed up slowly. It was evident she was a dingbat wearing all those damn clothes in 100-degree weather, but something about that message felt surreal.

She had a small bag clutched in her hands she had just pulled from her bosom. Stepping closer to him, she dumped the powdery contents into her hand and blew it on his clothing. "Don't ignore God's angel. I'm telling you what I know."

He jogged toward the garage, but he could hear her still shouting.

"I am the voice. I am the way, and you can't run from death."

Quamae got into his truck and went to meet up with Dirty. On his way there, he didn't play any music. The car was completely silent. Everything about that encounter was bad, and he could still feel her clammy hands on his skin. Whatever she threw on him wasn't visible.

He arrived quickly at the trap house, and like always Dirty was sitting on the porch in his favorite chair. He walked up and sat across from him with a spooked look on his face. Dirty peeped it right away.

"What's up, my G? You looking crazy as fuck."

"Bruh, some crazy shit just happened to me."

"What's that?"

Quamae replayed everything that happened with the dingbat lady, including the dust she blew on him. Dirty sat there looking crazy as hell, scratching his head.

"That's some wild shit, my G. You scared?"

"Hell nah, but I ain't gon' lie, she spooked the fuck out ya boy." He laughed it off. "But I don't believe in that voodoo shit, so it's all good."

Dirty's eyes shifted toward the road at the car coming up the street. "Don't be mad at me, my G."

"About what?"

He nodded toward the car when it got closer. "About who pulling up." Things hadn't been the same since their fallout, and he was hoping he could get them to squash the beef. A crew torn apart in the midst of a war was a crew destined to fall. They still had unresolved beef with the niggas from the east, and now was not the time for inside beef.

"So you set this shit up?" He was the last person he wanted to see.

"Yeah, man, just be cool. The man wanted to holla at you about the shit, but he know you ain't fuckin' with him."

"You muthafuckin' right I ain't. Fuck that nigga."

Chauncey walked up toward the porch, but stopped when he saw Quamae rise to his feet. Today was not the day he would catch him off guard. Dirty inched a little closer to make sure no blows were thrown. He placed his hand on Quamae's shoulder.

"Ain't no fighting today. I called y'all both here to clear the air and squash the beef."

"I ain't squashing shit with this bitch-ass nigga," Quamae spat. "Loyalty don't mean shit to him, and I don't trust this muthafucka."

Chauncey nodded his head and let him get that anger off his chest before he responded. "Come on now, Q, you know I ain't no bitch-ass nigga. We grew up together, so you know what it is. I understand you mad, but ain't no need to get out of pocket with the disrespect. I fucked up. I know I did. I should've never hit your wife, and believe me, it wasn't on purpose."

"You damn right you fucked up, nigga, and I'm calling it like I see it."

Chauncey put his hand on his chest. "Oh, so I'm a bitch now?" he chuckled a little bit. Not because it was funny, but because he insulted him once again. "Well, maybe if you didn't wife that ho we wouldn't be having this conversation right now."

That was a low blow, and Chauncey knew it. Quamae reached for the pistol tucked in his waistband, and so did Chauncey. It happened quickly, like some shit off a western movie. They aimed to fire at each other.

This had Dirty astounded. He backed up a little bit in case they decided to open fire.

"Come on, man, y'all boys put that heat down."

They both ignored his pleas for peacemaking. Their eyes were locked on one another, waiting for the moment to see who would blast first. They were once friends, but quickly turned into enemies. Nobody flinched 'cause if they did, that meant lights out.

Chauncey broke the silence. "Nigga this how you wanna do this? You gone let that ho mess up what we had."

Dirty peeped a truck coming up the street. "Put those guns down, man, somebody coming up the block."

Quamae gritted his teeth and eased his finger on the trigger, never taking his eyes off the man he would've given a kidney to. "Nigga, you messed up what we had."

Boca! Boca! Boca! Boca!

***

"Mr. Joyner, the doctor is signing off on the paperwork for her release."

Blue smiled at the nurse. "Thanks. I really appreciate all you've done."

"You're very welcome. I'll be back soon with the discharge papers." She turned on her heel and exited the room.

Sasha stepped from the bathroom after changing her clothes. "Are you excited about going home with me?"

She approached him, stood in between his legs, and ran her hands through his dreads. "I'm ecstatic. Are you happy I'm coming home to you?"

"Hell yeah." He blushed, running his hands up her thighs and stopping in between her legs to rub her fat cat. "Damn, I can't wait to get in this."

That made her giggle. "You are so nasty."

"Nah, I'm so damn horny. It's been a whole month since I got some pussy."

She pulled his hair gently, raising his head to hers. "You sure about that?"

"Hell yeah."

Meeting him halfway, she kissed him on his soft lips. "Better be."

"Now, I did have a bitch trying to give me some pussy, but I turned the bitch down. That ho wasn't worth the trouble." He was referring to Carmen. Sasha was oblivious to the fact her so-called friend was trying to fuck her man.

A knock on the door put an end to his confession. "Come in," she yelled.

An officer walked into the room and Blue was pissed instantly. He was about to put an end to the bullshit early. "We're not answering anymore questions, so please let yourself out."

The officer ignored Blue and focused on the woman in front of him. "Sasha Banks."

"Yes."

He passed her a manila envelope, and as soon as it touched her hand, he nodded. "You've been served."

"What?"

"Have a nice day, ma'am." The officer left the room quickly.

"What is that?" Blue asked.

"I don't know." She opened the envelope and pulled out the paperwork. Her eyes were moving back and forth across the paper. Blue looked on until her eyes stopped moving. She exhaled and placed the papers back into the envelope.

"What does it say?"

"They're divorce papers. Quamae filed for divorce."

Sadness took over her happy moment when it shouldn't have. If her memory was intact, she would've been rejoicing at the good news. Blue was aware she hadn't regained her memory, but he didn't like the fact her mood shifted the way it did. Dealing with her situation was going to require a lot of patience, because clearly she forgot a divorce was on the way before the accident. He took a deep breath and put his feelings on the backburner. That was the only way he could help her remember her past.

He lifted her chin. "Are you okay?"

"Yeah, just surprised, that's all."

"Don't be. This was already in the making before the accident. Remember, this is what you wanted. You had already made the decision to leave and to move out the house."

"But isn't that where they found me?"

"Yes, but you wasn't living there."

Sasha tilted her head to the side. "So why was I there?"

The day had Blue in his feelings, and he definitely didn't want to bring that back up, but he didn't have a choice. "That's what I was trying to figure out myself. I went there to look for you, and when I saw your car there, I flipped out. I was beating on the door, but no one answered." He shrugged his shoulders. "I guess you were already in the hospital at that time."

"Is my car still there?"

"I guess so. I haven't been back over there to check."

"Do you have my keys?"

"No. I think Carmen has that stuff, so you might want to call her and get it back."

"Can we go today?"

"You don't need to be driving in your condition, but we can get it at a later date."

"Okay." She agreed.

The nurse was just returning with the discharge papers and instructions. She handed them to Blue. "She may need psychotherapy to help her get through the trauma she suffered. We provided some of those services, but we are limited to what we can do here. I'm pretty sure her nightmares will continue to surface. We would normally prescribe medicine for pain, sleep, anxiety and PTSD, but since she's preganant, all she can take is Tylenol and Benadryl."

"What is PTSD?"

"Post Traumatic Stress Disorder. It's when someone suffers from a life-threatening episode, such as what she went through. If her symptoms worsen, bring her back to the ER."

"Okay, I will, thanks."

"You're welcome." She gave Sasha a hug. "Get better, sweetie."

"I'll try."

On the way outside, Sasha held onto Blue's arm tightly, as if he was about to run away. "Are you okay?" he asked.

"Will you always protect me?"

"Of course I will. You don't have to ask that."

"You promise?"

"Yes. What's wrong? You afraid of that nigga?"

She nodded her head up and down. "He's capable of doing a lot of damage to me."

"You don't have to worry about that nigga from this day on, and that's a promise." Blue's phone vibrated in his pocket. "Hold up, bae, let me get this." He dug in his pocket to answer the call. "What's up?" They continued walking until they made it to his truck. "Everything good?" he asked, waiting on a response. "A'ight, bet. Holla at me when it's done."

Sasha waited until he was off the phone. "Can I use your phone?"

"Who you calling?"

"Carmen."

He frowned. "For what?"

"I need to see if she has my keys."

Blue passed her the phone. "Block my number, 'cause I don't need her calling me."

Sasha dialed the number and waited on her to pick up.

"Hello?" Carmen answered.

"Are you at home?"

"Who is this?"

"Sasha."

"Oh, hey boo. Yes, I'm home. What's up?"

"Do you have the keys to my car?" She was hoping she hadn't lost them, but who knows because she couldn't remember a damn thing.

"Yeah, and I got your purse, too."

"Okay, I'm on my way to get it."

"You're out the hospital?"

"They just discharged me."

"Oh, that is so good to hear. I missed you like crazy."

"Well, why haven't you been back to see me?"

"That's another story that we'll talk about later."

"Alright, I'll be there in like 30 minutes."

"Okay."

After they hung up, Blue had an attitude, but he couldn't let her see it because that would only create questions he wasn't prepared to answer.

Sasha passed him back the phone. "She lives in Pembroke Pines, not too far from where I used to live."

"Yeah."

Blue wasn't too happy about seeing Carmen's face, especially after she pulled that ho stunt. All he could do was suck it up at the moment, but after today he wouldn't have to worry about them ever crossing paths, and he would make sure of that.

When they finally reached Carmen's place, he parked the truck and kept it running as an indication they wouldn't be staying long. He looked over at her. "Grab your stuff and come right back. I need to get you in the house."

"Alright."

Sasha noticed Carmen was standing outside talking to a very tall, handsome, well dressed white man. Blue shook his head.

"This ho gotta be selling pussy," he mumbled under his breath.

Sasha got out of the truck and approached them. She was greeted with a hug. "Stan, this is my sister, Sasha."

"Nice to meet you," he replied.

"Likewise," she smiled.

Stan grabbed Carmen's hand. "I will see you tonight."

Carmen was blushing big time. "You surely will."

"Okay, I must get going. I have a business meeting at two. It was nice to finally meet you, Sasha."

"Same here," she lied. Carmen had never told her about Stan, but it was clear she had been a part of their pillow talk. They watched as Stan got into his black Maserati and took off. Sasha couldn't wait to question her.

"Who was that?"

"This guy I met at the courthouse while I was paying my ticket. He's a lawyer."

"Clearly."

"I think I like him."

"Yeah, right. You never like anybody."

"Un-uh, Sasha, he's different and divorced."

Sasha tooted up her nose. "Really?"

"Yes. I think I may keep this one."

"We'll see, 'cause you change men like you change your drawers." Their small talk was cut short when Blue honked the horn. Sasha looked back and held up one finger. "I'll call you later, because somebody is ready to go."

Carmen gave her another hug. "Yeah, I can see that somebody is a little impatient."

"He is trying to get me in the house."

Carmen laughed. "I bet. That man want some ass, as long as he been waiting on you to get out the hospital."

Sasha walked away. "I love you."

"I love you, too."

Chapter 9

Dirty hit the pavement when more gunshots rang out. *Boca! Boca! Boca!* Looking across at Quamae, he knew his eyes were playing tricks on him. He and Chauncey were huddled in the corner together, letting off rounds toward the street. When Dirty peeked from behind the short brick wall that served as his shield, he recognized the truck behind all that gunfire.

"Man, who the fuck is these niggas?" Quamae spat.

"I don' know," Chauncey replied. "Probably Dred's peoples. You knew it wouldn't take long to figure this shit out."

"Them niggas don't know 'bout this spot, though." Quamae looked toward the truck to see if he could recognize any faces. The sun was halfway down, making it difficult to make out a face.

"When the shots stop, we need to hit it indoors." Dirty was ready to make a mad dash inside. He left his piece sitting on the counter.

"Fuck that; when I start shooting, y'all hit it in the house." Chauncey slid over to the edge and opened fire so Quamae and Dirty could get inside. The men in the truck took cover, then Chauncey slid in after them.

Dirty peeped through the blinds and saw two bodies get out of the truck toting some big shit — a machine gun, to be exact. The figures in the dark were familiar. Everything about their stature made them recognizable, even in the dark. "These niggas got a machine gun."

"What niggas?" Quamae needed answers.

As soon as he backed away from the window, a hail of bullets came through, shattering the windows and the front door. One of the bullets whizzed by Quamae's head, putting a hole in the flat screen. He stretched out on the floor.

The drive-by lasted for all of three minutes, but it felt like forever when the rabbit had the gun. The shots finally came to an end and all that could be heard were tires burning rubber leaving the scene.

"Who was the niggas?" Chauncey got up off the floor and brushed his pants off.

"That nigga Blue's homeboy." Dirty headed toward the door and peeped outside. "He did this shit. I saw him and the nigga that robbed me at Dred's house."

Quamae's wheels were turning in his head. "What the fuck him and that nigga doing together?"

"I don' know, my G."

"That's how them niggas knew where to find us." Chauncey put the blame on Dirty. "That's yo' muthafuckin' homeboy. Ol' friendly-ass nigga."

"Fuck you, nigga. I ain't friendly." The whole situation was fucking with his head, but he couldn't let them see him sweat. "So, what y'all gon' do?"

"What the fuck you mean *y'all*, nigga?" Chauncey didn't like the sound of that shit. "You mean we, nigga. What, you scared of these niggas?"

"Bruh, I ain't scared of no nigga that bleed like me."

"Well, act like it, then." He walked away to calm himself down. "The fuck you mean *y'all?* Like you don't know these muthafuckas."

"We gon' pull up on these niggas. Simple as that, but first I gotta call Freeman." Quamae pulled out his phone and hit him up. "Aye, we got a problem over here."

"Yeah, I heard. I'm headed over there now. Don't talk until I get there." Freeman had already gotten the call and was headed in that direction. "Don't forget the spot check. That place is about to be swarming with cops."

"A'ight." He hung the phone up and slid it back in his pocket. "Spot check troll on the way."

Dirty packed up their guns and the little bit of drugs left over in a duffle bag and took it to the next door neighbor's house. An old lady lived there, and because he always looked out for her, she allowed him to utilize her shed.

By the time he returned, Freeman and the gang were there, looking for evidence and asking questions about the shooter. Freeman pulled Quamae to the side to talk to him in private while the other two were hemmed up by the cops.

"Since the last meeting I have been doing a little research on Dred, and when I went to the hospital to question your wife I ran up on something interesting." He escorted Quamae toward his patrol car.

"And what's that?"

"Do you know somebody name Darian?"

"Nah," he had no idea who the hell he was talking about. "But what does that have to do with this?"

"Darian is your wife's boyfriend, and also Dred's nephew. I had a little run-in with him at the hospital. He took a swing at me, so I looked him up after the incident to see who he was. I don't know if any of this ties together, but we'll find out."

That name did not ring a bell for him at all. "What does he look like?"

"There's a folder in my backseat, but you know I can't hand it to you. So I'm going to place you back there and you can take a look."

Freeman opened the door and let him in. "I'll be back in five minutes."

"Yeah." Quamae sat down on the hard seat and closed the door. The suspense was killing him because Dred had never mentioned a nephew to him.

When he grabbed the folder and opened it, the first page was a complete shocker. Staring back at him on the mugshot was a picture of none other than Blue himself. "What the fuck?" he mumbled. "This ho sleeping with the enemy."

After being let out of the uncomfortable seat, he walked up to deliver the news to the boys. They were standing on the sidewalk so ballistics could collect the shell casings. "Y'all won't believe this knowledge I'm 'bout to drop." He looked around to make sure no one was listening. "That nigga Blue is Dred's nephew."

"Get the fuck outta here," Chauncey replied.

"No bullshit. I just saw the shit in the folder Freeman showed me." Then he looked at Dirty. "You knew that shit?"

"Hell nah. That shit new to me. Me and the nigga never talked about business or any other personal shit," he continued to ramble on. "I didn't even know about him and Sasha until you told me."

Chauncey didn't believe one word the nigga was saying. He mugged him. "So you mean to tell me this nigga sat with you and gambled all fuckin' day and not once did he mention Dred being his uncle?"

"Nah, man, the nigga was private like that."

Chauncey smirked. "Yeah, I bet he was." He looked over at Quamae. "Listen, bruh, I know you mad at me and I don't blame you, but right now ain't the time for it. I fucked up, like I said earlier, and I'm sorry. You gotta believe me on that. We was fucked up after you got shot." He placed his hand on his shoulder. "We were trying to comfort each other, and one thing led to another. It was wrong, and if I could take it back, I would."

The words seemed sincere, but that video said different. *If it were truly a mistake, then why the extra affection on the porch?* Quamae thought to himself, but he didn't have the answer to that question. For now he would let that go because Blue was trying to take him out, and he wasn't going out like that. He needed his fake homies in his corner to take Blue out first.

"I'ma let that shit ride for now because we got bigger issues than someone I don't want. We'll address that shit another day, but as of right now we gotta find this nigga."

The two of them embraced in a brotherly hug. Dirty sat back and watched with nothing to say.

"Oh yeah, I got the address of them niggas who shot me in the sports bar. The niggas from Opa-Locka."

"Well, let's run down on them pussies, then." Chauncey was hyped. "And I'm talkin' 'bout tonight." He clapped his hands together. "You wit' it?"

Quamae didn't hesitate. "Hell yeah, let's roll. Dirty, go grab our shit out the neighbor's yard. It's about to be Fourth of July in Dade once again."

As soon as Dirty disappeared behind the bushes, Chauncey looked at Quamae and spoke loud enough for only him to hear. "We need to watch that nigga. Something about this impromptu meeting for me and you ain't sitting right with me."

"Yeah I know. I was thinking the same thing. The trap house fucked up and he don't have nowhere to go, so I'ma take the nigga to the crib and keep an eye out on him."

"Good, and if you notice anything funny, I'm taking the nigga out with no explanation."

They fist bumped. "No doubt. Ain't no room for snakes in this camp."

"Damn right, nigga, and it's time to cut the grass."

"As a matter of fact, let's wait on hitting them niggas up. I got a plan."

"Okay. Whatever you say, I'm wit' it."

"Cool."

As promised, Quamae took Dirty back to his home to keep an eye on him. That was the only way to get the truth behind the shooting.

"You straight, bruh?" Quamae asked while standing at the bar in his den, fixing a drink. Dirty appeared to be in deep thought and too quiet for comfort.

"Yeah, I'm cool," he huffed. "It's been a crazy night, that's all."

"You right about that." He took a shot. "You want one?"

"Yeah."

He slid him a miniature glass filled almost to the rim and Dirty downed it. "You think this had something to do with Dred?"

"Shit, I thought it was until yo' homeboy upped that fie. I don't know what to think now, but I will say it's some foul shit going on."

The stare he gave Dirty was cold as ice, causing him to look away. He was intimidated by Quamae's gangsta nature. He knew he could be ruthless when necessary. It was like Quamae could see straight through the bullshit. Apprehension shook his body like a stripper's first night on a pole. "I ain't have nothing to do with that. You know that, right?" He looked in his direction, but not at his face.

"I ain't say you did." Quamae sat back and observed his every move. What was amazing was the fact he couldn't look in his eyes. Not even once. They had been friends long enough to know he was feeling guilty about something. Snakes and fakes couldn't handle eye contact. "But if you need to get something off ya' chest, then say it." Quamae wanted him to come clean about anything he was keeping a secret. He felt it deep in his gut, and nine times out of ten his gut was right on the money.

"Nah, we good. We just gotta get to the bottom of this shit."

"Dat part." He cut his eyes and headed to his room. "Sleep easy."

"You, too."

Quamae went to his room and locked the door behind him. One thing he couldn't stand was a lying-ass, snake-ass nigga, and his boy was on the radar. He could deal with a thief on any given day because he knew what to expect. Liars, on the other hand, couldn't be trusted, and he never knew what to expect.

Sitting down on the edge of the bed, he sat his gun on the nightstand. "Nigga, you better be praying to God I don't find out he was involved in this shit."

To him, Dirty wasn't a threat, but right now be couldn't be trusted either.

Sleep was hit-and-miss that night. It was impossible to sleep under the same roof as your frienemy.

***

Sasha lazily blinked her eyes and saw a dark shadow staring at her. She was too shocked to open her mouth because she couldn't believe her eyes.

"What's wrong, baby? You act like you just seen a ghost."

Afraid of what might happen next, she reached for her phone, but Quamae snatched it quickly.

"No, no, no. You won't be needing this. What's wrong?" he smirked. "I came to check on you. You know, to see how you were doing. From the look of things, it doesn't seem like you're doing too well." Quamae stroked her hair and it sent chills down her spine. Her heart began to race and her breathing picked up heavily. Sasha felt like she was about to go into cardiac arrest at any moment. She was scared to death, fearing what he would do to her.

"Calm down before you have a panic attack," he whispered softly. "Do you know why I'm here?"

Sasha shook her head no, then he leaned in closer to her. "I'm sorry, but I can't hear you. Could you speak up please?" He was really getting a kick out of seeing her sweat.

"No," she replied.

"How is my daughter?"

"What daughter?"

"The one you carrying." He rubbed her stomach, causing her to cringe. "You claimed it was mine."

"And you said it wasn't. Just leave me the fuck alone and go worry about that bitch Gigi and her baby, because my baby has a daddy."

He cut her off quickly. "Shut up, ho! It's your fault you're in the predicament you're in now. If you weren't busy fucking every nigga that spoke to your slimy-ass, none of this shit would have happened. But no, you had to open your legs for every Tom, Chauncey and Blue."

"Fuck you," she shouted. "She ain't your baby."

Quamae reached into his waistband and placed the barrel of his pistol on top of her forehead. "Ho, who the fuck you think you talking to? I will splatter your brain all over this pillow."

She knew he wouldn't hesitate at the chance to kill her because she had come so close in the past, but the location was too risky. There was no way he would risk getting caught.

"So, you gon' shoot me?"

"Ho, do I look stupid to you?" He put his gun away, then stepped in closer and placed both hands around her neck. Quamae squeezed her tight, using every muscle in his body. Sasha kicked her legs and tried to release his hands from the base of her neck by biting him. Strength like the hulk came from somewhere, because she was able to get free long enough to let out a deadly scream.

Blue shook Sasha from her nightmare. "Baby, relax, relax. It was just a dream."

Her forehead was dripping in sweat and her heart was beating out of whack. Blue pulled her close and rocked her gently. "It's okay, baby. I'm here. I'm not gon' let anything happen to you. I promise."

"It's like he was in here, and he was trying to kill me. I was so scared," she whined.

"You don't have to worry about him ever putting his hands on you. I'll kill that nigga before I let him hurt you again."

After getting her to relax, he got up to get her Benadryl and bottled water from the kitchen. Back in the room, he was prepared to take care of his girl. "Come on, bae. Get up and take your medicine so you can get some sleep."

Sasha sat up and did as she was instructed, and thirty minutes later she was out cold. Blue cuddled up behind her so she wouldn't feel alone. For him, this was the worst feeling, to watch her go through something so traumatic and he couldn't do anything to stop it. The only thing he could do was help her get through it. There wasn't a doubt in his mind about who was responsible, but he already had that taken care of. He just needed confirmation.

The following afternoon Blue and Quint were sitting out back by the pool. This had become their new meeting spot so they could talk in private.

"Did you handle that business? I didn't get a call, so I'm in the dark right now."

"Yeah, but it wasn't a successful hit."

Blue's eyebrows slanted down. "What the fuck is that supposed to mean?"

"It was a miss."

"Damn, what the fuck? Y'all niggas need target practice or some shit?"

"Shit was crazy."

"Damn, I gotta do the shit myself."

"Somebody gotta be praying for them niggas, 'cause there is no way they was supposed to survive."

Blue was past pissed off, and it showed on his distraught face. "Or that nigga tipped 'em off."

"Bruh, chill. It's gon' get done."

"Facts." The whole cat and mouse game was getting out of hand, and he was ready to put that shit to an end.

The sliding glass door caught their attention. It was Sasha, walking toward them with a plate of food on a tray. "Sorry to interrupt, baby, but your food is done." She had prepared his favorite meal: steak, shrimp, and a loaded baked potato.

Quint hollered as if a joke was just told. "Damn, my nigga, you got it like that?"

"Damn right, nigga. I take care of home."

Sasha smiled and sat the tray in front of him. "Yes, he does. Hey, Quint."

"What's up, sis? This nigga got you slaving over the stove, huh?"

"I gotta feed my man. You want a plate?"

"Hell yeah. That shit smells good as fuck."

"Bae, you can't be feeding this nigga. He like a stray dog. Feed 'im one time and he won't leave."

"There's an extra room he can sleep in."

Quint laughed. "Tell his ass."

She placed her hand on her stomach. "I'll be right back."

"You ready to have that baby yet?"

"I wish," she replied before walking away.

Blue looked over his shoulder. "Bae, bring me something to drink, please."

"Okay." Sasha closed the door behind her.

"Bruh, you got ya'self a real one."

Blue blushed, showing all of his teeth. "That's that baby."

Quint squinted his eyes and got up in Blue's face, taking him by surprise.

"What the hell you doing?" He stuck a shrimp in his mouth.

"Every time you talk about her you get this twinkle in your eyes."

"Get the fuck outta here with that shit."

"Naw, dawg, I'm serious." He observed him once more. "You in love, ain't it?" This was a side of him that had yet to be seen. Out of all the years they'd been friends, he never acted this way toward any female. He was too busy sticking and moving, not giving a fuck about feelings.

"Hell yeah. I love that girl."

"Aww, that's so cute." He reached up to touch him, but Blue slapped his hand away.

"Man, g'on with that gay shit." He joked around because his hitter was far from gay.

"Damn, she gotta be sucking the skin off that dick, licking balls and ass."

Blue responded with a mouth full of food. "I don' play those ass games."

"On a serious note, though, how she doing?"

"She's okay. I can't get her to sit down and rest."

"Yeah, 'cause I was about to say she shouldn't be cooking."

"She won't sit still."

"Oh."

Sasha walked over and handed Quint a tray as well. She looked at her man and he was demolishing his food. "Is it good, bae?"

"Hell yeah. Did you eat yet?"

"No."

"You need to go and feed my baby."

"We're about to eat now."

They cleaned their plates, leaving nothing behind except for the bone, shrimp tails, and potato skins. Blue stretched. "Damn, that hit the spot."

Quint didn't respond because he was in deep thought. "You think that's yo' baby?"

"I don' know. It's a strong possibility. I was hittin' her raw out the gate."

"Bullshit." If he didn't know anything else, he knew Blue wasn't raw-dogging nothing. Unsafe sex wasn't his thing. "I know you strapped up, Magnum King."

He twisted one of his dreads. "G-shit, bruh. The first time I hit her I had on one, but I snatched that bitch off when the shit got good."

"You had to be feeling her."

"Had to 'cause she was still with her nigga, but they wasn't fucking, though."

"Yeah, right. All females say that shit that live with a nigga."

That comment brought him back to reality. Blue sighed. "I want the baby, so I ain't stressing."

"You gon' get a test done, right?"

"It is what it is. I'ma still be with her, regardless."

"I just don't want to see you hurt if she ain't yours." He objected to the fact he didn't want to get tested, but he wanted to be supportive to his friend, so he left it alone.

"Bruh, I don't see myself leaving her. So, technically it don't matter if she mine or not. I love the mama, so I gotta love the baby."

"That's real, nah. Whatevea makes you happy, bruh, I'm all for it."

"I appreaciate that."

"It's all love."

"I'm 'bout to clear it. I got a lil' baddie I'm 'bout to slide up in." They both stood up and did their handshake once more.

"Nigga, you ain't the only one with a baddie. Mine in the house and I got a baby to feed when I get in there." They both laughed.

"I'll get up wit' you later."

"Fo' sho."

Chapter 10
Two weeks later

Sasha lay in bed and watched the *Criminal Minds* marathon while she waited on Blue to get home. The transition was rough at first, but he made sure she was comfortable. She was slowly remembering things, and some were hard pills to swallow. She pulled the comforter over her body and dialed Carmen's number, thinking she could put things in perspective.

"What's up, chick?" There were some rustling noises in the background.

"What are you doing?"

Carmen held the phone with her ear so she could retrieve her keys from her purse. "Walking out the store."

"What store?"

"7-Eleven." She managed to get the keys out and unlock the car door.

"Where are you going, home?" Sasha asked.

"I have a few errands to run and then I'll be finished. Why?" Carmen threw the bags onto the passenger seat and got in the car.

"I haven't heard from you in a while. What's up with that?"

"Well, every time I did call you, paw patrol said you were asleep."

"Who the hell is paw patrol?" she laughed.

"Your boyfriend. Have you talked to India yet?" There was some juicy shit she needed to find out about, and she didn't want to elaborate on Blue.

"No." She paused and spoke slowly. "Why was I supposed to talk to her?"

"I'll let her tell you."

"Tell me what?"

"She said she called you, but you didn't answer."

"Well, let me call her, 'cause you acting like you can't say nothing."

"You know, she wanted you to be the first to know. Besides, she'll kill me if she knew I told you. So call her now. Smooches." Carmen ended the call quickly.

Sasha was anxious to find out what was going on, so she called India right away. India picked up on the first ring. "Bitch, where have you been? I've been calling you all morning."

"I was asleep."

"Girl, I'm so pissed I can fuck a bitch up right now." There was a lot of hostility in her voice.

"What happened?"

"Okay, Steve spent the night with me last night. So this morning I dropped my car off to get an oil change at the dealership. After we left there, we went by my shop. While we are sitting in there some lady walks in throwing a fit. Now, of course I'm lost, but Steve looked like he saw a fucking ghost. She slapped him and was like *is she the reason you can't come home at night?* So I step in and say *hold the fuck up, what the hell is going on? Better yet, who the fuck are you?* She says she is his wife."

Sasha let out a slight scream while cupping her hand over her mouth. "Hell no!" She couldn't believe Steve was married and little miss prissy didn't know it.

"Yes, bitch! Then this motherfucka had the nerve to just sit there looking stupid."

"So he didn't say shit?"

"Hell no. Then this crazy bitch talking about how she been following him and she knows where I live and all this crazy shit. I told both of those crazy bitches to get the fuck out of my shop before I catch a case."

"Girl, I can't believe Steve. Are you okay?"

"Yes, I'm fine. It's no big deal."

She knew India was lying and very good at hiding her feelings, so she had to ask her again just to make sure. "Quit trying to be so tough all the time and holding stuff in." There was silence on the phone. "India!" she yelled.

"I'm still here."

Sasha knew she was trying to keep from crying, but she could hear it in her voice. "Are you still at the shop?"

"No, I'm home."

"What about your appointments for today?"

"Peaches is going to take care of everything for me."

"Okay, well, sit tight. I'm on my way over there."

"Are you sure you can drive?"

"Yeah, bitch, I ain't brain dead."

"Alright, I'll be here."

An hour later Sasha and Carmen were on India's front porch, waiting on her to open the door. The sun was beaming and they were getting impatient. She finally staggered to the door and opened it.

"Damn, girl, took long enough. All this chocolate is about to melt," Carmen said as she barged in. "And I know you not sitting around here moping. I say we get up and go kick his ass."

"Hell yeah!" Sasha agreed while giving her a high five, knowing damn well she was in no shape to cause any trouble.

"Don't worry, sis, we'll think of a master plan to make you feel better," Carmen added.

India sat on the couch Indian-style. "He's been blowing up my cell phone and house phone. He is driving me crazy trying to apologize and justify the situation."

"That's bullshit, and don't fall for it, either." Carmen had zero tolerance for the lies, and she would dismiss a nigga quickly for it. She wasn't afraid to drop one and move on to the next one.

India folded her arms. "I'm not fucking with him after all of this shit." Tears started to build up in her eyes. "I didn't even know he was married."

India sobbed and cried for 15 minutes straight before Carmen grew irritated.

"Fuck that shit! India, get over it, okay? So what if he's fucking married? You'll live. You act like he was the only piece of dick in the universe." She stood up and paced the floor. "Crying over spilled milk and shit."

She looked up at Carmen with the most evil look, and if looks could kill, Carmen would've been laid out on the floor. "Fuck you, Carmen. You always have some slick shit to say."

"No, bitch, don't fuck me, fuck that no-good married nigga."

Sasha intervened because she knew her girl could be insensitive at times. "Stop it, Carmen, you know that's not right. We are supposed to be helping her through this."

"I'm sick of this bullshit. She always parading around like she found herself a gold fucking medal, but ended up with a piece of shit. Now, if you want to fuck up his world, then let's do it. If not, shut the fuck up."

"Bitch, if you don't shut up…"

"*What?* What the fuck you gon' do? I will drag your ass all up and through here."

Sasha was getting sick of her mouth. "Carmen, shut up before I slap the shit out of you. This is really pissing me off, and I'm not in the mood." Sasha sat back down and so did Carmen.

"See, this is why I don't have a man. I don't have time for heartbreaks and all that stupid shit that comes with it," Carmen continued to rant and rave.

India retaliated. "No, you don't have a man because you too busy fucking everybody else's man."

"Damn right, but let me tell you the difference between me and you. I fuck and get paid. You fucked and got played. After he done with you, he goes home to his wife and kids. Now what?"

Those words cut her deep, and she didn't know what to say. Before she knew it, India hauled off and slapped the hell out of her. Carmen slapped her back, and they wrestled with one another. Sasha jumped in the middle of them to stop them from fighting.

By the time she got them to calm down and relax, which was an hour later, they were able to come up with the perfect plan to execute. When they finished with Steve, he'd be divorced before he knew what hit him.

The first thing they did was buy a pregnancy test and have Sasha pee on it. He was gonna pay severely for the pain he had caused.

India then handwrote a letter to his wife telling her about her husband's baby she was carrying. The letter also included she would be expecting child support, and they could discuss paternity matters with her attorney. The only thing left to do was sit back and watch her plan unfold. She wasn't about to be the only one with a broken heart.

***

"It's a girl," Dr. Joyner shouted.

Quamae hung his head in disappointment. He just knew it was going to be a boy. Gigi, on the other hand, didn't care if it was a boy or girl, as long as it was a healthy baby from her man.

All he could do was rub his head and pout like baby. "Doc, you gotta be kidding me."

"What's wrong, daddy? You're not happy with the news?" Dr. Joyner asked.

Gigi wiped the blue gel off of her stomach and tried to sit up on the table. "He's upset it's a girl."

Dr. Joyner laughed and gave Gigi a hand as she struggled to get up. "I can relate to that. My daddy had four girls and one boy. And we gave him a run for his money. Me, on the other hand, I have one son and he's 22. I thank God every day that he gave me a son."

Quamae smiled. "I'm not upset because we can just try again." He winked at Gigi. From the sounds of it, it looked like their relationship was going to be a promising one. "I'm just thinking about how all three of my girls are going to drive me insane."

She scratched her head and immediately thought he had other kids. If her memory served her correctly, this was her patient's first pregnancy. "Oh, you have other kids?"

"No, ma'am. I'm talking about her," he pointed at Gigi, "our baby, and my baby sister. A boy would've carried my name and legacy. All girls want to do is get married and drop their daddy's name."

Gigi looked at Quamae with googly eyes. She was so in love with that man, and now they could work on their relationship.

"It's going to be okay."

"I can't argue with that," she laughed.

During the car ride home, Quamae appeared to be in deep thought, and that was because he hadn't been honest with Gigi about what had been going on. He tried pushing the thought out of his head, but it continued to resurface. When he stopped at the red light, he turned off the music.

"There's something I need to tell you that I haven't been honest with you about."

Fear immediately stepped in to dampen her perfectly good day. She shifted in her seat and folded her arms. She was ready to go off like the missing link. "It better not be about that bitch," she warned.

"Nah, man, it ain't nothing like that." Her response caused him to have second thoughts, but in the event something happened to him, he didn't want her in the blind. "About two weeks ago I was leaving my attorney's office and this weird old lady grabbed my hand and said someone close was trying to kill me. She blew some dust on me and I walked off. Not even an hour later I get to the trap house to holla at Dirty and some niggas started shooting at us."

A concerned looked appeared on her face. She was upset it took so long for him to tell her, but nevertheless he was telling her, and that meant a lot. "Why didn't you tell me this weeks ago?"

"I didn't want you to panic. I don't need you stressing every time I walk out the door."

"But you're telling me now, so what's the difference?"

"You need to know just in case something happens to me. I'm just telling you to be on the safe side."

"So you think that lady put something on you?"

"I know she did. I just don't know what. Out of all the bullets that hit the house, none of them touched me." The light changed, so he pulled off. "Shit crazy, bae."

"Why don't we go and see my old pastor. I haven't been to church in a while, but we can stop by." She grabbed his hand and rubbed it. "Don't keep nothing like this away from me again, please. I've endured this pain with you before, in case you forgot. And I have gone through a lot to get you back, and now that I have you I refuse to lose you to street violence."

"Oh, so getting pregnant was the way to get me back?"

"No, we went half on this baby."

Quamae hadn't hustled on the dope tip for a while due to the current circumstances. He was missing out on money, but he definitely didn't lose any from his own pockets. If it wasn't for the weed plug, no income would be generating. It didn't bother him one way or the other since he was about to call it quits and go legit. The loyalty amongst his closest comrades was at stake. So his focus was on opening up a restaurant and lounge in order to clean that dirty money and walk the straight and narrow path. He managed to stash away 15 million dollars, so he was set.

After getting dressed, he headed out into the cool breeze to meet up with his financial consultant. It was time to make some changes for the greater good and his new family. There were two things guaranteed in the dope game: death or prison for life. Over the years he dodged both with a fine-toothed comb, but these days he felt like his luck was finally running out. He locked up the house and placed recording devices in the guestroom and den, since Dirty wasn't there, and went to handle his business. He was determined to get to the bottom of the shooting. Downtown Ft. Lauderdale was extremely crowded during the week. The courthouse was smack dead in the middle, so plenty of people were in and out all day. He parked in front of the tall glass building where the bank was located and put his money in the meter before heading inside to the visitor station.

"I'm here to see Jonathan. My appointment is at ten." The security guard gave him a visitor's badge and pointed him in the direction of the elevators.

Quamae stepped from the elevator when he reached the sixth floor, looking like a distinguished gentleman. He was wearing a three-piece Armani suit and dress shoes. Everything about him screamed success. The receptionist eyed his chocolate skin like she wanted a sample.

Her cheeks were flushed red as she stumbled over her words, trying to form a complete sentence. "Um. Hi. Hello. I mean, good morning. You must be Mr. Banks?"

"That would be me." He smiled.

"Mr. Silverstein is awaiting your arrival."

"Good," he smirked while adjusting his tie.

"Come on, right this way." She pranced down the hallway, putting an extra swish in her itty-bitty hips.

Quamae followed behind her, snickering on the inside. She was definitely not his cup of tea with her pale skin and flat booty, but he appreciated the flattery. She opened the door, then stepped to the side.

"Mr. Banks has arrived."

Mr. Silverstein waved his hand, signaling her to close the door. He ended the call he was on to acknowledge Quamae.

"What's up, my brother?" They shook hands. On the outside Jonathan was as white as could be, but on the inside lived a hood nigga. He stood at 5'11" with jet-black hair and blue eyes. From his appearance, no one would ever suspect he grew up in the projects.

"Shit, I can't call it. Ready to clean this money, though." He took a seat on the black leather chair.

"I know you are." He picked up a folder from the desk. "I have all the paperwork for the property, and all you have to do is sign."

He grabbed the folder and thumbed through the papers. "That easy, huh?"

"Hell yeah." He rubbed his chin. "You see this face? I get shit done," he joked. "All I had to do was create an inheritance letter saying you came into a large sum of money and that muthafucka's eyes lit up like he was on a molly."

"For the love of the dough, huh?" If Jonathan couldn't get it done, then it couldn't be done. That's how good he was at white-collar crimes.

"You got-damn right. I can sell a hooker this dick. That's how strong my game is."

Quamae cracked up. "Yo' mama should've never raised you in the hood."

"Shit, she couldn't help it. She got one piece of that black Mandingo and couldn't concentrate." He rocked in his chair with his hands behind his head. "There is one other thing. I don't think it's a good idea to pay cash for the place, so I put in a loan request for you, and they approved you for two hundred thousand." He paused when he saw the mug on Quamae's face and held his hand up. "Now, before you say anything, I did that to keep the feds off our asses. If this shit blows up, you and me will be in a federal penitentiary."

"Okay, that makes sense. Besides, I trust your judgement."

"Good, because I've never steered you wrong."

"Did you find out about the property?" Dirty was only there for two weeks, and he was ready for him to bounce. He didn't feel comfortable sleeping under the same roof with a potential traitor.

"Oh yeah, the owner lost the place due to a foreclosure, and you can grab that now if you like."

"What's the asking price?"

"They want one hundred thousand, but I think I can get them to sell it for eighty cash."

"Yeah, do that, and give me the forms to fill out."

He grabbed another folder and passed it to him. "It's already done, and the check for 25K is in there with it."

Quamae smiled and nodded his head. "I see you ain't fuckin' off."

"Nah, I know what you trying to do, so I pulled every string I could grab and made it happen."

Quamae grabbed a pen from his desk and signed his name on the promissory note. "I would love to stay and chop it up with you, but I'm on a mission." He stood up and shook Jonathan's hand. "The first bottle is on me when the spot opens up."

"I'm holding you to it."

He picked up the folder and headed out of the office. "I'll send back the forms when they are signed." He waved the folder in the air.

"Love you, man."

"Love you too, bruh."

***

When he arrived at Gigi's place, she was dressed and ready to go, staring at herself in the mirror. She was quite pleased at the way her pregnancy made her skin glow and filled her out in the right places. Quamae walked up behind her, placed both hands on her hips, and kissed her on the neck.

"Damn, you fine, bae. I wanna snatch this dress up off yo' ass right now."

She blushed and tilted her head back for a kiss. "Not right now, we have someplace to be."

"I have a surprise for you."

She turned around quickly. "Where is it?"

"In the truck." He looked down at her neck, admiring the fine piece of jewelry he purchased for her a few months back. "I love the necklace. It's about time you wear it."

"You do?" she played along. "My man bought it for me."

Downstairs in the truck, he grabbed the folder from the backseat and handed it to her. "Surprise."

She grabbed it, but she was hesitant about opening it. "Is this what I think it is?" Gigi was hoping it was the finalization of his divorce.

"I don't know. Why don't you open it and see."

Gigi opened the folder and examined the papers. She was confused when she saw her name. "Quamae, what is this?"

"I thought you went to college?" he chuckled.

"I did," she giggled, slapping his arm. "I see my name, but what does it mean?"

"That's the paperwork to your duplexes. You own them."

Gigi was ecstatic. "Are you serious? Don't play with me right now." She bounced up and down in the seat.

"G shit. I have to make sure you and baby are straight if anything happens to me."

"Don't talk like that. You ain't going nowhere."

"I have something else for you." He passed her an envelope.

When Gigi opened it up, she thought she would pass out at any moment. She pulled out a check with her name on it written in the sum of twenty-five thousand dollars. "Oh my God, you are the best, baby." She leaned over and gave him a kiss. "What did I do to deserve this?"

"Being the mother of my child." He grabbed her hand and kissed it. "Now you can quit your job. I told you I would take care of you. All you have to do is sign those papers, get you some tenants, and collect your rent money."

"You keep saying me. Isn't this our property?"

"Nope, that's all you. I don't get a cut. I bought this for you, so you don't have to worry about working anymore."

She thought about it long and hard, then stared into his brown eyes. "I'll put in my two weeks' notice when I go back to work."

"That's all I wanted to hear."

Thirty minutes later they pulled up in the church parking lot and got out. They held hands as they stood in front of the door. She looked up at him to gain his approval. "You ready to do this?"

"Ready as can be."

Quamae held the door open so she could walk in. They were greeted by Pastor Green as he walked down the aisle. "Gianni, how are you doing these days? I've been missing you at service."

The moment he kissed her on the cheek, Quamae's forehead wrinkled up while he cut his eyes at Gigi.

"Yeah, I know. I've been sinning, as you can see," she said while rubbing her belly.

"Well, babies are blessings, and we all fall short of the glory sometimes, but that doesn't mean we stop listening to his word or praising his name."

"I know, and I will do better. I promise"

"Good, 'cause there is always a place for you here. A place that does not judge and welcomes all sinners."

She turned her attention to her man. "Pastor Green, this is my boyfriend, Quamae."

They shook hands. "Nice to see you again, son. I see the two of you are back together. Hopefully I will be marrying you two real soon." He glanced at Gigi's round belly.

"We're working on it."

"I hope it's sooner than later, 'cause my God-daughter deserves the best." He turned around and escorted them to his office. "Follow me."

The Pastor's chamber was exquisite. It was furnished with cherry wood furniture, a matching desk and bookshelf. Quamae scoped the scene before pulling out a chair for Gigi, then sitting down beside her. Pastor Green folded his hands and placed them on the desk.

"From my understanding, Gianni tells me you are concerned about some hoodoo?"

"That's correct. I'm not a believer, but it did rattle me just a bit."

"Okay, so tell me what happened."

Quamae spent the next ten minutes giving the pastor the run-down on the dingbat with the powder and the edited version of the drive-by. There was no way he was sharing the real details with a man of the cloth. For all he knew, Quamae was a walking saint.

The pastor held this star-struck look on his face. "It sounds like she was trying to perform some type of hoodoo magic on you to serve as protection."

"You believe in that shit?" The pastor's eyes grew wide due to the slip of his tongue. Gigi slapped his leg. "I'm sorry for the language, but this is nerve-wracking for me," he apologized.

"It's okay, but no, I don't believe in that. I believe in the power of my Lord and savior, Jesus Christ." He rose to his feet to drop some knowledge on the couple. "Hoodoo magic is something that many people believe will protect you from malevolent energies. What she threw on you was something called Cascarillo powder."

"Okay, so how do we get that off of me?" Whatever hex, voodoo, or hoodoo she put on him, he didn't give a damn what it was called as long as it was off of him.

"I have some holy oil, and we can indulge in some prayer to get rid of any bad spirits around you." He stared down at him. "Including your friends with hidden agendas." The pastor paused. "And based on the company you keep, you need it. I will also give you a book on spiritual warfare." He handed him a thick pamphlet. "Read the prayer in it every day, and a little church wouldn't hurt the both of you."

The pastor pulled out some holy oil from his desk and approached him with it. "Come on stand with me." He dabbed a little on his finger and traced a cross on Quamae's forehead.

A million thoughts were running through his head because he had never experienced anything like that before. He stood there with his hands at his sides, his eyes closed, and let the pastor work his very own magic in silence.

He placed his palm on his head and closed his eyes. Gigi did the same. "Father God, we come to you in a time of need to guide this man and protect this man in your precious name. Protect him from his friends and enemies, Lord, and anyone who is seeking to harm him. Heavenly Father, I ask that you place your armor on his body, be the helmet of salvation, the breastplate of righteousness, the shield of faith, the shoes of the gospel of peace, the belt of truth, and the sword of the spirit to resist the enemy so he will flee. I ask that you summon your warrior angels to fight on Quamae's behalf. And if it is your will for him to confront the enemies directly, then guide him and protect him. Give this man a resolute spirit so he will be consistent in his prayer and steadfast with his resistance. Grant him the wisdom to stay alert, even when it seems the enemy has moved on and ended his attack on him. We praise you, Lord, for your victory over the enemy, his defeat, and that victory will be Quamae's. In your precious name, we pray. Amen."

"Amen," Quamae and Gigi shouted in unison. He opened his eyes and wiped away his tears. The feeling that came over his body was something he never felt before. It was like an out-of-body experience. He felt cleansed from his sins and pure like the day he was born. With his newly-gotten armor, he was ready for war.

Chapter 11

Chauncey held Monica in his arms while escorting her to his car. Tears were sliding down her cheeks as she held her head low to the ground. She shivered from the cold morning wind.

"I got you, baby, come on."

There was no response. The pain, agony, and heartbreak made her want to lay down and die. Everything that she went through had been for nothing. Today was the day she said goodbye to *her* unborn baby. The saying "momma's baby and daddy's maybe" was proven to be a fact. He finally made her get the abortion he had been screaming about. He helped her into the front seat and buckled her in, closing the door afterward.

As he drove through traffic, she gazed out the window, having a mental meltdown. The car was rocking constantly due to the shaking of her body.

Chauncey tried to comfort her. "Baby, please relax. Just lay back and sleep. I promise we will get through this together."

Monica's eyes spit venom when she stared him down. That was the last thing she needed to hear from his lying-ass lips. "If you didn't make me have an abortion, there wouldn't be anything to get through." She folded her arms across her chest and sobbed louder.

"So you think a baby would've made our situation better?"

"No, you were supposed to make it better. If you wasn't so busy trying to fuck every bitch with a pussy, you would've had time to work on your family."

"I mean, if you feel like that, then why bring a baby into the equation? You already saying I ain't shit, so I don't understand what the problem is." He scratched the top of his head. "You know how a nigga rockin', so don't get amnesia all of a sudden."

"You right," she sniffled. "I'm just a fuck for you. You only wanna parade me around and fuck me when it's convenient for you."

"You need to cut that shit out."

"Fuck you, Chauncey!" she screamed. "I hate you. Just take me home and leave me the fuck alone." She turned back to face the window and watch everything fly by as he increased his speed.

Her constant whimpering was slowly pushing his patience out the window, so he turned the volume up on the stereo. The vibration from his pocket made him jump. He pulled his phone out and saw he had just gotten a text from Ayesha.

Ayesha: *I want to see you today*
Chauncey: *Be there in a hour*
Ayesha: *I'll be waiting*

He slid the phone back in his pocket and focused on the road. When he pulled up in Monica's complex, he helped her out of the car. She snatched away from him.

"Don't fuckin' touch me; you've done enough. Thank you."

He didn't bother replying because that was one argument he wasn't going to win. As soon as they got to the front door, he walked her to the bed and tucked her in. Instead of complaining, she went with the flow.

"I'm about to hit it. I'll be back." Monica ignored him and closed her eyes, so he walked out without saying another word, feeling the villain. No matter how he felt, he was happy her pregnancy was behind them.

In his mind he knew that it was going to take a while before things got back to normal, but until it did, he had Ayesha as a replacement. The doctor made it very clear she couldn't have sex for the next three weeks, but that didn't apply to him. He was ready to knock the lining out of li'l mama's pussy for the next few weeks, and that's exactly where he was headed.

***

It had been a while since Nate dropped by to check on his son. Although their first encounter was everything but pleasant, he couldn't find it in his heart to walk away so easily. His heart was already disabled permanently thanks to his baby mama. He lost 15 years and his woman; there was no way he was about to lose his son to the streets. The timeframe it was going to take to build a relationship didn't matter. He was willing to do anything to make it work. The task wasn't going to be easy because NJ was tough as nails with alligator skin. The prayer he dropped to the man upstairs was to snatch his son from the death grip the streets of Lauderdale had on him.

Nate pulled up and parked in front of the duplexes that sat adjacent to where NJ lived. He sat in the car with the radio off, trying to figure out a different way to approach his junior without failing again. Nate was determined to give his son something he never had, and that was a father. The streets were dark, but he could spot him with the little bit of light coming from the light post. Watching him bust lick after lick made him aware his business was booming. The fiends didn't stop coming.

Suddenly two shadows caught his attention. Two males walked up toward NJ wearing hoodies, so he paid close attention to their demeanors. From the looks of things he could see they were exchanging words. Right after that one of the boys removed something from his pocket. It didn't take a college degree to figure out what was going on.

Nate slipped out of the car like a thief in the night and crept across the street unnoticed. Once he was close enough, he was able to hear every word being said.

"Run them pockets, nigga, and them Jay's on your feet. I'm glad you went and stood in line for them shits."

NJ wasn't a punk by a long shot, but he knew he was outnumbered by one body. Two things he learned in life were to pick and choose his battles and know when to hold him tongue. That would determine if he lived to see another day to get that revenge.

"This shit ain't over, nigga. You got me right now." He nodded his head and bit down on his lip, feeling defeated. That night he let his guard down and slipped up on some rookie jack boys. He bent over to untie his shoes when he was smacked over the head with the butt of a gun.

"Shut the fuck up, nigga."

"Argh," he grabbed the back of his bloody head.

The rabbit holding the gun wasn't paying attention, and that's when Nate crept up behind him and placed that cold piece of steel to the back of his skull. "Gimme that gun, nigga."

The young boy held his hands in the air and Nate snatched the piece from him and put it in his back pocket. He then returned the favor and knocked him over the head with his Glock. His friend stood there spooked as he held his head in his hands.

NJ was dazed. He squinted his eyes, trying to zoom in on his savior, and that's when he recognized the face as his alleged father.

"Turn around and look at me." Before they could turn to face the opposite direction, NJ hit them both with a two-piece, bringing them both to their knees. His hands were lethal like Muhammed Ali, so he was a force to be reckoned with.

Nate kicked both of them. "Get your punk asses up and look at me." They staggered and followed the directions given. "I just did 15 years for a murder, and I don't mind going back for burying y'all asses." He leaned in closer to make sure they got the message. "I'ma say this one time, and one time only. Don't fuck with my son, or next time I will kill you and yo' homie. You got that?"

They shook their heads up and down.

NJ looked at the stranger with a new-found respect. If it wasn't for him, he probably would've been outlined in chalk when the sun came up the next morning. He knew how his generation got down. They didn't give a damn about human life and wouldn't hesitate to pull the trigger. His foster mother loved to quote her favorite lines whenever a homicide occurred:

I don't know what's wrong with y'all twentieth century babies. You don't respect your elders or authority, and all y'all wanna do is sip lean, pop pills, and smoke flocka. Y'all need daddies, that's the problem with y'all generation.

He could hear her voice loud and clear. She wasn't wrong, but he often wondered what was her problem and if she would be sniffing powder if she had her daddy in her life. The funny thing about it was how she could talk about Jesus when she sniffed more lines than a barcode.

Nate shook him from his thoughts when he placed a hand on his shoulders. "You straight?"

"Yeah, I'm cool. Thanks, man."

He put his heat in his back pocket and looked at his son while he held a shirt to his head to stop the bleeding. "No need to thank me. I just did what any other father would do for his child."

He wanted to contest what he just said, but decided against it. The least he could do was apologize about his reaction a few weeks back. He looked Nate square in the eyes and manned up. "I want to apologize about the way I handled shit the first time around. That shit wasn't kosher, and I was outta line."

Nate's lips spread corner-to-corner and produced a smile. "All is forgiven if you could forgive me for being absent from your life. I know it won't happen overnight, but I want the chance to explain everything that happened between me and yo' mama. If you just hear me out, then you would understand the hand you were dealt in this game of life." He paused for a second. "Can you do that for me?"

He nodded his head. "Yeah, we can do that. Let's go inside."

Nate followed behind his junior as he escorted him to his living quarters. Compared to the outside, the inside was immaculate. When he stepped into his room, the first thing he noticed was the huge picture of Al Pacino on his wall. His eyes wandered to his king size bed, then to the 50-inch flat screen and PlayStation 4. NJ walked to the closet and opened it to stash his drugs and money in a small safe. Nate was amused by his shoe collection that contained every sneaker Michael Jordan dropped and every boot by Timberland.

"I see the game been good to you."

NJ smirked at his comment. "Yeah, I do alright." He closed the closet door back. He pulled the chair from the computer desk. "Here, have a seat." Then he walked over to his bed and sat down on it. "So you did a 15-year bid, huh?"

"Yeah."

"So, what's the story behind you and my mom?"

Nate took a deep breath and prepared to tell him everything. The good, the bad, and the ugly. He started off with how they met, what brought them closer, Frank's murder, his conviction, and how Sasha left him in prison and failing to mention she was pregnant with him. He could see the glassiness in his eyes, but he knew he was fighting the urge to cry in front of him. There was a knock on the door.

"NJ!" his foster mother yelled. "Watchu doing?"

He exhaled deeply. "Come in."

As soon as she walked in, she didn't hesitate to bring up the reason she was looking for him. "Watchu got for me?" She never noticed Nate sitting scoping her out.

NJ reached into his pocket, pulled out a baggie of coke, and placed it in her palm.

"Thanks, son," she smiled. She only called him that when he was giving her something. She took a step back to exit the room, and that's when she noticed Nate. "Oh, I'm so rude. Who is this?"

"I'm Nate." She walked over and extended her hand.

"Ms. Walker, but you can call me Angela, handsome."

He chuckled a little. "Thanks."

She continued holding his hand. "Aren't you a little too old to be hanging with NJ?" She assumed he was one of the older hustlers from around the way, but he corrected her quickly as he took his hand from hers.

"Nah, I'm his father."

She was confused, because to her knowledge he didn't have one of those. "Father?"

"Yes, father. My name is Nathaniel Josiah Black." He pointed at NJ. "The same exact name as his."

She looked at her foster son for confirmation. "Is this true?"

He nodded his yes. "He just got out of prison. He didn't know about me."

"This is one hell of a surprise." She placed her hand on her chest like she was about to have a heart attack. "Now I see where you get your good looks from. Well, I'll leave you two alone." She rushed out of the bedroom quickly so she could fill her nose with that white girl.

"How does she treat you? Do you like living here?"

He wasn't slow, and he knew he was referring to her drug use. "It's cool and all. She never mistreated a nigga, you know. She pretty much let me do anything as long as I supply her habit."

"I know it's a li'l early in the play to say this, but I would like for you to come live with me when I get my place."

"Nah, that's cool. I would love to get from around this shit."

"Good." He didn't hide his excitement. "And there's a lot I need to teach you about the game if you gon' be in it."

"There's always room for knowledge."

They sat and talked for hours until the break of dawn with no restrictions on the conversation. They learned a lot about each other, and that was the beginning of a new relationship. NJ learned they had similar ways and finally understood where his temper came from: like father, like son.

***

For the past two hours Chauncey and Ayesha rode around all over Broward County, drinking and smoking. Monica was steadily blowing up his phone, but he kept sending her to voicemail. He was using that time to get to know his new piece since they jumped into sex head-first. There was no time to argue with her about a baby he didn't want. Blaring through the speakers was Eazy-E. He bopped to the music, and Ayesha was doing the same.

Chauncey laughed, looking at how crunk she was off the classic album. "You don't know shit about Eazy," he joked.

"Yes, I do," she assured him.

"This was before your time, youngin'."

"So, I saw the movie." She continued to bounce in her seat. "I've been playing his music ever since."

"Rap for me, then." He turned the radio down just a smidgen to amp her up by saying Dr. Dre's part. *"Wait a minute, wait a minute, cut this shit. Aye, yo, yella boy, why don't you rewind it."*

She took a sip from her drink and cleared her throat.

"Niggaz don't see I'm a 100% legit,
And you know it ain't about all that bullshit.
It's about fuckin' this bitch and that bitch,
But not the bitch with the seven-day itch, like that ho
Just throwin' me the pussy. She says she wants to do it like a doggy.
She's bad, nobody is badder,
But she got more crabs than a seafood platter."

She was rocking side-to-side and pointing her fingers in the air.

Chauncey was amused by her little performance and knowledge of the lyrics. "A'ight, I see you over there. I guess you know a lil' something."

"I know a lot. I was just joking about the movie thing. I grew up with my brother, and this is all he listened to."

"Oh, okay, you got some gangsta in you. That shit sexy as fuck." He licked his lips and gripped his dick in his hand. "And when we get to my place, you gon' have a lot of gangsta up in you."

"You are so nasty." She loved his thug mannerisms. It was such a turn on. She licked her lips and winked at him. "I'm feeling it already."

"I'ma puncture your lungs tonight."

"Damn, that just made my pussy wet."

"Let me see."

Ayesha opened her legs and placed one foot on the dash board. She lifted her dress, exposing her bare pussy. Using her right hand, she placed two fingers on her clit and rubbed it. "Ah." She moaned and bit down on her bottom lip.

Chauncey damn near lost control of his car trying to watch. He jumped on I-95 and put it on cruise control. "Damn, shawty, I love that freaky shit." He kept one eye on the road and the other eye on the prize. "Turn this way so I can see."

With no hesitation she turned to face him, placing one leg over the seat and her back against the door. "That's better for you, baby?"

"Hell yeah." Taking one hand off the steering wheel, he reached over and rubbed her clit before sliding in two fingers. He finger-fucked her slowly.

"Ss. Ahh. Mm." She put two fingers in her mouth and sucked them. Her hips rocked evenly with his strokes. It was nothing like the real thing, but it would do until they arrived at their destination.

"Yeah, she ready. I'm putting that ass to sleep."

"Please do," she moaned again, but this time she held the note like she was singing in the church choir.

He moved his hand and put his fingers in his mouth, tasting her juices. "Nah, hold that shit in. I don't need you tappin' out before you get the dick."

As soon as they made it inside Chauncey's bachelor pad, they didn't waste any time getting naked, leaving a trail of clothing to the bedroom. Ayesha was about to climb into bed when he stopped her.

"Ain't no laying down. Put your hands on the bed and spread them legs."

She complied. He stood up behind her, rubbed the head up and down her slit, and plunged that meat in her once she was nice and wet. "Uh," she groaned in a high-pitched voice.

"Damn, girl." He squeezed her ass and sank in deep until he felt her ass was against his pelvis. Pumping in and out of those guts, he pulled out slowly and glanced down at her juices glazing his wood, giving it a shine. "Ss. Ooh."

She wiggled her hips. "Do it faster."

He smacked her ass. "Throw it back." He smacked it again. "Bounce on it."

The stinging sensation sent chills over her body, awakening a sleeping giant. She closed her eyes and pretended she was on stage, dancing to her favorite song. She bent her knees and bounced on it just the way he wanted it.

"Grr," he grunted. "Yeah, just like that."

Their strokes were in rhythm for the next few minutes. The slapping sound filled the room, along with pleasurable moans. "Fuck me harder," she demanded.

Chauncey obliged and put the smack down on that ass. He rammed every inch of his pole into her slippery hole and hammered away for the next five minutes. "This dick good to you?"

"Ooh. Ow," she answered in between each breath she took. "Yes. Ow. Mm."

His next move was the best when he grabbed her legs and put her thighs on his shoulders, holding her upside down. When he was face-to-face with her shaved peach, he put his mouth on it and slurped the juices. "Shit." She was in heaven, because this was something she never experienced.

He came up for air. "Suck that dick."

With her hands still planted on the bed, she moved her head and took his erect penis into her mouth and went to work. The movement of her head was rapid-fire. Five minutes in he could feel his knees buckle, followed by a tingling sensation, but that didn't stop him from eating her up. "Argh. I'm cummin'," he grunted. She continued to suck him up until semen oozed from the tip, swallowing it all.

It was three in the morning when Chauncey and Ayesha were woken by loud screaming. When he opened his eyes, he wished he was dreaming. Standing over him crying was a deranged Monica wielding a switch-blade. He jumped up from the bed, butt-ass naked.

"What the fuck you doing here?" he yelled.

"What the fuck you doing with a bitch in the bed?"

Ayesha looked at Monica with a cold stare, but she didn't say anything. She decided to let Chauncey handle the crazy bitch.

He grabbed the basketball shorts folded on the dresser and slipped them on. "Man, just go home with all that crazy shit."

"No wonder you been sending me to the voicemail. I'm at home suffering from a fuckin' abortion and you over here fucking some random-ass ho."

"I gotcha ho. You better address him and not me, 'cause you don't know me." Ayesha wrapped herself in the sheet just in case Monica tried something. "I advise you to go home and heal from that baby."

Chauncey looked in her direction and held up one hand to quiet her. "Chill, I got this." Then he stood face-to-face with Monica. "Put that shit up before you hurt yourself."

"Trust and believe I will not hurt me, but I will hurt you."

"I swear to God, if you touch me with that I will fuck you up, and I mean that shit."

She took a swing, trying to cut him, but he jumped back and grabbed her arm. Snatching the blade from her hand, he threw it on the bed so Ayesha could retrieve it. He bent her wrist back, bringing her down to her knees.

"I told you not to try me."

"Chauncey, stop," she cried. "Let me go."

"Nah, 'cause I told you not to try me. And how the fuck did you get in here?"

"A key. How the fuck do you think?"

"I didn't give it to you." He wanted to beat the snot out of her, but he couldn't do it. "Come on, let's go. Now isn't the time or place for this shit. Just go home and I'll talk to you later."

"So this how you gon' treat me? Like I don't mean shit to you?"

"Monica, we are not together, and you know this. But you wonder why I never took that step with you?" Chauncey escorted Monica out of the bedroom and into the living room.

Ayesha stayed put until she heard a scuffle and glass breaking. She jumped up from the bed, still wearing the sheet. When she made it into the living room, she could see Chauncey and Monica fighting. She stood there for a minute until he had her on the couch, choking her.

"Get the fuck off of me. You just mad because you got caught."

"You can't get caught when you not in a relationship."

She screamed, "Fuck you, Chauncey, you ain't shit. Only a fuck-nigga would hit a female."

He slapped her in the mouth, drawing blood. "Yo' daddy a fuck-nigga, you pussy-ass ho."

Ayesha finally jumped in and pulled him off of her. "Bae, just let her go." She never called him bae before, but after he fucked her soul and ate that pussy like it was a competition, she had to put a handle on that.

"Get the fuck outta here." He grabbed the single key from the floor that she used to gain entrance and pushed her out onto the porch.

"Whatever you thought this was, it's over. Don't hit my shit no more, either."

He watched her get up and pull a phone from her pocket. She walked away slowly dialing a number. He couldn't hear her, but the person on the phone picked up and said, "911 what's your emergency?"

Chapter 12

Sasha stood in front of the mirror brushing her hair while listening to Blue shout out 25 reasons why she should stay in the house. For the life of her she couldn't understand why he was so livid.

"You need to stay in the house and rehabilitate. Why do you keep driving up there?"

She rolled her eyes. "Because she can't come here."

"You damn right she can't."

"Why do you hate Carmen so much?" She sat the brush down and turned to face him. "What did she do to you for you to act this way toward her?" She folded her arms, waiting for an answer.

"Just listen to what I'm telling you." He didn't want to tell her about the incident at the hospital, but if she didn't back away soon, he was gonna put it out there. "Your girl got a lot going on, and you don't need to be around her."

"You don't even know her to say that."

"Apparently you don't know her either." He turned his back to her and walked over to the bed. "You think that ho is your friend," he mumbled under his breath and took a seat on the edge of the bed.

"What did you say?" She genuinely couldn't make out what he said.

"Nothing, man, just go to your girl house." He lay back with his hands behind his head and looked up at the ceiling.

"Not until you tell me what you said."

"Well, I guess you staying home, 'cause I ain't repeating shit."

"Fine." She walked over to him and stood between his legs. "I don't want to argue with you about something so trivial."

"Well, stop being so defiant and listen to what I'm telling you."

She leaned down toward him. She tried kissing his lips, but he moved his head. "Bae, come on and stop making a big deal out of nothing. I promise I won't be gone long."

"You're missing the point of what I'm telling you, but go ahead." He pushed her gently. "Let me up."

Sasha backed away. "Are you serious right now? You're that upset?"

"Nah, I'm good. That's on you. Keep walkin' 'round like shit sweet. You don't even know who attacked you, but you stay in the streets." Blue grabbed his keys and walked out of the room. "I won't be here when you get back," he said, slamming the door behind him.

Sasha sat down on the bed and thought back to that day, but nothing surfaced. Her memory of that day was blank. Sadness came over her because she wanted to know what happened and who would do such a thing. There were so many questions that needed answers, and she knew just who to call.

After storming from the house, Blue drove to Opa-Locka to meet up with his crew. Sasha had him heated, so he needed to go to a place where he could take his mind off the situation at hand. Just the idea of her being around Carmen was head-boggling. He could only imagine how many times she pulled that stunt on her girl's man. A fraction of him wanted to expose her for the fraud ho she was, but he was too worried about hurting his girl in the process. Because as long as they were together, she never had to worry about him blessing her with the dick.

When he hit the block, there were kids playing football in the street. Every little boy from the hood had a dream of going pro. He whipped into the driveway and stepped from the truck. Blue stood in front of the door, adjusting his piece before he knocked.

"Who is it?" someone shouted.

"Blue, nigga. Look out the fuckin' window, lazy-ass nigga." He hated to announce himself at the door.

The door opened and TJ stepped aside to let him in. "Calm down, angry-ass nigga."

"Suck my dick." He walked past TJ and slapped hands with Quint. "What's up, my nigga?"

Quint giggled. He was clearly high as the afternoon sun. "Boolin' on this yack."

Blue took a seat on the leather sofa. "That's all y'all niggas do in this bitch."

TJ laughed. "Nigga, you sound like you need a muthafuckin' cup or a huge one. You all uptight and shit."

"Get off my nigga's back." Quint passed Blue the bottle. "Fix you one and tell yo' boy what's up."

TJ was higher than a giraffe's pussy and was in the mood to play. "I'll tell you what's wrong with that nigga." He stood next to Blue and put his hand on his shoulder. "That cougar pussy got him in his feelings and shit."

Blue knocked TJ's hand off his shoulder. "Fuck you, nigga."

Quint squinted. "Nah, blood, say it ain't so."

TJ laughed louder. "Oh, nigga, it's so. She got this young nigga wrapped around those French-tipped nails of hers."

"Y'all think the shit funny. Fuck both of y'all niggas." Blue sat back, folded his arms, and sat the bottle next to him.

"Come on, holla atcha boys, man. You know we just bullshittin' around." Quint needed the scoop.

Blue picked the bottle up and removed the top, taking a huge gulp. "A'ight." He held the bottle in his hands. "I ain't never tell you, TJ, that she was pregnant and shit."

TJ couldn't wait. "So, hold up, you nutted in something and made a baby, nigga?"

"I don' know if it's mine, though. It could be that nigga's baby."

"The nigga I shot in the bar?" TJ asked.

"Yeah."

Quint shook his head. "Damn, blood, you still sweating that? I thought you wasn't worried about that. What you gon' do?"

"I wanna be with her, regardless. It don't matter if the baby mine or not." He felt kind of lame for saying that in front of TJ, but he couldn't deny his feelings for her. Quint already knew how he felt about her.

"Damn, she must got kryptonite in that pussy," TJ teased Blue at his own expense.

"That ain't even the problem. When she was in the hospital, her homegirl was trying to fuck me in the parking lot."

Quint looked puzzled. "So you ain't fuck her?"

"Hell nah."

"You must love her, 'cause the Blue I know wouldn't give a damn if they was real sisters." Quint and TJ slapped hands. "On God."

"It ain't like that with her. I want this shit to work, but I don't know if I should tell her or not."

Quint stopped joking when he saw his right-hand was serious. "That's tough, my nigga. You think her girl gon' say something?"

"I don' know. She ain't said shit yet."

"If you tell her, that will definitely cause problems. But if you don't and the friend do, then you have a bigger problem," Quint added.

TJ looked at them both like they were crazy. "Both of y'all muthafuckas smoking dope. Don't tell her shit. You didn't fuck her, so that's all that matters. If it ain't broke, don't fix it."

"Yeah, I hear that, but I told her I didn't want her around her."

TJ was the oldest among them, and he had a little more experience than they did. "Did she ask you why?"

"Yeah, but I didn't tell her."

"Now she gon' have that shit on her mind forever. You know these females petty nowadays."

Quint picked up a blunt from the table. "Fuck all that. Let's smoke to get that shit off your mind."

The sunny skies turned into darkness and they were still at it. Blue was finally where he needed to be: stress free. The loud and yack had him feeling lovely. All he wanted to do was go home and fuck the shit out of his girl.

A text message came through his phone, and it was the very person he was thinking about.

Bae: *It's late. Where are you?*

My Forever: *Opalocka*

Bae: *What time are you coming home?*

My Forever: *Y?*

Bae: *Because we need to talk*

My Forever: *I'll be there soon*

Bae: *Kk*

Blue sat the phone on his lap and looked up at Quint. "That was her. She said we need to talk."

"You think she knows?"

"Man, I don't know. I guess I'll see when I get home." Sasha had his mind racing like he was competing for the gold in the Olympics. If she knew, that meant he had a lot of explaining to do. He sat back on the sofa and thought of a million ways to defend himself. Because if Carmen told it first, there was no telling how she flipped the story. "Roll another blunt before I go. I don't know what the fuck I'm walking into."

***

Quamae waited until after midnight to leave the house. He was dressed in black sweatpants and a hoodie. He grabbed two bangers, one for his hip and the other for his ankle. She watched him get strapped up and prepared for war. Trepidation settled in on her heart, making it hard for her to breathe.

"Do you have to do this?" Her voice trembled. She already knew there was nothing she could do to change his mind, but it was worth a try. "I'm afraid you won't come back to me and the baby."

It hurt his soul to hear the fear in her voice, but he had to handle his business. "These the same niggas that tried to take me away from you and my baby. I'm not letting that go, and you shouldn't either. I promise I'll be back, though." He kissed her on the forehead. "I love you."

Tears filled her eyes. "I love you, too." She knew there was nothing she could say to make him change his mind once it was made up.

He walked downstairs to meet his boys waiting in the den for their departure. "Let's ride."

The night was still as the full moon lit up the sky. Quamae, Chauncey, Dirty, and Amp checked their surroundings as they sat in the infamous Opa-locka neighborhood. When the coast was clear, they emerged from the car and headed toward the house. As they got closer, they could hear music playing. They peeped through the windows and observed their assailants sitting on the sofa, drinking and passing a blunt, looking as if they were about to pass out at any given moment. They crept around to the back door for a blitz attack. Amp used a screwdriver to jimmy the locks open. He pulled the door open slowly and they crept in one-by-one, tiptoeing through the house unnoticed until they were standing in the living room.

"Y'all know what it is; get on the floor." Quamae aimed his piece in their direction.

"What the fuck?" TJ shouted as Quamae took long strides toward him until he was face-to-face with the barrel of his gun.

Dirty inched closer, scoping out the room. "Who else in this muthafucka?"

"Nobody," TJ replied.

Dirty recognized the familiar face. "Quint? What the fuck you doing here?"

He didn't say a word.

"Get on the floor, nigga." Quamae made him lay face-down on the floor. He looked at Quint. "Get yo' ass down here, too." Quamae stood over him and removed his hoodie. "Remember me, nigga?"

TJ stared at him for a long time before he answered him, and then terror took over. "I'm sorry, man. I ain't wanna do it. Blue had a hit out on you." He babbled, begged and snitched for his life.

Quint already knew he was about to die, so there was no point in snitching or begging for his life. He looked over at TJ. "You soft-ass nigga, shut up."

"What the fuck did you say?" Quamae heard that name loud and clear.

"Blue said y'all was beefing and to off you. Man, I swear, I ain't wanna pull that trigger. I got kids, man."

Chauncey looked down at Quint. "So, y'all shot up the trap house too, huh?"

"I ain't got shit to say," Quint answered coolly, as if he didn't have a banger pointed at him.

Chauncey stomped on his head twice. "Oh, you ain't snitchin' like your boy, huh?"

Quint ignored the instant headache from his boot. "If you gon' kill me, muthafucka, pull the trigger, 'cause I ain't going out like that nigga over there."

"Dat part!" Chauncey put the barrel to the back of Quint's head and pulled the trigger. Blood leaked onto the carpet. He looked at Quamae and said, "Smoke that nigga and let's ride."

"Please, don't kill me. I said I was sorry."

"God forgives. I don't."

Before he could pull the trigger, a noise from behind startled them and, on instinct, Dirty turned around with no hesitation and let off a round. The body of a child hit the floor with a loud thud.

"Oh shit!" Amp shouted. "That's a kid, man."

The dude Quamae was talking to let out a painful howl as he looked back to see the unthinkable. "You killed my son," he cried. His son was laid out on the floor with a bullet hole in his head.

Quamae turned back around and shot him, execution-style. Chauncey tucked his piece. "Come on, let's get the fuck outta here." They made a break for the door and ran to the car. Once they made it to the highway, Quamae looked at Dirty. He could tell it was bothering him by the expression on his face. "Man, what the hell happened back there?"

He shook his head. "Man, I don't know. The shit happened so fast. I ain't even see the git. All I heard was a noise, and I reacted on impulse."

"Damn, man, that's fucked up." He grunted and hit the dashboard. "Fuck!"

Chauncey looked over at his boy. "It was an accident, man. You know he didn't do that on purpose."

"Yeah, I know. But did you hear the nigga say Blue put the hit out on me? And that ho sleeping with the enemy."

Chauncey switched lanes on the interstate. "Don't worry, bruh, we gon' get that nigga, too."

Quamae sat back in deep thought. He couldn't believe he was responsible for the death of a child. He had no intention for things to play out the way they did, but now that was something he would have to deal with, because that child's blood was on his hands. He may not have pulled the trigger, but he was just as guilty as Dirty. It was his beef that landed them there in the first place.

***

When Blue made it home, he was tipsy and horny. There was no way he was about to have a deep conversation that night. He walked into the room and Sasha was in a sound sleep, from what he could hear by the light snoring. The room was dark, but he managed to walk over to the bed and remove his clothing. That yack had him feeling like the Incredible Hulk with the way he yanked her pajama bottoms off. Sasha had to be tired because she didn't move.

Blue grabbed her by the legs and pulled her to the edge of the bed. The sudden movement startled her. "What are you doing?"

He completely ignored her question and placed his head between her legs. She understood exactly what he was doing and closed her eyes. The warmth of his tongue made her melt. Waking up to some head was better than breakfast in bed.

"Mm." She rubbed her hands through his dreds and twirled her hips. Blue was young, but he knew what to do to the female body. As he sucked on her clit, he used two fingers to penetrate her. "Uh. Uh. Uh. Ss." She opened her legs wider so he could indulge in his favorite spot. He put his thumb on her clit and rubbed it. "Uh. Ooh, yeah. Right there."

"You like how I eat that pussy, don't you?"

"Mm. Yes."

Blue raised his head and wiped his mouth before taking that dive to feed his baby. He rubbed the head against her wet pussy until he found the opening and sank in. With one leg on his shoulder and the other around his waist, he concentrated on hitting every corner. With every stroke he lost all control, ramming every inch of him inside the warmth of her walls. "Damn, this pussy hot. Shit."

Sasha let out a few high-pitched screams. "Ah. Ah. Ugh."

He put his fingers in her mouth to quiet her down to keep her from being embarrassed by his mom. Blue wasn't worried because his ol' girl already knew he was fucking the air out of her ass every night. She had heard Sasha on a few separate occasions.

Blue gripped her hips and plunged in and out. "Grr," he grunted. "Shit." He stabbed her insides over and over with mad aggression, causing her to scream. Sasha was a little too loud, so he covered her mouth with his hand. There were no plans to ease up on her. He was on a thousand with his built-up anger, liquor, and weed. He couldn't put his hands on her, so her pussy had to pay the price.

Chapter 13

The next morning Quamae walked into the bedroom to find Gigi watching the news and crying. She turned around when she felt his presence. "Did you did this?" Her face was flushed from the constant waterfall flowing from her eyes.

"Do what?" he played dumb. He knew exactly what she was talking about. Quamae closed the door and leaned against it.

She pointed to the television. "That? Did you do it?" she screamed.

He looked in the direction of her finger in silence, and on the screen was the home they ran up in the night before. A picture of the little boy that was shot and killed flashed across the screen. He was only six years old. Reality set in on him and gripped his heart tight. He opened his mouth to speak, but nothing came out.

"Answer me, dammit. Did you do that shit?"

He shook his head no. He didn't lie, but he wasn't telling the truth either.

She stood up and walked over to him so she could look in his eyes. "Don't lie to me."

He looked away from her because he couldn't stand to look at her and lie so blatantly. "I didn't do it."

She grabbed his face with her hand and turned it toward her. "I can tell when you're lying, Quamae. You have a baby on the way. How could you do that to a child? What if that happened to us? Somebody running up in this bitch and killing your family."

Tears managed to break the dam and stream down his face. "I'm sorry, I didn't mean for that to happen. It was an accident." With his back against the wall, he slid down until he was seated on the floor. He cried into his hands and Gigi bent down to comfort him.

"Baby, tell me what happened."

Quamae recited the incident play-by-play, and by the time he was finished, Gigi was emotional all over again. She felt his pain, but her heart went out to the family.

"It happened so fast. I couldn't stop it if I wanted to."

"I know, baby. I know." She held him in her arms and rocked back and forth.

For the duration of the day they stayed indoors while torment and shame floated around the house like clouds in the sky. Quamae couldn't eat or sleep, and Hennessey became his voice of reason. The liquor caused him to think heavy, and all he could hear was TJ's voice. *"I'm sorry, man. I ain't wanna do it. Blue had a hit out on you."* Those words were unsettling, and he wondered if Sasha had anything to do with the hit. He was certain he saw the bruises on her, and he wondered if that caused the attempt on his life. Whatever the case, maybe Blue wasn't going to be around much longer. Sasha either.

Quamae rolled a blunt to take the edge off, and that caused him to think further into the situation. Quint's presence in the trap house let him know Blue was also behind the drive-by. The only thing left to do was for him to find out if Dirty had anything to do with it. The fact he and Chauncey were called over right before it led him to believe it was a setup from the jump.

After killing Blue's boys, Dirty had them to drop him off at his baby mother's house, so that gave him the chance to sit back and listen to the recordings.

He picked up the two devices from the guestroom and den and plugged in the earphones. Placing the buds in his ears, he pressed play and lay back on the couch to get comfortable.

***

Blue was sprawled out across the middle of the bed, knocked out cold. Sasha knew he consumed too much alcohol the night before. He wasn't a stone-cold drinker, but he was fucked up last night, especially after the way he beat her down. Her middle was still sore from the thrashing he put on it.

She watched him sleep, admiring how sexy he looked with a hangover. The love she had for him was real, and no one or nothing could change that. If someone told her she would be in love with someone else, she would've called them a liar. Sadly, she was in love and pregnant without a clue as to who her baby's father was. There were more questions about how she ended up there, but she never received an honest answer.

Sasha decided to reach out to Chauncey in hopes he could shed some light on her situation. She shot him a quick text.

Sis: *Are u busy?*

Brother: *Nah what's good*

Sis: *I texted you the other day but you didn't respond*

Brother: *My bad I was busy. I meant to text you back but shit got crazy*

Sis: *I need to ask you a question*

Brother: *Shoot*

Sis: *What happened with me and Qua? I don't remember*

Bro: *He found out we slept together when he was in the hospital*

Sis: *Damn (crying emoji) how did he find out?*

Brother: *Idk. He showed me a video of me and you standing on the porch the morning after it happened. I don't know who recorded it*

Sis: *Damn what did he say?*

Brother: *A lot but I explained everything to him and let him know it only happened once by accident. We cool now*

Sis: *Do you think he did this to me?*

Brother: *At first I did but now I'm not sure*

Sis: *Thanks*

Brother: *You're welcome take care*

Sis: *I will*

Sasha sat on the floor Indian-style, trying to figure out what happened to her. All she wanted was her memory back, and not the stories she was being fed. She was determined to get the truth one way or another. With her eyes full of tears, Sasha sat and cried, rocking back and forth, praying God would give her the strength to remember that fateful day.

In the middle of her prayer, a loud vibration broke her concentration. She looked up to see where the sound was coming from. It had to be Blue's phone, because hers was facedown on the floor next to her. She ignored it and went back into prayer. His phone continued to vibrate back-to-back. After listening for a few minutes, she got up to check, because whoever was calling wanted to speak to him badly.

Sasha grabbed the edge of the bed to pull herself up. All the extra weight she gained made the task a little more strenuous.

"Shit, maybe I shouldn't have sat my big ass down there," she giggled.

Picking the phone up from the dresser, she swiped the screen to gain access. There were eight missed calls and a text message: *Some shit went down hit me back.*

"Blue," she called out, walking toward the bed. "Get up." When he didn't move, she shook him. "Bae, get up, something's wrong."

"Huh?" he mumbled while turning over.

"Get up. Something happened, and you need to get up now."

"What?"

"Here, check your phone." She put the phone in his hand. "Open your eyes so you can see."

Blue blinked a few times before putting the phone in front of his face. He focused on the text for a few seconds before dialing the number and putting the phone to his ear.

"What's up, woe?" he asked.

Sasha couldn't hear the context of the conversation, but judging by his facial expressions, it wasn't good news he was receiving.

"What the fuck happened?" He pushed the covers halfway off of himself and sat up. "Nah, man, not my muthafuckin' nigga. Come on, man, tell me this shit ain't true?" He put the phone on speaker and put his hands on his head.

"I wish I could tell you that shit, blood, but crime scene all over this muthafucka."

"Damn, my nigga gone." The hurt he felt was indescribable. Quint was his right-hand, his go-to man, and his voice of reasoning. "I was there last night. That shit had to go down right after a nigga left."

"Damn, man, I'm glad you wasn't there for that shit. And whoever did the shit killed TJ's son, too."

"That's fucked up, man. These niggas gon' pay for that shit."

"We don't know who did it, though."

"I think I know who behind the shit. I'm on my way."

"A'ight, blood. I'll be here."

Blue slung the covers off of him completely and jumped out of bed. Sasha was standing there to receive him with open arms. "Bae, you okay?"

He shook his head. "Nah."

"Come here." She reached for him and held him tight around the waist since he was taller than her. "It's gon' be okay. I'm here."

"They killed my nigga, Quint," he sobbed. Crying in front of a woman was a first. He always displayed this tough, bad boy image, but they hit him where it hurt, and somebody was gonna have to straighten him.

"I know, baby, and I'm sorry." She rubbed the small of his back, shedding tears with him because his pain was her pain. Over a short period of time she had grown to like Quint, and it was a tragedy that he was gone.

"I have to get over there." She released him so he could get dressed. Once he was finished, he grabbed his keys. "I'll be back."

Sasha took the keys from his hand. "No, I'm going with you, because you don't need to drive."

On the way to Opa-locka, Blue gave her directions on how to get there. The closer they got to the neighborhood, the tighter his chest became. His anxiety level was at an all-time high, and he was certain he would pass out at any given moment. Blue wiped his sweaty palms on his jeans out of fear of what he was about to encounter. Hearing about his boy was one thing, but to see him in a body bag was another story.

Sasha had to park a few houses down because the block was on Crenshaw. Everybody and their mammy was trying to see what was going on. Blue got out of the truck, and she followed suit. The crime scene van, Miami PD, and Channel 7 news were among the crowd trying to get answers. As they walked up, they noticed a few people holding up their cellphones, going live for Facebook.

She glanced at the fake reporters. "People will do anything for Facebook likes. No privacy whatsoever with their disrespectful asses."

Blue spotted his boy who made the call immediately and walked up on him. They embraced in a tight G hug. "Have they brought the bodies out yet?"

"Nah, they still in there."

He extended his arm to the left of him in Sasha's direction. "Dee, this my ol' lady, Sasha."

Dee looked her over and noticed she was pregnant. "Nice to meet you."

She held out her hand. "Same here."

"I don't shake women's hands. I give hugs." He smiled, showing a full set of gold teeth.

Sasha laughed. "Oh, okay. I didn't know." She leaned forward and gave him a granny hug.

Dee turned to Blue. "I see you got a baby on the way that you failed to mention, my boy."

He put his arm around her. "Yeah, I got a li'l one on the way."

Sasha blushed at the fact he put claim on her baby without knowing if it was really his child. That gave her hope he would be there, no matter what the test said.

"Congrats, fam."

"Thanks."

After standing in the crowd for a good fifteen minutes the authorities came out wheeling three gurneys carrying the body bags. Blue caught sight of it and ran in their direction.

"Quint," he yelled, causing everyone to look in his direction.

Sasha wobbled behind him as fast as she could. "Blue," she screamed. "Come back."

Blue grabbed the gurney Quint was on, which wasn't hard to determine since TJ was a bigger dude. "I need to see my brother. Y'all made a mistake. This is not my brother."

The officer placed his hand on his chest. "Sir, I need you step back."

He swatted his hand off of him. "Get the fuck off of me. I need to see my brother."

"Sir, you're gonna have to calm down and come down to the morgue and identify the body."

He pushed past the officer, grabbed hold of one of the bars, and unzipped the bag. "Quint, you can't leave me, man." His screams were painful. "Come back, bruh. Please don't leave me."

Sasha stood and watched him fall apart. Dee snatched him up. There was nothing she could do to tame him. Dee grabbed Blue and pushed him in the direction of his truck. "He already gone, man." He then looked at Sasha. "Come on and take him home."

She shook her head and climbed into the truck, waiting for him to get Blue in. Once he was seated, he punched the glove compartment, startling Sasha.

"I'ma kill that nigga, and that's on God."

***

One week had passed, and Blue stood on the wet pavement in an all-white linen suit and dark shades to cover his red eyes. His dreadlocks were twisted into an elegant bun. Sasha was by his side, wearing a white dress, holding his hand while he said his final goodbye to Quint. The preacher was saying his final prayer.

"Father God, we thank you for the twenty-two years of life you gave to Quinton Jackson. You saw fit to bring him home, so we will not question you. I ask that you heal the hearts of his loved ones. In the midst of this storm, let them cherish his precious memories, which will sustain them. Let them find peace, strength, and the courage to move on as he takes his final rest. God, wrap your loving arms around them and comfort them. Amen."

As Quinton's casket was placed into the wall, Blue held his head low. He couldn't believe his brother was really gone and he would never see him again. The cries from the crowd were loud, but there was one in particular that stood out from the rest.

"No, Quint, what am I supposed to do without you?" a female screamed.

When Blue looked up to see who it was, he recognized her as Quint's ex-girlfriend. She ran up to the wall and dropped to her knees with her hands pressed against the wall. "I never got the chance to tell you I'm pregnant. You're supposed to be here to help raise our child."

One of Quint's cousins walked up and picked her up off the ground and escorted her back to the limo. She was bucking and screaming, so someone else had to come and help him carry her to the car.

Blue waited until everyone went back to their cars before he squatted in front of the tombstone. He removed his shades and wiped the tears from his eyes.

"Damn, bruh, you about to be a father, and you didn't even know it." He chuckled a little. He was far from happy, but the moment was bittersweet. "I promise you, bruh, that your shorty will know who you were and will never go without anything as long as I'm breathing." Blue roared loudly, like the king of the jungle, and it echoed like thunder. "Damn, it wasn't supposed to go down like this, my nigga. I was supposed to be there with you. We was supposed to hit Vegas for our 23rd birthday."

Sasha stood behind him, rubbing his shoulders. "He's in a better place, baby."

He shook his head. "Selfish as this may sound, I don't think so. We were just starting to live life. He's supposed to be here with me right now."

"God don't make no mistakes."

Blue's gloomy eyes met Sasha's. "God made a mistake when he took my boy." Tears rolled down his face. "This shit hurts."

She tugged at his arm. "I know, baby. Come on."

He resisted at first, but then he gave in. "I love you, bruh, forever."

Blue stood up and walked away, feeling defeated. He was supposed to be there to save Quint, and he would never forgive himself for his death. If he had stayed a little bit longer, he would still be alive.

He helped Sasha into the truck and walked around to the driver's side. During the ride home, Blue rapped and cried.

"Life's ups and downs, they come and go.
When I die, I hope I live in the sky.
All my folks who ain't alive, hope they live in the sky.
Pray to God when I die that I live in the sky.
Its true what goes around comes back, you know.
So when I die, hope I live in the sky.
All my folks who ain't survive, may they live in the sky.
Tell God I wanna fly, let me live in the sky."

Blue reached into the backseat to grab the bottle of Remy he picked up before the funeral. He sat the bottle between his legs and broke the seal before turning it up in his mouth. Since Quint's death he had been going hard on the drinking, and it scared Sasha to death. She feared he would go out and do something stupid to land himself in jail, or worse, next to Quint.

Back at the house, Sasha left Blue in the room to drown his sorrows in liquor while she took a shower. In the bathroom she cried because she didn't know what to do with him. He had become so depressed they hadn't slept together since the night he left Opa-locka. He barely left the house, and he stayed in bed most days.

After her shower, she went back into the room, and what she saw was enough to give her a heart attack. She screamed as the horror scene was about to unfold in front of her eyes. "Blue, please don't do this."

"It's over. I can't sleep, eat, or function. It's better this way, Sasha. I love you. I loved you from the first time I laid eyes on you at the gas station." He closed his eyes. "I have a little over $300,000 saved, and it's yours. Live your life, baby girl. Don't worry about me."

"I love you, too. I need you, Blue, please don't leave me like this." Sasha walked over to him slowly and carefully so she didn't set him off. "We have a baby on the way, and so does Quint. Baby, you just made him a promise you were going to take care of his child."

Sasha knelt down in front of him with tears in her eyes. Her heart was about to beat out of her chest, fearing his reaction. She grabbed the gun he was holding under his chin. With no resistance, he let it go and she removed the clip.

"When I moved here from the Bahamas, Quint was the first friend I made. I'll never forget that day." He wiped his face with his shirt. "It was my first week of school, and I was fresh every day. There were some boys who were jealous of me, and they tried to jump me after school and take my shoes. Quint showed up, stepped to the ringleader, and hit him in his shit."

Blue laughed, reminiscing about his trip down memory lane. "He told them I was his brother, and if they stepped to me again, he was gon' murder them." He shook his head. "They never tried me again. Me and Quint became best friends that day, and we've been joined at the hip ever since then. That was twelve years ago." He paused before he continued. "My life will never be the same without him."

"Just hold on to those memories, and I promise I will help you get through this."

"You promise?" His eyes were dark and sad.

"I promise." Sasha hugged him tight. "I'll be here forever, and I mean that."

Chapter 14

Over the past few weeks, Nate and NJ had been working on their relationship. It wasn't perfect, but they were making progress. NJ still had abandonment issues, and there was only one person who could put everything in perspective, and that was his mother.

He sat in the passenger seat while his dad drove through the city. "So, where are we headed?"

"I think it's time we paid your mother a visit so she could tell you her side to the story. I can only give you my side because, honestly, I don't know why she gave you up. She didn't even tell me she was pregnant."

"You know where she lives?"

"Yeah, Slim got the address for me."

NJ sat back and thought about all the questions he was going to ask. Growing up, he always wondered what she looked like and what type of person she was. No one in the foster care system bothered to help him gain info on her whereabouts. They told him they had no records of her, so he gave up on finding out. Every emotion he could think of was present in him. Anger, anxiety, fear, excitement, and happiness consumed his fifteen-year-old brain.

"What if she gets upset we popped up out of the blue?"

His eyes remained on the road, but he could see him from his peripheral vision. "I don't care how she feels. I've been mad for fifteen years, so she could miss me with that. I lost fifteen years behind her. Those years could've been spent getting to know you."

Nate hopped onto I-95 South and turned on the stereo. He couldn't wait to see the expression on her face when he arrived. An old-school jam by Teddy Pendergrass came on, and NJ frowned.

"Man, what you got us listening to?"

"Music with meaning, but you wouldn't know nothing about that."

NJ grabbed the aux cord. "Man, you lame-vibin', and I can't ride like that." He hooked the phone up. "I got something for you to jam to." He put on something up-to-date.

"What the hell is this *Purple Reign* shit?"

"That's Future."

"He need to be in the past, because Prince owns *Purple Rain*."

"Pops, stop lame-vibin', 'cause he the truth." He had become comfortable enough to address him as Pops, especially since he acted like an old man.

"That's a lie. Prince is the truth."

"Well, Prince ain't here no more, so you need to cut it. You gon' like him, watch what I tell you."

"I don't think so. This generation of rappers is gay. Everybody wearing these tight-ass pants. Nigga's nuts can't even breathe."

NJ cracked up. "Would it be better if they wore oversized jeans and white tee's like y'all did back in the day?"

"That was the style back then."

"That shit was whack back then."

Twenty-five minutes later they were pulling into the driveway. "Damn, this a nice-ass house she live in," NJ admired the scenery. "They must got that guape, living out here."

"Tell me about it." Nate was disgusted she was living the high life while their son was stuck in the hood hustling. He turned the car off. "Come on."

They walked up to the door and rang the bell. A pregnant woman answered the door, but it wasn't Sasha. Nate looked confused. "Um. Hello. Is Sasha here?"

Gigi rolled eyes and put her hands on her hips. "She don't live here anymore."

Nate wasn't feeling her attitude, but he ignored it. "She used to live here?"

"Yeah."

"Well, do you know how to get in contact with her?"

"No, I don't." She held her hand up. "Wait a minute, who are you?"

"I'm Nate, and this is our son, NJ. He wanted to see his mother."

Gigi was blown away by what she just heard. "Sasha is his mother?"

"That's what I said."

NJ was aggravated with her bitchy attitude. "Listen, man, do you know where to find her or not? 'Cause we ain't with the twenty question bullshit."

Gigi rolled her neck. "Excuse me?"

"You heard me."

Nate had to calm his junior down if they were going to get the answers they needed. "Relax, son, I got this."

"Hold on." She closed the door.

"That bitch don't know me. She will get slapped in her mouth, fuckin' with me," NJ spat.

"Stay cool, man, she pregnant. She probably all hormonal and shit."

"She probably his side bitch or some shit."

The door opened and Nate recognized Quamae from the Facebook post Slim showed him. "How you doing, man? I'm Nate, and this is my son, NJ. Do you know where I can find Sasha?"

Quamae looked at Nate and then NJ. They definitely were father and son. He just couldn't believe they were standing on his front porch. "Um. Yeah, but she don't live here anymore."

"Do you have a number for her?"

"Yeah."

"You're her husband, right? No disrespect, but my son wants to see his mother."

"Nah, it's cool. We're going through a divorce right now." Quamae stepped to the side. "Let's chop it up real quick. Come in."

Nate and NJ walked into the house with him and followed him into the living room. "Here, have a seat."

Quamae was finally face-to-face with two of Sasha's many secrets. He sat across from them. "So, you are the infamous Nate Sr. and NJ? This is some wild shit." He grinned.

NJ was confused. "Why is that some wild shit?"

He leaned forward and folded his hands. "I was with your mother for four years, and not once did she mention she had a child. I didn't find out about you until a few months ago when your grandmother paid me a visit."

NJ was hurt, to say the least. "So she never mentioned me at all?"

"Sasha is very," he tapped the side of his head. "How can I put this? She is very secretive. There were a lot of things I didn't know about her."

"You right about that shit. I just got out after doing fifteen years, and she never told me she was pregnant."

"That's fucked up." He looked at NJ and felt sorry for him. Sasha wasn't fit to be a mother back then, and she definitely didn't deserve to be one now. "Sorry, man, about everything you went through. I know that has to be a tough pill to swallow." Quamae gave Nate her phone number.

Nate stood up. "We won't hold you up any longer than we already have. Thanks for everything. We appreciate it."

"No problem." They shook hands, then Quamae escorted them out the door.

As soon as they made it to the car, Nate dialed her number and put it on the loud speaker. The phone rang a few times before she picked up.

"Hello." She answered with a lot of hesitation in her voice. He figured it was because he didn't have a local number.

"Can I speak to Sasha?"

"This is her, who's calling?"

She sounded so mature since the last time he heard her voice. But that was to be expected since he hadn't heard it in years. "It's been a long time, Sasha."

"Who is this?"

"Nate." He waited for her to respond, but she was silent. "The Nate that did 15 for you."

"Oh gosh, you're out?" She never thought she would hear from him again, but boy was she wrong about that.

"In the flesh, and I need to see you ASAP, so when can you meet me? I just left your husband's house, and I have someone who wants to meet you."

Chapter 15
Christmas Day

Quamae opened his eyes to a spectacular view of his woman slobbering on his knob. She was definitely in the holiday spirit, wearing a two-piece Christmas lingerie set that exposed her huge stomach. She looked sexy in a red ribbon halter-top and Santa pants made into booty shorts.

"'Tis the season to be jolly," he sang, placing both hands behind his head, seizing the moment.

She took her mouth off his stick and joined in, staring at him with those tantalizing eyes. "Fa-la-la la-la, la-la la la."

"Damn, you know how to wake a nigga up right." Gigi made him feel like a king at all times, and for that reason he had a special surprise for her. "You keep this up, ain't no telling what Santa might give you."

Gigi put her throat muscles into overdrive until his warm semen slid down her throat. She stood on the side of the bed and licked her lips. "Breakfast will be served in a moment, so wash up."

"I wanna eat you for breakfast."

"You will be patient. I promise I won't get cold." She winked.

"So you just gon' tease a nigga like that?"

"Yep." She swished her hips side-to-side and made her way into the kitchen.

Quamae went into the bathroom, flipped the seat up, and took a long, loud piss. He tilted his head back and released a thunderous roar like the king of the jungle, then stood in front of the mirror to brush his teeth and wash his face. When he was done, he grilled at himself in the mirror, admiring his pearly white teeth, and clicked off the light.

On his way back to the room, Gigi was prancing down the hallway carrying a serving tray. She followed him to the room and fed him breakfast in bed. She had already eaten earlier that morning, so she could cater to her man with no distractions from the big girl in her womb. After breakfast, she presented him with two nicely-wrapped gifts in brown wrapping paper with a gold bow.

"Merry Christmas, baby," she puckered up and planted a wet kiss on his thick, juicy lips.

"Thank you, baby."

He removed the bow and tore open the wrapper, revealing a jewelry box. When he opened it, he was surprised to a see a 30-inch Cuban link bracelet to match his necklace. The second box contained a gold Michael Kors watch with diamonds in the face. He wasn't expecting much from her, but she definitely went all-out for him, and he was definitely going to return the favor.

"Damn, baby, you went all-out for yo' nigga."

"I wanted to show you how much I appreciate you."

They engaged in a long, wet liplock. He took a moment to catch his breath. "Damn, I love you."

"I love you, too."

"I'm ready for dessert now."

"I know you are."

"Take off that costume and come sit on my face." He was anxious to devour that pussy.

Gigi turned her back toward him and pushed her shorts down seductively with her thumbs. Grabbing her ankles, she made her booty cheeks bounce with a slight twerk, exposing her pretty lips from the back.

Quamae admired the view while stroking his dick with his right hand. "Damn, bring that pretty shit over here."

She crawled onto the bed and mounted his face, easing down on his mouth. Holding the headboard, she closed her eyes and arched her back. A soft moan escaped her lips when he started to suck on her juicy peach.

Later on that evening, Quamae and Gigi got dressed in the attire he purchased for them. He was wearing an all-black tuxedo, white shirt, and a red tie while Gigi wore a solid red dress with black Christian Louboutin pumps and a black clutch. He stared at her like she was the most beautiful woman he had ever laid eyes on.

His cellphone rang, snapping him out of her trance. "Hello?" He listened to the caller on the other end before he responded. "We're coming down now." He looked at Gigi. "Are you ready, gorgeous?"

She blushed. "Yes, I am."

They left the apartment hand-in-hand as they walked into the parking lot. There was a Ferrari stretch limo parked in front of the building, waiting for them. Gigi shouted with glee. "Is this for me?"

"Yes, my love. I told you tonight was going to be special."

The chauffer opened the door and let them in. Once they were seated, he held Gigi's hand in his.

"I'm loving my surprise already."

"The best is yet to come."

Quamae fixed himself a glass of champagne and took a sip. It was fun watching her squirm in her seat, wondering what the surprise was. By the end of the night she was going to be the happiest woman on the planet. They traveled thirty minutes before they pulled up to a waterfront mansion in Fort Lauderdale. It looked as if there was a party going on. The house was immaculate and packed with cars. The driver opened the door and Quamae climbed out first. He turned around, grabbed Gigi by the hand, and ushered her up the walkway.

Once they were inside, her breath was taken away when she saw their families. Her godfather was even in attendance. She walked around and greeted everyone with a hug. She couldn't believe he had thrown her a surprise Christmas party. *When did he have time to plan all of this?* she wondered.

For dinner they served lobster tails, shrimp, filet mignon, potatoes, and different vegetables. Quamae, Gigi, and Emani sat at the closest table to the stage.

The host came up and grabbed the mic. "Today we have a special guest in the house, and he's here to perform a special song for a special lady. Everybody give a round of applause for Lyfe Jennings."

Gigi couldn't believe her favorite artist was about to grace her with his presence. She couldn't wait to get home and give Quamae the business. There was nothing she wouldn't do for him or to him tonight or in the future. "My favorite singer. You remembered."

"How could I forget? Merry Christmas, baby. I hope you're enjoying your surprise."

"Yes, I am, and when we get home, I'm going to show you how much I love it."

"I'm looking forward to that," he grinned.

Lyfe Jennings walked up on the stage and grabbed the mic. "Thank you for the love in the house. I want to dedicate this song to Gianni Gaddis, from Quamae Banks."

Gigi was ready to cry on the spot when he started to sing. Quamae grabbed her and they began to slow dance to his sweet melody. Every type of emotion filled her up. She held him tightly and listened to the lyrics.

Having someone you can grow old with
Until God calls y'all home
Must be nice
Having someone who understands
That a thug has feelings, too
Someone who loves you for sho'
You never let 'em go
Even when your hustling days are gone
She'll be by your side, still holding on
Even when those 20s stop spinning
And all those gold-digging women disappear
She'll still be here

The crowd clapped and screamed when he finished the song. By this time Quamae had let go of her hand. Her focus was on Lyfe, and when she finally turned around, he was down on one knee.

Gigi panicked, placing her hand over her heart. "What are you doing?"

"Something I should've done a long time ago."

He grabbed her hand and looked into her eyes as he poured his heart out to her. "Gianni Gaddis, I know that everything between us hasn't been a smooth ride, and I've even made some bad decisions and left you behind. But I promise from this day forward, if you promise to be my wife, I will make that happen and make you the happiest woman in this world."

The tears were pouring down her face heavily. She couldn't believe the day she had always dreamed of was finally happening.

"Gianni Gaddis, will you please be my wife?"

"Yes!" she shouted happily. She bent down and gave her future husband a kiss. Never in a million years did she think Quamae would get down on one knee and propose to her.

After the party was over and they returned home, Gigi forgot all about being pregnant and put the pussy on him like she had never done before.

She rode him ferociously while his toes threw up all types of gang signs. He gripped her waste tightly to apply more pressure as they grinded together in perfect harmony.

"Who's the man?" he asked in between breaths.

"You are, baby. You're the muthafuckin' man," she purred. Her goal was to leave his ass sucking his thumb and curled into the fetal position.

***

After receiving the most shocking news about Nate's release, Sasha knew it was time to be completely honest with Blue. She didn't want to be in another relationship carrying around a bunch of secrets, so she gave him her true story, raw and uncut.

There was so much he didn't know about her, and it was like a punch to the gut. Nevertheless, he didn't blow up on her the way Quamae did.

Unsure of what his response would be, she bit down her nails nervously. "Are you going to say something?"

"Yeah." He was in deep thought. "Remember that night on the beach when I said you could tell me anything and I wouldn't judge you?"

She nodded her head. "Yes."

"Well, I meant what I said. I'm glad you told me. I just wish it was much sooner."

Her heart skipped a beat, not knowing where he was headed with his words. "Does that change the way you feel about me?"

"Of course it doesn't."

"Are you about to break up with me?"

"Sasha, I don't know…." He hesitated to search for the right words to say, and she panicked. "How many times do I have to tell you I love you? That I loved you from day one?"

Her eyes grew wide because she was expecting to hear the worst, but as usual, he was the same ol' loving Blue. "I thought you were about to end this."

He grabbed her hand and kissed it. "It's going to take a lot more than your past to make me leave you. I'm not walking away that easily, and besides, our relationship is still fresh, so we have a lot more to learn about each other. It's all good, baby, don't worry."

She looked away. "What did I do to deserve someone like you?"

"Being yourself. I love your flaws and all. Now come on so we can go and meet *our* son."

One hour later, they were parking in front of Houston's. Sasha noticed Nate immediately, standing next to their son at the entrance.

NJ looked up and saw a woman walking in their direction, holding hands with her man. He elbowed Nate Sr. "Pops, you need to find you a bad bitch like that, but one that ain't pregnant, though," he joked.

Nate slapped him on the back of the head. "Boy, that's your mama."

"Damn, old girl fine." As they got closer, he recognized a familiar face and his mouth dropped.

"You don't have the sense God gave you. Stand up and stop playing all the time." NJ did as he was told. "And please be nice, 'cause that mouth of yours is nasty."

"What? I got anger issues, and that ain't my fault It's hers. And she with this nigga."

"You know him?" he mumbled under his breath.

"I fuck with his cousin, Jazz. I guess she got a thang for hustlers."

Sasha stopped in front of them. Their resemblance was crazy. NJ was the spitting image of his father. "Wow, you look just like your father."

"It's good to see you again, Sasha." Nate stepped up and gave her a hug. "It's been a very long time."

"Good to see you too, Nate."

"NJ, this is your mother, Sasha." He nudged his arm, signaling him to do the same.

"I don't have a mother. Never did." His thoughts went back to what Quamae said about her.

"NJ, what did I just—"

He was interrupted by Sasha. She put her hand up. "It's okay, Nate. I expect him to be upset. I don't blame him." She looked in NJ's direction. "There's a lot that happened to me, and that is the reason I gave you up, but just give me the chance to explain everything to you."

He sucked his teeth. "Yeah, a'ight."

Blue was standing behind her, waiting on either one of them to jump bad. No one was about to disrespect his woman in his presence. The old head wasn't gon' be a problem, but that young one would probably have to catch those hands.

Sasha grabbed Blue by his arm, shaking away his thoughts. "This is my boyfriend, Blue."

Blue and Nate Sr. slapped hands. "What's up, homie?"

"Just coolin'," Blue responded. Then he addressed NJ, but he mugged him a little, recognizing him from around the way. He knew he was fucking his little cousin. NJ also bought work from him before. "How you been, li'l homie?"

NJ laughed on the inside at the irony of how he was fucking Jazz and Blue was fucking his mama. "You know, just maintaining."

"Okay, are y'all ready to go inside?" Sasha asked.

"Yeah, let's go." Blue led the way and held the door. When they were out of earshot, he stepped to NJ. "My cousin told me you hit her."

NJ was shaken because he'd heard stories about Blue, and he didn't want those types of problems. He was definitely out of his league. Sucking his teeth, he responded. "Man, she hit me first."

He put his hand on his chest. "Listen, I'ma say this one time only: keep your hands off my cousin. If she tells me you hit her again, I promise you gon' have to see me. I'm sure you don't want me to put my hands on your ol' girl, 'cause you know how I get down."

"I got it, man. I won't touch her again."

"Good, and respect your mama. She went through a lot of shit, so giving you up was the best thing for you." He put his hand on his shoulder, making him flinch. "Relax, I'm yo' stepdaddy now," he laughed. "Let's go eat, 'cause I'm hungry as fuck."

During dinner, Blue sat back and observed the new cat at the table. He could tell Nate still had feelings for Sasha by the way he looked at her, but that shit was dead. He was the one and only man in her life. NJ was an exception to the rule.

NJ played with his silverware while looking Sasha in the eyes. "So, I keep hearing you did what was best for me. How was that?"

Sasha took a sip of water. "When I found out your daddy was going to be away for 15 years, I knew I couldn't take care of you. I could barely take care of myself without him."

"I'm sure life wouldn't have been that bad. You seem well off now, so why didn't you come back and get me?"

She peeped the slick remark and knew it was because of where she used to live and who she was married to. "I never told my husband about you." Blue cut his eyes at her. "I mean my ex-husband, and I didn't know how he would react to the news. I also felt it was best to stay away and not interfere with your life." Her eyes started to water, so Blue handed her a napkin.

"I get it. You didn't want to be a part of my life."

"The family I left you with didn't have kids, and they seemed like the perfect fit. What happened?"

"They're dead is what happened, and after that I bounced from home to home."

"I'm so sorry, NJ. I didn't know."

"How could you? You didn't bother to look for me."

"I can't change the past, but I can fix the future," she pleaded.

"Well, you seem like you are going to have your hands full in a few months, so I'm good. I got my dad."

The hurt was real. He completely shut her down.

Blue kicked his feet and tilted his head to remind him of what he told him earlier.

"I'm sorry, Sasha. I didn't mean for that to come out like that." NJ didn't like the way Blue was keeping him in check right at the table without being seen or vocal about it. "We can give it a try."

Blue picked up his glass of champagne and chugged it. If he had to catch up with NJ solo and snatch him up by the collar to make him repair his relationship with his mother, he was willing to do so.

After dinner was over, Blue paid the tab and they were all heading their separate ways. He smiled at NJ. "We'll be seeing you soon." NJ ignored him and walked behind Nate without a single rebuttal.

In the truck, Sasha sat in silence, rubbing her stomach. "Are you okay?" he asked.

"Yeah, I'm good." she smiled. "It actually went better than I thought it would. I'm just stuck on the fact he was quick to give Nate another chance versus me."

"That's probably because they both were in the blind about the situation. Don't worry, though, he'll come around and open up to you."

"Is that what you were talking to him about?"

"Yeah, I told him to give you a chance and not to shut you out. You had it bad, too, and you did what you thought was in his best interest."

"Thanks, baby. I really appreciate you being here for me."

"That's my job."

"I love you so much."

"I love you, too. Grab that box out of the glove compartment for me and open it."

Sasha pulled out the box, and when she opened it she was blinded by shiny diamonds. "Is this for me?"

"The one and only. Merry Christmas, baby."

"This necklace is beautiful." Sasha held it up in the air, admiring the expensive piece. After placing the box in her purse, she slid close to him and unbuckled his pants, freeing his dick. She stroked it a few times before making it disappear into her mouth.

Chapter 16

Chauncey and Ayesha lay in bed with their bodies drenched in sweat. She rubbed his bare chest with her hand. "You can't keep doing this to me."

"What?" he questioned.

"Sexing me like this. You know my weakness, and you just using it to your advantage. I'm mad with you."

He grinned. "No, you not. That's what you want me to believe. Besides, you the one who just tried to kill me. I haven't done anything to make you mad."

"Are you still fucking that crazy girl?" She could tell he was taken by surprise. "I want you to end it with her if you are." He still had a puzzled look on his face. "And stop looking stupid like you don't know what I'm talking about."

"That's because I don't know what you talking about."

"You fucking Monica."

"Man, go ahead with that crazy shit. You already know the answer to that. As much as you like to fuck, I don't have the energy to beat up another pussy."

"Don't play games with me, because I'm very stingy. I don't like to share."

"I'm stingy, too, so I guess we got something in common." He brushed it off because he knew she was just making assumptions. Good dick would make any chick go crazy, and besides, Monica was history.

"Just be honest, okay."

"Chill, bae. I ain't hittin' no other chicks besides you."

"Why she keep calling you, then?"

Chauncey grabbed his dick and laughed. "She miss this. She acting crazy like you are right now."

"That's not funny, and you better not give it to her, either."

Chauncey rapped a clip from Drake's song. "*You know this dick ain't free. I got girls that I should've made pay for it, got girls that I should've made wait for it.*" She was hooked, and he knew it.

"I'm glad you find this funny." She pouted and rolled over, turning her back to him.

"I'm just playing, ma. Calm down." He rolled her back over and straddled her. "I know what will make you feel better." Chauncey kissed her.

She placed her hands on his chest and pushed him. "That won't make it better."

"But this will." He pushed her legs apart and entered her.

"Ss," she moaned.

"That's all you want, is for me to keep this dick up in you."

She shook her head up and down. "I can't help it. I have to fuck you every day. That's my job."

"Mine, too."

***

The following morning, Quamae rolled over and stared Gigi in the face as she slept. A lot had changed about her facial features, and she was wearing that motherly glow well. He admired her beauty as he stroked her face with his hand. She was the epitome of a real woman.

"I love you so much," he whispered. "This is how it should've been years ago."

"Aw, baby, I love you, too," she replied, catching him off guard.

He smiled. "You playing possum on me, huh?"

She blinked her heavy eyelids a few times. "No."

"Did I make you happy last night?"

Her smile stretched her eyes. "More than you can imagine."

"So, are you going to move in with me?"

After the proposal last night, there was no way in hell she was saying no. "Yes, I will." She wiggled her ring finger and smiled. "Forever."

He was happy with her response, although he knew she would say yes off the strength of the engagement. "Good. I'm about to stop by the house real quick and run a few errands. I'll be back soon."

She nodded her head. Quamae dressed quickly in a pair of jeans and a bulletproof vest, which had become a part of his everyday wardrobe. After all the shit he'd been through, he had to be cautious in the streets. He pulled a black shirt over his head and covered himself in a lightweight, hooded faux-leather jacket. The temperature was surprisingly cold due to the sudden change in the weather, but he loved the change nonetheless.

"Why are you wearing a bulletproof vest?" she asked out of curiosity.

"I'd rather be safe than sorry."

That suddenly reminded her about the club incident. "Please be careful."

"I promise." He gave her a kiss on the forehead and headed out the door.

On the way out, he hit up Dirty. "What up, bruh?"

"You still need to get in the house?"

"Nah, I'm with my baby mama. Where you at?"

"Headed there in a few, but I gotta slide on that nigga in the plaza about my cash."

"Oh, a'ight. Hit me up if you need me."

"Yeah."

An hour later, Quamae was leaving the shop from collecting his money. As he walked through the parking lot, he noticed a truck creeping through slowly. He immediately secured his backpack and reached for his gun on his waist.

"I don't know who this is, but we can do this shit in broad daylight."

The back window rolled down and shots rang out. *Boca! Boca! Boca!*

He exchanged gunfire and took cover behind a car. Bullets were flying, shattering the windows. Glass was falling all over him. Whoever it was wanted him dead, and they wasn't stopping. He rose to his feet and let off a few more rounds when he was hit twice.

"Shit."

Quamae dropped to his knees and hit the pavement from the impact of the bullet. He had been hit in the shoulder and once in the chest, but the BPV stopped it. He lay on the ground and caught a glimpse of the license plate when they sped off. He grabbed his banger off the ground and let off another shot, shattering the back window. His truck was only a few feet away, but he knew he needed to move fast because a few people were watching him and asking if he was okay. He even heard one yell to call the cops.

Quamae got in the car and peeled off before removing the leather jacket and setting it down in the passenger seat. Examining the hole from the bullet, he dug in his pocket for his phone. He placed a call to his close friend and comrade.

"Hey, Doc. I need you, man."

Doc had served time in the army, so he was quite nifty with the needle and thread. "What happened?" Doc asked.

"I got shot in the shoulder."

"Where you at?"

"On my way home."

"A'ight, man, I'll be there in 10 minutes."

"Thanks, fam." He ended the call.

When he made it to his house, he removed the BPV and his shirt before running water over the wound. Quamae gritted his teeth from the intense burn. While waiting on Doc, he received a call from Freeman.

"What's up?"

"Do you know a young lady by the name of Monica?"

"Chauncey's girl? Her name is Monica."

"Well, I don't think that's his girl anymore. She called in on the tip line and dropped some info, saying he's a big-time distributor."

"You bullshittin'."

"I wish I was. Her allegations have sparked up an investigation, so steer clear of him, because he's on the radar now."

"Damn, this is fucked up."

"She didn't drop your name, so don't worry. You're in the clear."

The doorbell rang. "Good. Keep me posted. I gotta go."

"Will do."

Doc arrived promptly, just like he said he would. They went into the kitchen, where he set up shop.

"You might wanna take you a stiff shot of this moonshine," he warned. "This can make a grown man cry." He pulled the bottle from his duffle bag and handed it over. Quamae grabbed a glass, filled it to the rim and gulped it down.

"Fuck," he grunted from the burning sensation as it traveled through his system into the pit of his stomach.

"That shit strong, ain't it?" Doc laughed.

"Hell yeah."

Quamae took a seat at the table and allowed him to work his magic. Doc covered his mouth and nose with a surgical mask and pulled out a pair of surgical tweezers. "I need you to relax," he explained. "Whatever you do, be still and don't move a muscle."

Quamae relaxed his muscles and prepared himself for the pain he was about to endure. The instrument felt cold on his skin as Doc removed the bullet lodged in his shoulder. Once he placed the fragment on the table, he placed a towel under his arm and poured a tremendous amount of witch hazel on his wound. Quamae closed his eyes tightly as the tingling sensation began to pulsate his arm. After the wound was dry, Doc picked up the threaded needle and pierced his skin. The pain was unbearable and a real tear-jerker. He could feel the sting as the sharp tool tore into his flesh. Tears pricked his eyes, but he didn't let them fall. *You a G nigga, man up and stop whining like a bitch!* He gave himself a pep talk, clenched his fists tightly, and took it like a man.

When Doc finished, it was like a breath of fresh air. "Thanks, man, you a life saver."

"You know I got you." He washed his instruments in the sink and packed up. "I'm not gon' ask what happened. The less I know, the better. All I'm gon' say is be careful."

"Oh, no doubt."

"Keep that area dry for a week. The stitches will dissolve on their own, and you'll be good."

He handed Doc some cash and walked him to the door. "Thanks again, man."

"You got it."

Quamae went back into the kitchen to call Dirty, but his phone kept going straight to voicemail. He scratched his head whenever he was in deep thought. Then a thought crossed his mind and he ran for the steps.

When he made it the room, he grabbed the recorder and went down to the den. He sat down and pressed play while he fixed himself a drink. The pain from the stitches was throbbing, and he needed to numb the pain. After listening for what seemed like hours, he gave up and was about to press stop until he heard talking. Quamae held his glass in his hand and took a shot. Then, from nowhere, the conversation took a left turn. He was shocked, to say the least, and the glass he was holding slipped from his grip and crashed onto the floor.

"I can't believe this shit," he huffed.

Quamae dialed Chauncey's number. "What's up, bruh?"

"Aye, I need you to get to my house, like yesterday."

"What's up? Some shit just went down?"

"You can say that. How long before you get here?"

"Shit, I can be there in twenty minutes." Chauncey jumped out of bed quickly.

"I'll be here, waiting."

"Yeah."

Quamae sat for an hour and thirty minutes waiting on Chauncey to arrive, and when he did get there, he was in Gorilla mode.

"What's up bruh?" Chauncey asked.

"Damn, nigga, that was more than twenty minutes."

"I know, bruh, my bad. My girl was trippin' and shit. All she wanna do is fuck."

"Who, Monica?"

"Nah, I got a new li'l baby, Ayesha, and she is the truth. I had to drop something in her before I left."

Quamae shook his head. "Damn, she got you pussy whipped?"

"Hell nah. The pussy good as fuck, though."

"You talkin' 'bout Ayesha who strip?"

"Yeah. You know her?"

"I seen her around. But anyway, I got something you need to listen to, and some dirt on sweet ol' Monica." Quamae didn't want to spend too much time talking about his latest chick because he knew her, and he knew her very well.

"Let's hear it."

"Well, I got a call from Freeman, and let's just say that bitch Monica is foul as fuck. She dropped a tip saying you are a big distributor of coke and they need to investigate you."

"That bitch." He pounded on the table.

"We gotta walk light for now."

"Shit, we been walking light. We ain't been touching no dope." He rubbed his hand over his face. "She wanna play it like that? I got something for that ho."

"And now, here is the grand finale." Quamae sat the device on the counter and turned the volume up to the max. "We gon' have to kill this bitch."

Then he pressed play.

***

Sasha was still thinking about the dinner she had with Nate and NJ. Seeing him after all those years made those sweet memories resurface. There were times she had to catch herself from reminiscing in front of Blue. She was not trying to make him feel uncomfortable, although he had nothing to worry about. The love she had for Nate still existed because without him she wouldn't have gotten another chance at love or life. He exposed her to something she had never experienced in her first fifteen years at life, and that was affection. When the time presented itself, she was going to sit him down and apologize for leaving him alone for all those years. The apology would only serve as a good gesture because it did not make up for lost time. He needed to know how sorry she was. Fifteen years in prison for a crime he didn't commit was enough to drive anybody crazy.

She had to admit Nate did look good, and his body was just right. The weights and milk definitely did his body good. Flashbacks of their first time invaded her thoughts.

"Why you hiding up under the covers? You scared?" Nate asked while he stood at the side of the bed, getting undressed.

Sasha shook her head. "No."

She wanted to take the next step with him to see what love felt like. He was her protector, and she was prepared to satisfy his needs to keep him happy. When he dropped his boxers to the floor, her eyes widened at the thickness and the length of his dick. Crazy as it may sound, she was anxious to feel it. Nate caught her expression and smiled. "Don't worry, I'll take my time with you."

She smiled nervously, unsure of what to expect from him. Nate got up under the covers with her and slid down between her legs. Sasha was confused because she didn't understand why his face was down there.

"What are you doing?"

"You never had head before?" he asked.

"No."

"Well, just relax, and I promise you'll like it."

Sasha closed her eyes, while Nate went down on her. It felt weird when she felt his tongue circle on her clit. When he sucked on it, her body shivered and she was in ecstacy. Minutes later, a strange feeling came over her and she wiggled her body.

"Nate, wait, I have to pee."

Nate lifted his head. "No, you don't. You 'bout to nut. Just let it go."

She was confused. "What's that?"

He laughed at her inexperience with sex. "It's an orgasm, not pee."

Going back down, he sucked on her until she screamed and came in his mouth.

That was the first orgasm of many more to come. Nate took his time, as promised, and made slow, sweet, passionate love to her over and over again for the rest of the day until she couldn't take any more. Sasha never knew sex could feel so good, especially when it was done willingly.

From that day on, sex had become her new addiction. Nate taught her everything she needed to know about sex, including teaching her how to suck a mean dick, which she perfected quickly.

Sasha came back to reality and got out of the car to go inside Carmen's house. She knocked on the door and India let her in. "Took long enough. What you was outside doing?"

"So you knew I was out there and you still made me knock?"

India laughed. "I didn't feel like getting up. Is that okay with you?"

"Yep." Sasha brushed past her to get to the sofa. "See how you starting already?"

She played dumb and grabbed Sasha's ass. "I didn't do anything boo."

"Bruh, stop being so gay."

Carmen laughed at the both of them. "You know India gets gay and aggressive when she drinks."

"She better stop before I make her eat this pussy."

Carmen frowned. "You so nasty, make me think both of y'all hos' gay."

Sasha flopped down on the sofa next to Carmen. "You know I don't take nothing but dick."

India sat across from them. "Yeah, that's why you blowed up now."

"I know, right? And I can't wait to drop this load, 'cause I can't fuck how I want to."

"I'm sure you and Blue fucking on a daily basis," Carmen replied.

"Yeah, we do." She sucked her teeth. "But shit, all I can do is lay there while he beat it up. I like to participate, and I feel like he being a bedroom bully right now."

India giggled. "You play too much."

"I'm serious, sis. You know I like to be in control and shit." She scratched the top of her head. "I think he trying to dick-whip me or some shit."

Carmen rolled her eyes. "Girl, bye. He already did that, bae."

"I know, right? His li'l young ass be having me hollerin' and shit."

"Damn, he got it like that?" India asked.

"Hell yeah, he got a big-ass dick and a hurricane tongue."

Carmen snickered because she knew Sasha was telling the truth. If Blue wasn't so wrapped up into her friend, she would know what it felt like, too.

"Well, I'm glad we friends and don't want his ass, 'cause anybody else would be trying to sample that shit."

Carmen rolled her eyes and was immediately offended by the comment since she was trying to get a sample a while ago. Luckily no one knew what happened that day. However, India peeped the obvious eye roll and called her out.

"Why you rolling your eyes, Carmen? You want a young nigga to beat up the twat, too?"

"'Cause that is too much information." She wondered if Blue had said anything to her about their little situation, because she found it strange that she was going into great detail about their sex life.

Sasha cut her eyes at Carmen. "I know you ain't talking, because you love to tell us about your fuck fests."

"And she doesn't leave out one little detail," India added.

Carmen wanted to change the subject quickly. "Anyway, what happened at the dinner?"

"Yeah, how does Nate look now?" India added.

Sasha sat up in her seat and popped her lips together. "Girl, let's just say that Nate is real fine. He still looks the same, you know, just more mature now."

"You sound like you wanna fuck the nigga," India joked. "You want that fresh meat straight out the penitentiary." The girls cracked up.

"Gawd damn, suck 'im up," Carmen sung.

"I hate the both of y'all, just so you know." Sasha was in tears laughing from their jokes. She had to calm herself down in order to finish the story. "So anyway, NJ hates my guts, and I don't think he's interested in patching up our relationship."

"Why you say that?" India wanted all the tea.

"His attitude was so nonchalant, although he did act a little differently after Blue spoke to him. I don't know what he said to him, but he did lighten up with the attitude."

"Let me find out Blue trying to be a step-daddy," Carmen added.

India thought it was too early to pass judgement when that was only their first encounter. "You have to give him some time, especially since this was his first time seeing you in his life. This is something new to him, so just take things slow at first and don't rush it."

"Yeah, I know that, but he doesn't act like that toward Nate. He respects him, and I witnessed that firsthand." Sasha leaned back on the sofa and pouted. "That's not fair. He's giving him a chance, and they just met, too. I guess I'm the villain."

"Well, you did give him up and never went to see him. Maybe he can relate to his daddy more because they didn't know about each other, but you knew all along."

India rolled her eyes. "Shut up, Carmen."

"What? I'm just saying what it could be that's making him act that way. You always think a bitch trying to be funny."

"'Cause, bitch, you always trying to be funny."

"Not right now, I'm not. This is a serious matter."

"So, what you gon' do, Sasha?" India focused her attention back to her sister in need.

"I don't know. I want to fix it, but I don't know how."

"Start by opening up that line of communication. He has to be baby-stepped into this. Just put yourself in his shoes for a second and ask yourself how would you feel if your mom gave you up?"

Sasha frowned, shaking her head. "That's not a good example. I wished like hell my mama would've gave me away."

"Um. Yeah. That was a bad example." She paused for a second. "Okay, so pretend you had — fuck it. You just have to pretend that all of that pertained to you. Just put yourself in his shoes."

"I would be upset, probably."

India shook her head. "Un-uh, you would've been upset."

"Okay, okay, I get what you're saying. I'm going to just reach out to Nate and we'll go from there. I'll take him shopping or something, 'cause from what I can see, he dresses very well."

"He got that honest," Carmen replied.

"Yeah, he was rocking some expensive threads."

"Sounds like he selling dope." That was the first thought that popped into Carmen's head.

"Shit, he might be. Who knows?" Sasha shrugged her shoulders. "I'm going to step out and call Nate. I'll be right back." She got up and grabbed her cellphone.

"Why you can't talk right here?" Carmen wanted to know what was about to be said. "Don't go over there and let that man feed that baby. She come out looking like him, Blue gon' fuck you up."

"Shut up, Carmen." She walked outside and dialed Nate's number.

Chapter 17
New Year's Eve

India had just made it home from a long day of standing, sewing in bundles, perming, and coloring hair. She was beat, and all she wanted to do was take a long, hot bath and sleep for the rest of the evening. She ran herself a nice, hot bath and stuck one toe in to make sure her body could tolerate the heat. Satisfied with the temperature, she eased down in the water, lay back, and closed her eyes while the sound of Whitney Houston filled her ears.

Why does it hurt so bad
Why do I feel so sad
Thought I was over you
But I keep crying
When I don't love you

The beads of water pouring from her eyes soaked her face. She was still devastated from the news of Steve's marriage, and it was surely a hard pill to swallow. She was constantly putting up a front around her friends, but truthfully she was dying on the inside. He had been blowing up her phone all day and sending text messages, so she knew her little package had arrived at their address. She ignored every attempt he made to contact her.

As the bath water became tepid, she figured it was time to wash off. India scrubbed her body roughly, trying to scrub off any remnants of Steve embedded in her soul.

When she was done she felt clean, but her skin was tender from the wrath of her aggressive cleansing. She stepped from the tub and threw on a bathrobe, slipped her feet into her bedroom shoes, and headed to the kitchen. All she needed was a nightcap and she could snuggle alone in her warm bed. She opted on a glass of wine to reduce the anxiety she was feeling from the heartbreak.

India poured a glass of Pinot Grigio and took a long swig like it was water, then poured herself another. A knock on the door caused her to flinch, and an uneasy feeling grabbed her by the neck, causing a lump to form in her throat. She knew it was Steve, and for that reason she didn't want to answer the door, but she needed to be sure. When she looked through the peephole, she was surprised to see someone standing at the door holding a basket from Edible Arrangements.

On the inside she smiled at his persistence to win her over, but her face was balled up in disgust because there was no way she was taking his lying, married-ass back. She slung the door open, prepared to send the delivery person away, but suddenly became numb when she recognized the woman as Steve's wife. She pulled a small handgun from her pocket and aimed it at India's stomach.

"Back up, bitch, and let me in." She barged her way into the home without warning and backed India up against the couch.

"Please, don't kill me," she begged.

Steve's wife laughed hysterically as if India had just told some sort of joke. "Oh, what happened to the big, bad wolf I met in the shop weeks ago? Is the baby making you soft all of a sudden?" Her mockery was unsettling, and the look in her eyes made India's blood run cold. "You think you can come into our lives and threaten us with a paternity suit for your bastard child? Bitch, you are sadly mistaken, because I have worked too hard to turn that man into what he is today."

"No, please, I'm not really pregnant. I only lied because he hurt me. I wanted to make him suffer," she pleaded.

"Bitch, shut the fuck up!" she yelled. "Do you think I'm stupid or some shit? I saw the test, and you are going to die tonight."

India started quoting the scripture when Janine cocked the gun back. "The Lord is my shepherd, I shall not want. He maketh me to lie down in green pastures."

"Stop!" she shouted. "Did you pray to God when you were fucking my husband?" She snickered like she was on some type of medication and her lunacy had just kicked in. "Because he don't hear hos who commit adultery."

She fired two shots into India's stomach, and she hit the floor. Janine stood over her and laughed. "Now look what you made me do. Bitch, I'm off my meds, and I'm not responsible for what I did to you. Now, that should teach you a lesson about fucking with people's husbands."

She watched as India squirmed around on the floor, holding her stomach with tears in her eyes. "Don't cry. God might forgive you, but I sure as hell won't." She rubbed India's head. "You can finish your prayers now, 'cause I'm about to go home and fuck my husband while you die alone."

Janine locked the door on her way out and fled the scene with the fruit assortment in her hands. India lay on the floor and suffered until she took her final breath.

***

Carol sat on the bench at Holiday Park with great anticipation, waiting on Frank's son's arrival. A black Mercedes Benz pulled up and parked. A tall, handsome man stepped out and approached her. "Boy, you look just like your daddy."

He grinned, exposing his braces, because he had become accustomed to hearing that from everybody who knew Frank. "Tell me about it," he replied, taking a seat on the opposite side of her. "So, what's the good news I need to hear?"

She slid him a piece of paper. "That's the address to the bitch who had your father killed."

When he opened up the paper, there was a scribbled address on it. "Good looking out. I've been waiting on this day for a long-ass time."

She winked. "I know you have. I told you I would find out. Oh, and be careful. She has a dangerous-ass husband."

Mark reached into his pocket and peeled off five $100 bills and placed them in the palm of her hand. "Thanks for the info."

He stood up and walked away, plotting how he was going to avenge the death of his father. Those thoughts were in his mind for years, but he knew he couldn't get ahold of Nate because of his incarceration. So, when Carol tracked him down and said she was digging to find out who was behind it, he was gung ho about finally taking down whomever was responsible for his heinous death.

She sat and watched Mark as he drove away, thinking of her next plan to flee the area, if not the state altogether. The day she walked through the gates that separated her from her freedom, she knew she was returning to cause havoc in Sasha's life. *Oh yes, bitch, revenge is best served cold! I'll teach you about turning your back on me for a piece of dick. Ol' hot-pussy ho!* She put the money in her back pocket and left the park, whistling.

***

Sasha had just left her doctor's appointment when she received a call from Carmen.

"Hey, Carmen. What's up, girl?"

Carmen responded, but it sounded like jibberish.

"Hold on, 'cause I can't hear you." She put the receiver against her chest and looked at Blue. "Bae, turn the radio down."

He looked at her and turned it up.

She frowned. "Don't be rude."

"Hang up the phone," he demanded.

"She's crying, so stop being so mean." She put the phone back to her car. "What's wrong?"

"Sasha, it's bad."

Her heart started to beat harder in her chest. "What's bad?"

"She's gone, Sasha. She left us."

"Who left us?"

"India."

Confusion settled over her. "What do you mean? Where did she go?"

"She's dead, Sasha." She sobbed loudly into the phone.

"What did you say?" Her voice trembled.

"Somebody killed our sister."

Sasha screamed in agony and took her hand off the steering wheel, dropping her phone in the process. The car spun out of control, sliding across two lanes on the wet road and spinning in a full circle. Blue reached over and grabbed the wheel.

"Hit the brake. Hit the brake," he yelled.

She slammed on the brakes and they locked up. The tires skidded and the car stopped just in time next to a pole.

Blue threw the car in park and grabbed her hand. "You okay?"

"No," she cried, shaking her head.

"What happened?"

"My friend was killed." She opened the car door to look for her phone, and so did he.

He walked over to the driver's side and hugged her. "Baby, I'm so sorry."

A passerby pulled up next to them and got out. He was a tall, white, older man. "Are you two okay? I saw you lose control of the car."

Blue looked up. "Yeah, we're fine. Thanks."

"Are you sure? Does she need a medic?"

"She's just shaken up a bit."

"Okay." He turned to walk away, but Blue stopped him.

"Thanks, man. I appreciate your concern."

"Take care." Then he walked away.

Back at the house, Sasha sat on the phone with Carmen, crying nonstop while she explained the details of what she knew. Blue was getting aggravated because he didn't want her stressed out and felt talking to her was making it worse. He sympathized for the loss of her friend, but clearly the conversation was making it worse. He walked over to her and took the phone.

"What are you doing?" she asked.

"You need rest, and all she is doing is stressing you out more." He put the phone to his ear. "She will call you back, 'cause she don't need to be stressing out my baby."

Carmen was about to respond, but he didn't waste time giving her the dial tone. "Come lay down. I'm all you need right now."

Blue felt her pain, especially since he had just lost his very close friend not too long ago. The sobs and crying reopened his wound, and he began to shed tears for Quint. They cuddled under one another and fell asleep.

In the middle of the night, Blue was awakened by Sasha's crying and screaming. He jumped up and turned on the light. She wasn't in bed. It was coming from the bathroom. He felt a sense of panic come over him as he ran to her aid. He pushed the door open with force and found her on the floor, writhing in pain.

"What's wrong?" He was distraught.

"My water broke," she cried.

He didn't notice the puddle she was laying in. "I'm gon' take you to the hospital, so just relax."

He was trying to keep calm when he really felt like screaming his damn self. This was some scary shit, because he had never witnessed anything like this before. Out of all the nights, his mother was working the late shift when he needed her the most. Blue carried Sasha to the truck and they were off to the hospital.

After spending five hours in labor and delivery, she finally gave birth to a beautiful baby girl. Blue was in awe of her beauty as Sasha cradled her against her bosom.

"What's wrong?" she whispered.

"She's so beautiful."

"She is, isn't she?" She looked down at her new bundle of joy and smiled. "Her middle name is going to be India, after my friend."

"That's fine, baby. As long as you happy, I'm happy."

Watching a live birth made him want to be with her more than ever. He had never witnessed a pussy stretch so far to the point another human emerged from it. He never wanted to be a father until that very moment. Holding his baby girl in his arms, he felt a connection. As far as he was concerned, she belonged to him, no matter what the DNA test would reveal.

A few hours later, Blue was gone and Sasha had just gotten out of the shower before crawling back in the hospital bed. There were so many thoughts running through her head, and she needed someone to talk to, so she called Carmen.

"Hello."

"What are you doing?"

"Nothing. How are you feeling today? And whose number you calling me from?"

"I'm doing better now. I'm in the hospital, and I forgot my phone in Blue's truck."

"For what?"

"I thought I was having Braxton Hicks, but my water broke this morning, and I had the baby."

Carmen was excited as she shouted through the phone. "Yay! You had my godbaby!" Then she paused abruptly. "Okay, and who in the hell is Braxton Hicks? I know damn well you didn't name my baby that shit."

Sasha laughed. "You are foolish. Take off your blonde wig."

"Bitch, what's funny?"

"You."

"Why am I funny?"

"Because it's not an actual person, dumb-dumb." She couldn't believe Carmen was so clueless.

"Well, what the hell is it?"

"False labor."

She laughed as well. "Oh, you can have that?" she asked curiously.

"Duh! Girl, quit acting crazy."

"Oh no, baby, I'm not acting. I don't know shit about pregnancy or childbirth, and I'm not trying to find out, either," Carmen joked.

"You crazy," Sasha replied.

"Bitch, I'm dead-ass serious." She was adamant about not having kids. She was enjoying life and didn't want any distractions to interrupt her fun.

"I know, and that's the crazy part."

"What did you name her?"

"Dream India Joyner," she sniffled.

"Damn, we gon' miss her."

"I know."

Curiosity was killing her, and she needed the low-down on what was going on with her and her situation. They also needed to change the subject. "Did Quamae come up there?"

"No," she answered quickly.

"Did you call him?"

"I sent him a text, but he didn't respond."

"So, what are you gonna do? You already know he ain't gon do shit without a DNA test."

"Yeah, I know."

"Hold up. Fuck all that, why didn't you call me so I could come up there?"

"Because I didn't want any conflict between you and Blue."

"Really? So you gon' let him come between us?"

"No. I just thought it was best to keep you two at a distance until I find out what the real issue is."

Carmen tooted her lips up and rolled her eyes. "I guess, chil'. So, you told Chauncey, too?"

That question was out of left field for her. "What?"

"Did you tell Chauncey?"

"Why would I tell him?"

"What happened between y'all two?"

"Nothing," she lied.

Carmen took a deep breath before she dropped some knowledge on her. Their relationship was a little too close for nothing to have happened between them. "Sasha, just stop it. I know you and Chauncey were, in fact, fucking, and Ray Charles can see that. I'm supposed to be your sister, and you would lie to me? That ain't cool, I always have your back, no matter what." She refrained from saying anything further in hopes she would just come clean.

Sasha thought long and hard about being honest. It wasn't like she was going to tell Quamae about it. She closed her eyes and paced her breathing for the moment of truth. "You're right." She paused. "We were sleeping together."

"Damn, sis, that explains a lot. Is that why Quamae acted the way he did?"

"I don't know."

"So, now my next question: is Chauncey the father?"

Sasha froze before responding, *"I don't know."*

Chapter 18

Two weeks had passed since India was murdered in her home, and life wasn't getting any better for Sasha. The detectives on the case made no arrests, and she was losing her patience slowly, but surely. To make matters worse, Blue and Sasha were constantly down each other's throats and it was getting tiresome. She was two steps from moving out, because for the past few nights he was staying out late, just like Quamae used to do.

"What's going on with you?" She was apprehensive about hearing the truth, but she needed to know. "Are you fucking somebody else?"

He was holding the baby in his lap, but he looked up with an evil stare. "Don't go there."

"I'm asking a question, so you need to answer me."

"I don't have a reason to cheat."

"Somebody's keeping you out late at night."

"The streets." He looked into Dream's light brown eyes and smiled. "I have to take care of you, don't I, pretty girl? You understand where Daddy been, don't you." She cooed. "I know you do. You should talk to your mama."

"I heard that before." She folded her arms.

"Not from me you didn't, so you can stop comparing me to that fuck-nigga. I hustle, in case you forgot."

"I'm not comparing you to nobody, but ever since I came home you have had this nasty attitude toward me, and I haven't done shit to you."

"If you say so."

Sasha became irate and started to yell and scream. "What the fuck did I do? Apparently I didn't do shit, because you can't tell me. You are the fucking problem."

There was a knock on the door. "Is everything okay in there?" his mom asked.

"Yeah, Ma."

She opened the door. "Why y'all doing all this yelling and screaming around my grandbaby?"

Blue gave his mom eye contact. "Sorry about that."

"Give her to me." She grabbed the baby and left the room.

"So, you gon' tell me what I did to you?" Sasha stood in front of him.

"Nah, I'm straight. Back up off me, though."

"Fuck you," she spat. "You the one out here fucking and staying out late, and you wanna take that shit out on me because one of your hos made you mad."

Blue stood up. "Oh, it's *fuck me* now? Since you feel that way, let's put it out there, because you haven't been truthful."

"About what?" she shouted.

"You fucking Chauncey."

She froze.

"Nah, don't get quiet now. I know for a fact you fucked the nigga. I saw the texts in your phone." he walked up on her and leaned down in her face so she could look in his eyes. "Is that why the nigga was beating your ass? You was fucking his best friend right up under his nose."

Before he could say anything else, she reached out and slapped the words out of his mouth. Blue snatched her up by her shirt and pushed her against the wall.

"Don't put your fuckin' hands on me, and I mean that shit. I don't hit women, but I will fuck a bitch up."

She grabbed his hands. "Let me go."

"You must like for a nigga to put they hands on you. That shit make you feel loved or some shit?" She looked away. "I'll leave you before I beat you." He let her go.

"I'm sorry. It only happened once, and that was when he was in the hospital. I thought I was going to lose him, and—"

Blue cut her off. "Lose him? I'm confused, 'cause we were together then."

"That doesn't mean I wanted him to die. I was pregnant and emotional. I didn't know how we would turn out. Chauncey gave me a ride home. I was crying, and he was there to comfort me, and one thing led to another. I didn't mean to sleep with him. It just happened."

"So why didn't you call me to comfort you?"

She shrugged her shoulders. "I don't know. I'm sorry."

"And you didn't tell me. If you would've never left your phone, I wouldn't know shit."

"How was I supposed to just come out and say that to you?"

He grabbed his keys from the dresser. "I gotta get out of here."

Sasha grabbed his arm. "Blue, please don't leave. I'm sorry I didn't tell you."

He snatched away from her. "I'm out, man."

She ran to the door, blocking his path. "Don't go."

"I need to cool off before I do something I might regret. Give me my space."

"You want space now?"

"That's what I said."

Her feelings were hurt completely. She stepped to the side. "Go ahead and have your space. We'll be gone when you get back."

"You're not taking my baby anywhere."

"Don't argue with me about this. You said you need space, so I'll go. Carmen has an extra room for me and the baby."

Sasha pushed his last button. "I wish you wouldn't take my daughter around that ho."

"Why she gotta be all that? You don't even know her."

Blue pointed his finger in her face. "No, you don't know that ho."

"She's my only friend left, and you will not keep me away from her."

He laughed. "You think that ho is your friend? Well, let me enlighten you on your so-called friend. That day we left the hospital together, she tried to fuck me."

Sasha grabbed her chest and backed up so she could sit down. "Carmen wouldn't do that."

"Yeah, have a seat so you can hear this. We went to the liquor store so I could calm down, and when we came back, we sat in the truck and smoked a blunt. I was ready to get out, but she wanted to finish her drink. I dozed off for a few minutes, and when I got up she was jacking my dick. I told her to leave the hospital, and that's why she didn't come back up with me. So, like I said, that ho ain't your friend. I'm all you got, baby."

"I can't believe she would do that to me when she knows how I feel about you."

"Well, believe it. I was in need of comfort, too, but I didn't fuck your best friend. You see where I'm going with this?"

Blue headed for the door, but before he closed it, he looked back at her. "I'll see you when I get back, and you better not leave this house." He walked back into the room. "Better yet, give me your keys."

He left Sasha drowning in a sea of tears.

Blue was so pissed at Sasha that he ended up at one of his old side-bitch's houses. Red was a stripper at King of Diamonds.

"So, what brings you here? I thought you wasn't fuckin' with me no more?"

He stood at her front door, tipsy. "You gon' let me in or not?"

She stepped away. "Come in."

"Thank you, damn."

"Un-uh, don't come over here with that attitude."

"You already know how I am, so g'on with the bullshit."

"Yeah, I know. You wanna smoke?"

"I hope it ain't that Reggie Bush," he joked.

"Don't play, it's midgrade."

They sat on the couch and smoked. He was trying his best to ease his mind, but he kept thinking about Sasha and his baby.

Red could sense his mind was elsewhere. "You okay? You look like you got a lot on your mind."

"Nothing I can't handle."

She knelt down in front of him and unbuckled his pants. "Let me help you out."

Blue closed his eyes and let her do her thang. She was good with her mouth, but nothing compared to what he had at home. Tonight was the first time he ever cheated on Sasha, and he felt like she forced him into the situation. His phone grabbed his attention. It was Sasha, so he ignored her and focused on who was down below. Red got off of her knees and slipped a magnum over his piece. She already knew the rules with him: no glove, no love.

She eased down on him and rode him slowly, but he wasn't into it 'cause Sasha kept blowing his phone up. Looking down at the picture of his little girl's face made him feel guilty. He couldn't do that to her.

"Red, get up."

"Un-uh, this feel too good."

"I gotta go, get up."

When she didn't move, he pushed her off of him and snatched the rubber off. "I shouldn't have come here. My bad, shawty."

"So you just came here to smoke my weed and get some head, and a bitch can't get a fuckin' nut?"

He reached into his pocket, pulled out two twenties, and dropped them on the floor. "Get you some more. I gotta go."

"Don't come over here when you going through it with your bitch again."

Blue laughed it off. "I won't, it was a mistake."

On his way home, Red must have sent him a dozen messages, but he ignored them all. He had to go make things right with his baby. When he got there, Sasha was in bed crying, and Dream was in her bassinet, sleeping so peacefully. He sat down beside her.

"I'm sorry for blowing up on you earlier. I just held it in for so long, and I couldn't compose myself."

"I've been calling you for the past hour." She wiped her tears with her shirt.

"I know, and I apologize, but I need to tell you something." He stroked her face gently with his finger.

"What, you lied about what happened between you and Carmen?"

"No, that's the God's honest truth, and I put that on my Uncle Dred's grave." He took a deep breath. "Tonight I went by this chick's house I used to fuck with, thinking it would make me feel better, but it didn't."

"Did you fuck her?"

"Not really."

"What the hell do you mean, not really? You either fucked her or you didn't."

"She gave me head, and when she tried to ride me, I made her get up because I kept thinking of you and Dream."

She put her face in the pillow to muffle her cries. "How could you do this to me? You said you loved me and you wouldn't do that to me."

He rubbed her back. "Baby, I do love you, and that's why I left. You gotta believe me."

"You have a funny way of showing it."

"I came home and told you the truth when I could've lied about where I was." He took his phone from his pocket and opened up the messages.

"I'm not lying to you. Here." He moved the pillow from her face and handed her the phone. "Read the messages she sent me."

"I don't want to."

"Just read them so you'll know I'm not lying to you."

Sasha took the phone and read every last message she sent to him, then deleted them all. "Am I supposed to forgive you just like that?"

"Yes. We both made a mistake, and we have to move on."

"That's not fair. You cheated on purpose while I'm at home taking care of your baby. Mine was an accident. That wasn't supposed to happen. You went over there knowing you were gonna fuck her."

"Yes, I did, and I'm sorry. I acted out of anger, and I was wrong. The last thing I want to do is mess up our family." He pulled her toward him. "I love you, and I will never do anything to intentionally hurt you again."

"How can I be sure you won't get mad again and seek a revenge fuck?"

"Since we've been together, I haven't fucked another female. Even after you told me you were married. I still didn't. I could've fucked plenty hos, but I wanted to see where this would go between us."

"Promise me you won't hurt me again."

"I can't promise that I won't hurt you because I'm not perfect. But I can promise I won't let another bitch be the reason I hurt you."

"Yeah." She wasn't convinced one bit.

"You just don't know that I will kill for you." He meant that literally, and he would be happy when he finally got rid of Quamae for good. The last two attempts on his life were an epic fail, and he was starting to think his enemy was immortal. He had one last plan, and it needed to go smoothly this time around. If not, he was gonna have to kill the rat first, and then the ones he loved later.

**

Chauncey was cranked to ten after leaving the police station from being questioned for hours. It was dark when he reached Monica's apartment and sat in the parking lot. She wasn't home, so he sat and waited for her to get there. Since Quamae dropped the bomb on what was going on, he'd been out of it. Pills and liquor had become his new thing.

"This bitch is really trying to take me down, but I got something for her."

He sat and waited for hours before she finally pulled up and made her way to the elevator. When the doors opened, her heart dropped to the floor. She saw him standing there with a deranged look on his face. Chauncey pulled his gun out and showed it to her.

"You better not scream, or I promise I will kill you where you stand." He waved it in the direction of her apartment. "Let's go."

"I'm not, but can you please put that away." Monica did as she was told and walked slowly toward her door, letting him in.

"Bitch, you that bitter that you had to call the police on me?"

"Chauncey, I don't know what you're talking about."

"Bitch, don't play dumb. I heard the tape, and I know your voice. You called them the night you caught me."

"Oh, so now I caught you? I thought you couldn't be caught." She felt safe since he put his gun away.

"This is the wrong time to get slick."

Monica walked to her bedroom so she could sneakily call the police, but Chauncey was on her tail. "Don't walk away from me."

She needed to think fast if she was going to get rid of the maniac standing in her home. "I didn't do anything, so could you please leave?"

"Nah, not until you answer my muthafuckin' question."

She ignored him and removed her clothing as a distraction. Bending down, she slipped her cellphone on the floor and pressed the three digits for help. Chauncey eased over to see what she was doing.

"I wish you would press that muthafuckin' button." He grabbed the phone and backhanded her, making her hit the floor. Hovering over her, he snarled, "I should've known you wasn't shit, you dirty bitch. Trying to pretend like you love a nigga and shit."

"You're high and drunk, Chauncey. Please leave."

"Fuck you, bitch." He threw a few punches, catching her in the face and chest.

Monica lay out on the floor, crying and covering her face. "I hate you; get out!" she screamed.

"Fuck you, shit-eater." Chauncey turned around to leave.

Monica used the little bit of strength she had left and got up from the floor. She picked up her switchblade and followed him. He heard her footsteps, but before he could turn around she stabbed him in his shoulder blade. Chauncey yelped in pain and snatched the blade from his back.

"Bitch, you just stabbed me."

She took a few steps back after realizing what she had done before running back to her bedroom. She tried closing the door, but his foot was in the way. Chauncey kicked the door and was able to get in. Monica was afraid of what was about to happen, so she made another dash for the bathroom.

Chauncey grabbed her by the hair and slung her against the wall. "Bitch, you stabbed me?"

"I'm sorry, Chauncey. Please don't hit me," she begged.

Chauncey hit her in the face, and she slipped on a towel she left on the floor, hitting her head against the tub. Blood oozed from her head, as she lay there with her eyes open.

He ran to her and dropped to her knees. "Monica, get up." He shook her over and over again, but she didn't move. "Monica, wake up, please. I'm sorry for everything. Please, get up."

After realizing she was dead, he closed her eyes, went into her room, and got a blanket to cover her up. He kissed her on the cheek, cleaned up his blood, and left the scene. On his way home, he tossed the switchblade in the canal.

Chapter 19
February 14th, 5:00 a.m.

Beep! Beep! Beep! The sound of the alarm alerted the sleeping couple it was time for Gigi to bring their bundle of joy into the world. She had to meet her doctor in one hour so she could have her labor induced. Quamae reached over, silenced the alarm, and flicked the switch on the lamp. He rubbed her stomach gently. He couldn't wait to lay eyes on his beautiful daughter.

"Bae, get up, it's time to get dressed." He kissed her softly on her eyelids.

"But we just went to bed. I'm tired," she whined.

"I know, but you wanted to do the nasty," he joked.

"You did, too," she whispered.

"Hell yeah. 'Cause who knows the next time I'll be able to get some of your goodies."

Quamae helped her out of bed and watched her as she headed to the bathroom to shower and handle her hygiene. He couldn't believe that in several hours he would officially be a father. Gigi had finally terminated the lease to her apartment and moved into his house once Dirty moved out. They prepared for this special day over the past few weeks and had completely turned one of the bedrooms into a nursery.

Once they were dressed, he grabbed her overnight bag, the baby bag, and headed out the door.

As soon as they arrived at Memorial Hospital, Dr. Joyner was waiting for them. She had Gigi fill out some paperwork and set her up in the delivery room. She was timid and ecstatic at the same time about experiencing this for the first time, but her fiancés presence made it that much easier.

The doctor hooked an IV through her arm and connected a drip bag that would dispense a certain amount of Pitocin per hour to trigger the contractions.

"Okay, Gianni and daddy, I'll be right back. I have another baby to deliver. When I return, I will check your cervix and see how far you've dilated, okay?"

"Okay," they responded.

Quamae smiled at her. "You scared?"

"A little bit."

"Yo' scaredy-ass," he laughed.

"We'll see who passes out when it starts," she replied.

"Grown men don't pass out. I'm built to see this gruesome shit." They went back and forth, making jokes until Quamae found something on the television to watch.

A few hours had passed, and out of the blue Gigi started to rock back and forth, crying.

"Gianni, baby, what's wrong?" he panicked.

"I'm in pain. Please, call the doctor." She pointed in the direction of the remote. He pressed the button, and shortly after one of the nurses came in. The nurse rushed over to her.

"Are you having contractions?" She shook her up and down, indicating yes. "Okay, I'm going to check your cervix to see how far you've dilated to determine if you're ready to push."

Quamae stood and watched as the nurse put on a pair of latex gloves and inserted two fingers into Gigi's vagina. The nurse looked over at him and nodded her head. "She's ready." She removed the gloves and tossed them in the trash. "I'm going to go and page the doctor. Keep her calm and relaxed until I return."

He walked over and began rubbing her stomach. "Everything gon' be okay. We got this," he encouraged her. "I'm going to get you a rag to clean your face. Sit tight."

The faucet ran for a brief second, and he returned with a cold rag and wiped her face with it. "Try and relax. Here, hold my hand." Another contraction kicked in and she squeezed the hell out of his hand. "Damn, you strong," he teased. "I need to record this, because this is how you act when that meat up in you." That caused her to laugh.

"Shut up, stupid. I'm in pain."

"Yeah, I know. I have you in pain, too."

Dr. Joyner walked into the room, ending his dirty talk, and handed him a gown and a surgical mask. "Put this on, daddy. It's time to push."

He quickly put on his delivery attire and handed one of the nurses his phone. "Could you record this for me, please?"

She looked at him and smiled. "Sure, I can."

He walked back over to the bed and held her hand. The doctor instructed her to push over and over again. She was sweating profusely and applying pressure to his hand, making it go numb, but that didn't bother him one bit. "Come on, baby, you can do it. Push for daddy."

"It hurts."

"I know, baby, just keep pushing."

There was a high-pitched scream. "Get this thing out of me."

Quamae laughed.

"It's not funny," she yelled.

Dr. Joyner shouted out in excitement, "Come on, daddy, you want to see this."

He rushed over to the foot of the bed where her legs were spread wide in the stirrups and gasped when he saw how wide her vagina stretched. He couldn't believe that something so tight, which gripped his dick to perfection, could open up like a garage door. He was amused, to say the least.

He watched closely as his little girl forced her way out of the birth canal head-first. The doctor held her head and shouted for Gigi to push again. She did. That one push ejected her out fully, and her cries echoed in the room like a set of bass drums. He was filled with so much joy as tears filled his eyes. "Cut the umbilical cord, daddy."

He used the scissors to cut the cord, and that was the best moment of his life.

The doctor was walking over to clean the baby off when she was distracted by a loud, piercing scream from Gigi. She turned around quickly. "What's wrong?"

"Help! This shit hurts."

Dr. Joyner rushed back over to her to see what was going on, and when she glanced between her legs she noticed another head crowning. "It's another baby!" she shouted. "Push, Gianni, push."

"What?" Quamae was floored by the news. He walked over to see what was going on, and to his surprise another baby was indeed coming through the birth canal. "Get the fuck outta here."

"You got the boy you wanted so badly, daddy. I hope you're happy."

"Oh, I am." He cut the cord for the second time and walked over to Gigi and kissed her on the lips. "You just gave me two babies."

To say that he was happy was an understatement. Having a set of twins was never even a thought for them. Gigi breathed heavily as she tried to come to terms that she had just pushed out two bundles of joy. The nurse walked over and handed her the baby girl, as Quamae held on to his junior. After months of waiting to meet his baby girl, he had the pleasure of welcoming an unexpected visitor.

They named the twins Giavanni Malia Banks and Quamae Malik Banks Jr. This was most definitely the happiest day of his life. It trumped everything he had ever accomplished in life, and he was prepared to give his lady and his babies the world on a silver platter.

***

Blue walked around the round table and eyed everybody in his presence. "I know you're all wondering why I called this meeting, and it's because we have failed to kill Quamae on too many occasions. I have my personal reasons as to why I want him dead, and you should, too. He killed Quint, my uncle Dred, TJ, and his six-year-old son."

One of his soldiers spoke up. "Well, we all know one of us in here is friends with the nigga, so why don't you ask him?"

"I'm asking all y'all muthafuckin' asses."

"I'm just saying, the first time we touched him he didn't die, but the last two attempts we didn't touch him, point-blank period, and he steadily killing off our peeps."

Blue stood behind Dirty. "Yeah, why is that? Have you been tipping the nigga off or something?"

"Nah, man, I'm working with y'all."

"Well, tell me how in the fuck did he know about the spot in Opa-locka?"

"I don't know, man, the nigga is smart. He's a planner, and he also got the law in his pocket, so that's probably how he knows."

"And you just telling me this shit? I don't know, Dirty, I'm starting to think you got that name for a reason."

"I'll take care of it."

"Oh, I know you will." He held up two fingers and motioned for his bodyguard, who had been watching the door, to join him. The big, stocky dude walked over and handed him a Swiss Army knife.

Blue held the knife in his hand. "Dirty, which hand do you shoot with?"

He was afraid to speak. "I. I. My right hand," he stuttered.

"Put your left hand on the table."

Blue stuck the knife through the back of his hand. "Fuck!" he screamed. "I said I'ma take care of it."

He applied pressure, sinking the blade deeper in his hand. "Oh, I know you are, 'cause if you don't, I will kill you myself."

"I got it, man."

Blue looked at his bodyguard. "You can have your knife back."

He stepped up and yanked the blade from his hand. "Argh," he screamed, holding his bloody hand in his lap.

"Now, this is the last time we gon' meet about this nigga. I want the job done ASAP. I don't give a fuck if you have to kidnap his bitch for him to come to you. Get the shit done."

"We killing the bitch, too?" someone asked.

"Nah, let the bitch live. Kill her nigga, though." He gave Dirty a cold stare. "Who's life is more important, yours or his? Think about it."

Dirty didn't speak. He simply replied with a head nod.

"I'm leaving the number to my hotel room just in case there is an emergency. Do not call me for anything other than that." Blue picked up his keys from the table. "A'ight, I'm out. It's Valentine's Day, and Puerto Rico is waiting on me and my lady. I will see y'all when I return in a week, and I expect to hear good news when I get back. Go enjoy your ladies."

He whispered to his guard. "Keep an eye out on that nigga, and if he tries anything shady, off his ass with no hesitation."

"Got it." He dapped him up and left the house.

When Blue arrived home, Sasha was waiting with open arms. "About time you showed up."

"Took longer than I expected, but I'm here now. Are you ready?"

"Yep. I can't wait to get there and let this hair down."

"Well, let's go. The car service should be outside in a few."

At the airport, they boarded their flight, leaving all of their troubles behind. It was time to get their relationship back on track and create some memories.

Sasha and Blue had just arrived in San Juan, Puerto Rico and checked into the Ritz Carlton hotel. Amazed at the luxurious hotel, she couldn't stop cheesing as they walked hand-in-hand to their room. Blue opened the door, stepping to the side.

"Ladies first," he smiled. A week-long vacation was something they both needed, especially with all of the sudden deaths around them and their petty fights. Blue knew this would help get their relationship back on track. Things had definitely changed since the birth of their baby.

"Oh my gosh," she gasped. "This is so beautiful." The king size bed was covered in rose petals in the shape of a heart. A bottle of champagne was chilling on ice, and the patio faced a private swimming pool and a view of the beach. She could literally walk out on the patio and touch the pool water. Sasha faced Blue and pecked him on the lips. "You are the best man a woman could ever ask for, and for the next week I'm going to show you how grateful I am."

"That's sweet, bae, but being here with you is a present of its own."

"So you don't want any special treatment?"

Blue pulled her close. "Oh no! I never said that."

"Just checking. But in the meantime, I'm ready to explore this island and have a few drinks." She rubbed her hand over his chest. "Then, late at night, we can go skinny dipping."

"Sounds like a plan to me."

After they were dressed in their beach attire, they headed out to sight see and find a nice bar on the island. It was like a breath of fresh air. The wind was blowing slightly, causing the tree leaves to shimmy to its beat. During their stroll, they ran into the perfect spot, the Ocean Bar and Grill. Blue pulled out a chair for her to sit on before taking the seat next to her.

"Are you hungry?" he asked.

"You know I am."

The bartender greeted them and provided them with two menus. After placing their drink and dinner orders, they sat back and listened to the music playing. Minutes later, the drinks arrived. Blue was still mesmerized by Sasha's beauty, even after all she'd been through. There was a small scar on her cheekbone, but it didn't stand out that much, and he couldn't keep his eyes off of her. When she finally looked in his direction, she blushed. He still had that effect on her.

"What?"

"You just don't know how much I love you." He grabbed her hand and kissed it. "All I want to do is make things go back to the way they were. I know I hurt you, and I'm sorry."

Tears pricked her eyes. "I love you, too, and I'm sorry that I wasn't forthcoming about what I did."

"I understand, baby, and I forgive you. Everything we did in the past is where I want it to stay. We just need to promise each other that if we're having problems, we will let each other know. I don't want us pointing the finger because we are in this together, forever."

"I promise."

"I promise, too," he responded before sealing the deal with a kiss.

When dinner was over, they headed back to the room for a more intimate setting. Sasha grabbed the bottle of champagne and two wine glasses. "Are you ready to skinny dip?"

Blue grinned and removed his shorts. "I been ready." He grabbed the bottle and glasses from her hand. "What' chu waitin' on?"

"You are a mess." Sasha removed her clothing as well and allowed them to fall on the floor. "Let's go."

Opening the sliding door, she allowed him to walk through first since his hands were full. "Kings first." Sasha slapped his butt when he walked past, and he jumped.

"Baby, don't slap my ass, that's gay as fuck."

She giggled. "But you can slap mine, though."

"Hell yeah." He sat the bottle on the edge of the pool. "Men's asses were not meant to be slapped or touched. If you wanna touch something, grab this dick."

Sasha stuck her toe in the pool before easing down into the water slowly. "Oh, I will. Don't worry about that."

"That water ain't cold?"

"It's not freezing. You can step in it."

Blue popped the top on the bottle and it bubbled. "Time to celebrate baby." After pouring them a glass, he stepped into the water and handed her one. "I would like to propose a toast." They held their glasses up. "I have never been so happy with one woman before in my life, and I can't wait to see what the future holds for us." They clinked their glasses together.

"Aw, baby, do you really mean that?"

"Hell yeah!" he shouted. "You're like Jordan's on Saturdays."

"So, I'm a hot commodity, huh?"

"I gotta have ya."

Blue downed his drink and sat the glass down on the pavement before going underwater. Sasha sipped hers slowly and watched as he swam to the other end of the pool. Coming up out of the water, he shook his dreads and wiped his face. "You too cute to swim?"

"No."

"Oh, you can't swim?"

"Yes, I can. I just don't want too."

"Let me guess. You don't want to get your hair wet." He laughed.

"Yep. That is correct."

"So you came across the water just to keep your hair dry?" He shook his head. "We could've went to Orlando if that was the case."

"You know black women don't get their hair wet."

"So I need to get a Becky with the good hair?" he joked.

Sasha folded her arms. "I'll fuck you and Becky up."

He laughed again. "Keep calm. It was a joke."

Blue went back under the water and swam back to her, stopping once he was close enough to tease her with his tongue. He came up for air with a huge smile on his face.

"You so nasty. Somebody probably pissed in this water," she joked.

Shrugging his shoulders, he replied, "I gotta die from something." He grabbed her by the waist and pulled her underneath the water with him.

They spent the next hour playing around in the water, Sasha couldn't remember the last time she had that much fun. Being with Blue made her feel young and spontaneous. It gave her a chance to get in touch with her inner childlike behavior. Being forced to grow up fast made her miss out on a lot, and she loved him more for that.

Blue shook her thoughts away when he scooped her up in his arms and slipped his tongue into her mouth. She wrapped her arms around his neck, her legs around his waist, and reciprocated the kiss. He backed her up against the wall and reached for his stiff piece, sliding it in her. A soft moan escaped her lips from the penetration. Her mouth found his neck and she sucked down on it viciously, leaving passion marks. The champagne had them buzzed and feeling lovely. Their bodies moved swiftly in the water, making light splashes.

She could always tell when Blue was about to cum by the aggressiveness he quickly possessed. He slipped his arms under her legs, placing them on his forearms, and pushed deeply into her. She almost lost her balance, but she grabbed the wall, scraping her elbow in the process and held on for dear life.

"Cum with me, bae," he moaned.

"I'm trying to." She replied.

After round one was over, Blue wasn't finished just yet. They moved the next few scenes to the bedroom, where they made love until the sun came up. Since the baby arrived, going round-after-round was not really an option. Therefore, they were making up for lost time, even though she hadn't had her six-week check-up yet.

Destiny Skai

Chapter 20

Two weeks later

Chauncey was really going through the motions since he killed Monica, and sleep had not been an option for him. As much as he hated what she did to him, he didn't want to kill her. He kept telling himself it was an accident. According to the news, they had no leads or suspects and were treating the case as a homicide. They questioned the neighbors, but no one heard any commotion the night of the murder. The guilt was weighing him down like an anchor. He needed someone to talk to. Someone he trusted.

"What's up, bruh?" Quamae answered.

"I need to talk to you."

"Are you okay? Where are you?"

"Home."

"I can stop by in a few hours."

"No, I need you to come now. It's urgent." He wiped his eyes. "Please, bruh, come now. I'm begging you."

He knew it was urgent by the way he was acting. "I'm on my way; sit tight."

Quamae had a little over an hour to spare before his meeting, so whatever was going on, he had to make it quick.

Twenty minutes later, he pulled into Chauncey's complex and checked his surroundings. He could never be sure if he was walking into a setup or if he knew what he did to him. Stepping from the car, he tucked his piece into his lower back and put his coat on.

When Chauncey opened the door, he knew it was serious. "You look like shit, dawg. What's going on?"

"I feel like it, too."

Seeing him so emotional wasn't normal, so he assumed he got the bad news early. "Did something happen to you?"

"It's Monica. She's dead." He plopped down on the sofa. "I killed her, man."

"What?"

"It was an accident."

"Aw, man." Quamae sat down beside him. "What happened?"

"I went over there to confront her about what she did. She tried to call the cops, and we started fighting. I was trying to leave, but she stabbed me in the shoulder." Chauncey broke down as he went over her final moments of life. "She ran in the bathroom, and when I hit her she hit her head on the tub. She's dead, man. I killed her."

"Damn, C."

"What we gon' do?"

Quamae patted his shoulder. "I'll think of something, bruh. Don't leave this house for nothing, and I do mean nothing. I will see what's going on."

"I need to go to her funeral."

"No, you can't. The police will be waiting on you, probably. Did you clean up behind yourself, or did you leave anything behind that can place you in her apartment?"

"I don't think so. I took the knife she stabbed me with and I cleaned up my blood."

"Listen, you gotta lay low until I tell you it's safe."

"I got it."

"I have a meeting to get to, but I will check on you later."

"A'ight."

"And if Dirty calls, you don't answer. Don't pick up from anybody except for me, and pack you a bag. It won't be much longer before they find you here."

"Thanks, man. I appreciate you being here after all we've been through."

"It's all good. We've all made mistakes."

Quamae went back to his car, and he almost felt bad for what his boy was going through, but karma was a bitch. He removed his phone from his coat and placed a call.

A woman picked up. "Mission complete?"

"Nah, aborted."

"What happened?" she asked.

"He's going to take himself out sooner or later, so he won't need your help getting through the pearly gates of Heaven or the fiery pits of Hell."

"What happened?"

"All I can say is keep your eyes on the news and you will find out."
She was going to have to find that out on her own.

"Well, my mission been completed, and to think I actually liked the dude."

"He wouldn't feel the same way if he found out."

"Yeah, I'm sure. So, when can I meet you for the pick-up?"

"I'll get up with you in a couple of days."

"Good, 'cause I might need a gun now."

Quamae laughed. "I got'chu. I'll be in touch with the final payment."

"I'll be waiting."

"I know you will."

"Can I ask you a question?" She twirled her hair with her finger, not knowing the answer she was about to receive.

"What's that?"

"Why did you do it?"

"Loyalty is everything to me, and once you cross me, it can never be repaired. Any nigga that bites the hand that feeds them has to be dealt with, and that's why he will die a slow, painful death."

"I understand."

"I knew you would."

"Okay, I'll be waiting on your call."

"I bet you will," he laughed.

"Hush, boy. Bye."

"Thanks, ma."

"Always, baby."

***

Gigi had just gotten home from the hospital, thanks to her high blood pressure and the slow weight gain of one of the twins. She was sitting in the rocking chair, preparing to feed the babies. Quamae was sitting there, watching her with a kool-aid smile on his face.

"So, you about to breast feed them?"

"Yeah, I want us to have a special bond."

"Can I be next?" he grinned. "'Cause we need to work on our bond, too."

"Of course you can."

"So, how are they gon' eat when you not here?"

"You gon' feed them. How else are they gonna eat?"

"I don't have titties, and fuckin' with me, they'll be eating from the table."

Gigi laughed. "You are not feeding my babies anything besides milk." She lifted her shirt and positioned the baby on her breast. "Oh, bae, do me a favor."

"What?"

"Go look in my baby box in the den and get that breast pump out for me."

Quamae left the room in search of the box. When he made it to the den, he saw two boxes stacked on top of each other. One said *baby*, and the other said *Gigi's things*. Grabbing the first box, he tossed it onto the sofa and the contents spilled out. He ignored it, opened up the other box, and pulled out the pump. After closing the box, he went to the sofa to clean up the mess he made.

"Now, she know she could've put some of this shit in the trash," he mumbled while picking up the items. There was a diary with a familiar picture sticking out that caught his attention, so he opened it. The photo peeking from inside was of him and Sasha. He had to blink a few times to make sure his eyes were seeing correctly. Sure enough, it was a picture of them on their wedding day, but Sasha's face was missing. Gigi had replaced it with her own face.

"What the fuck?" he mumbled.

Quamae sat the photo down and read the passage:

Today is the day that I will make her pay. I'm going to take her husband and the life she has been living will finally belong to me. I swiped a few ovulation kits to make sure I get pregnant by my one true love. It may sound crazy, but I will do anything to get him back. So since he always wanted kids, I will give him what his slut-bag wife couldn't. I don't know if the ho is barren or not, but apparently she is since she could never give him a baby. I don't understand why he would leave me for her when she has nothing going on for herself. At least I got my degree to be a nurse. All she wanted was his money, and he was too blind and stupid to see it. In the end, he will be MINE!!!!

Quamae slammed the diary closed and put it in his pocket, along with the picture. Betrayal and karma had reared their ugly heads again, and this bitch was gon' pay. He took long, quick steps up the stairs until he reached the nursery. When he walked in, Gigi was smiling like shit was sweet. Little did she know he was about to unleash the beast on her sneaky-ass.

"You couldn't find it?"

"Give me the baby," he demanded.

"Why? What happened?"

He cut her off. "Give me the fuckin' baby." She handed the baby over and he placed her in the crib. Quamae stood in front of her and took out the picture and diary. "What the fuck is this shit?" he barked, causing her to jump and the babies to cry.

"Um. Um. It's." She stumbled over her words, trying to explain. Before she could formulate a sentence, he hit her in the face and she screamed as blood oozed from her nose. She used the baby blanket to catch the blood.

Quamae snatched it from her hand and threw it on the floor. "Fuck yo' nose, ho." He snatched her up by the collar and slung her up against the wall. "So, you been planning and plotting this shit for a while now?"

"Quamae, I love you," she cried.

"That word don't mean shit to me coming from you. That's just another four-letter word like fuck, shit, and piss. You only wanted me back to prove to Sasha you could take me back. That shit been dead between us, and I was too caught up in the bullshit to see it. This shit over, though, so you might as well pack yo' shit and leave, 'cause I'm bringing my muthafuckin' wife back home."

He squeezed her neck while she struggled to pry his fingers off of her. Gigi became lightheaded and slid to the floor. Quamae released his grip and punched her repeatedly. "You knew I wouldn't leave my wife on my own, so you got pregnant on purpose. You a slimy-ass ho for that one."

Gigi was screaming, and so were the twins, but Quamae ignored all cries. He was just about to hit her again when he felt someone grab his arm.

"Quamae, stop it." It was the nanny. "What are you doing? You don't hit a woman, and definitely not the mother of your children."

"No disrespect, but fuck this ho. She been lying and scheming on me all this time. Fuck her!" he spat while poking her in the forehead. "She better thank God I ain't pump her ass with some hot lead."

"Is that gon' make you feel better, killing her?" She placed her hand on his shoulder. "You go down for murder, and then your kids won't have either parent in their lives. Is that what you want?"

Quamae bit down on his lip and mean-mugged Gigi. "I'm outta here."

"Quamae, please don't leave," Gigi shouted as he headed toward the door.

"He needs some fresh air, let him go," the nanny said as she helped her from the floor. "I don't know what you did to him, but you better fix it. I've never seen him act that way before."

Gigi felt stupid for not securing those items, but with everything that had been going on, it slipped her mind. She walked over by the chair slowly, picked up the blood-stained blanket, and went to the bathroom to clean herself up.

Quamae had really taken her by surprise when he put his hands on her. Standing in the mirror, she cried from the mental and physical pain. Between the after-effects of childbirth and his punches, she couldn't decipher which one was hurting her the most. Then it dawned on her, what if Sasha went through the same thing? This was definitely a side of him she never witnessed before. The old Quamae would never act in such a manner.

Chapter 21

Quamae sped out of the driveway without checking his mirrors. Good thing no one was coming up the street, or they would've been dead on arrival. There was nothing nobody could say or do at that moment to calm him down. His hands gripped the steering wheel tightly as he gritted his teeth and rocked back and forth.

"That ho be lucky I ain't break her fuckin' neck."

There was nowhere to go and no one to trust with such sensitive information, so he cruised for all of ten minutes before stopping at the 24-hour liquor store in Hallandale. Quamae moved swiftly in and out of the store with his bottle in hand. There was a group of gits on the outside, but they didn't want that pressure if they tried him. Robbing season was year round in the Broward, but he stayed strapped.

Quamae drove through the local strip clubs in his feelings before he realized he missed his best friend. The sound of Musiq brought him to tears, as he sang along.

See, I'll love you when your hair turns gray, girl.
I'll still want you if you gain a little weight, yeah.
The way I feel for you will always be the same
Just as long as your love don't change, no.
I was meant for you and you were meant for me, yeah.
And I'll make sure that I'll be everything you need, yeah.
Girl, the way we are is how it's gonna be
Just as long as your love don't change.

Quamae contemplated calling her, but he didn't know what to expect on the other end of that receiver. Deep down he needed her to pick up that phone. He did a few quick breathing exercises before he grabbed his iPhone and made the call. The constant ringing discouraged him, and he was just about to hang up when he heard her voice. It was as sweet as he could remember when shit was sweet.

"Hello."

"Sasha."

She sucked her teeth. "What?"

"I need to talk to you."

Sasha was aggravated immediately because she knew she shouldn't have answered his call. "We don't have anything to talk about." Being married to him made her aware he was tipsy, and right now was not the time for the bull.

"Please, Sasha, don't be like me. Don't shut me out, please," he begged.

Hearing him in that state of mind also let her know he was emotional, and she could've sworn she heard a sniffle. "Quamae, are you okay?"

"No. I need you, like right now."

"Like what?" she questioned.

"I need to talk to someone I can trust, and you're the only one."

The memories of her begging him not to leave resurfaced, and she figured now it was her time to give him her ass to kiss.

"Hold on." Sasha walked outside so she could curse him out without disturbing her baby. "Listen to me, okay?"

"Yeah," he replied.

"You —," but then she paused. The music in the background erased every evil thought she had in her head. Loud and booming through the speaker was none-other than their wedding song. Sasha put her hand to her mouth and took slow breaths to collect her thoughts.

"Sasha, did you hang up?" He paused and looked at his phone to confirm if she had disconnected the call. "Hello?"

"No. I'm still here. I just."

"You just what?"

"Where are you?"

"I'm at the Hampton Inn by the pines."

"Quamae, I'm not sleeping with you if that's why you're calling."

"I know that, and I don't expect you to."

"Okay, I'm leaving my house now."

"A'ight."

Two hours later Quamae was still in his room alone. He texted her the room number, but Sasha never showed up. He continued to drink because he figured she was a no-show, but he brought that upon himself. His one and only chance to see her was shot to hell. Something inside of him wanted to call her, but he couldn't disappoint himself again. Finally giving up, he crawled into the bed and closed his eyes. Drifting into a light sleep, he heard a tap at the door, but he was sure it was just a dream. Seconds later there was a harder knock at the door, causing him to jump.

Quamae jumped up and walked to the door, anticipating Sasha on the opposite side of it. When he opened the door, it was indeed her, but she brought company with her. His heart dropped because this was the last person he expected to see. A huge lump formed in his throat, and for once he had nothing to say. Stepping back from the door, he gave them entrance.

Sasha walked over to the bed and sat down. Quamae followed and stood in front of her. It had been a while since he last saw her, and he must admit the baby made her body reach its full potential. She was sexier than ever. The way those jeans hugged her hips and ass made his dick jump.

Taking his eyes off of her, he looked down and observed the sleeping beauty lying snugly in her seat.

"Is this my baby?" he asked.

"No," she answered quickly, although it was never proven.

Quamae took a knee so he could get a better view of the baby. "Stop lying, 'cause this girl look just like me." He looked up at Sasha to get confirmation on his assumption.

"She looks like her mother."

"And her daddy."

Sasha was not about to waste anymore time playing this game. "Quamae, what did you call me for?"

"We need to talk, and I need to apologize for not answering the phone when you were in labor."

"Quamae, that was over a month ago."

"Listen." He sat down beside her. "I know that I fucked up, and I can't take that back. I made a big mistake, and I'm sorry."

She rolled her eyes. "I wonder why?"

"Sasha, please, let me talk."

"Go right ahead."

"I'm sorry for everything I did to you. I just get so crazy and I lose control of myself."

She rolled her eyes and sucked her teeth. "You think?"

"I'm serious." He grabbed her hand. "I fucked up big time. This whole thing was a plot from the beginning."

"What do you mean?"

"I found this diary that she been writing in with plans to trap me and take me away from you."

She snatched her hand away and folded her arms across her chest. "Well, she succeeded."

"That's not even the worst part. This crazy-ass bitch had a picture of us at our wedding, and she cut your face out and put hers in your place."

"Well, Quamae, that's what you wanted."

"No, it's not. I was only there because she said she was pregnant."

"That's funny, because I told you I was pregnant and you didn't care. You didn't go to any of my appointments, but I bet you went for that ho."

Sasha looked down at her sleeping baby and choked up a bit. The reality was it could very well be his baby, and he missed out on seeing her being brought into this world. A few tears cascaded down her face, and Quamae caught them quickly.

"Don't cry, Sasha, please. I'm so sorry for the hell I put you through. I just want to make things right between us. Can we just start over, please?"

"No, we can't. You really hurt me, and I can't forgive you right now."

Quamae shook his head. "What do I have to do? I'll do anything."

"Why, Quamae? Is it because the grass wasn't greener on the other side? You chose that bitch over me, and now look at you."

"I know." He placed his head in his hands.

"Is this the only reason you called me here?" She waited for an answer, but he didn't say anything. "Quamae, I have to go."

Quamae could feel her attempt to get up, so he rose and pushed her back down on the bed with a little force. "Sasha, please, don't go."

"No, I need to leave."

"Sasha, I love you, and we need to raise our baby together," he shouted, startling the baby. "I'm sorry for waking her up," he apologized quickly, not realizing he was so loud.

"You need to calm down." Sasha leaned down, unstrapped her from the seat, and picked her up. "I'm sorry, mama, for the noise." She cut her eyes at Quamae. "He didn't mean to scare you."

"What's her name?" he asked.

"Dream."

He smiled. "Dream, huh?"

"Yep."

"What's her whole name?"

Sasha hesitated, unsure of how he would react to the baby having Blue's last name without a paternity test determining whose name she should have. "Dream India Joyner."

Disappointment was thick on his face, like casket-sharp makeup. "You gave my baby that nigga last name? Damn, Sasha, that's fucked up. You didn't give a nigga a chance."

"He was there throughout my whole pregnancy, so I don't know what you expected me to do. And besides, you served me with divorce papers. Did you forget that?"

Quamae stood up in front of her and observed the baby closely. The last thing he wanted to do was start an argument, or upset her for that matter. In the meantime, he would let that go and address that issue later.

"You right, but don't sign them. Can I hold her?"

Sasha just knew he was about to start an argument, so she was prepared to leave with no hesitation. "What did you say? I'm right?"

"Yes."

"Oh, wow!" she exclaimed. "That's a first." She handed the baby to him. "I can't believe you just said that. And for the record, I signed them already."

Quamae held the baby in his arms and rocked her. He didn't want to believe she really signed them. "Damn, she is beautiful."

"Thank you."

"We made a beautiful baby."

Sasha sat and watched him talk and bond with Dream. It melted her heart to see him take to her so quickly, and the thought of him really being her father flashed in her mind. For the sake of Blue, she didn't want to find out the truth. Quamae made the decision he wasn't her father before she was even born.

"I'm sorry I wasn't there for you when you were born, but I'll be here starting now," he promised.

Quamae held Dream in his arms until she fell asleep. Walking over to her seat, he sat her down and covered her with the blanket. He turned to face Sasha and stared into her eyes before he said anything.

"Sasha, I miss you so much. I just want my family back."

"Quamae, how can you miss something you never had?"

He completely ignored her question, leaned down, and kissed her on the mouth. The aggression he displayed threw her off as she tried to push him off of her.

"Quamae, stop," she mumbled.

"Don't fight it, just let it happen."

Pushing her back on the bed, he eased between her legs and continued to kiss her. His hand crept up her thigh, caressing her spot. Her juices began to flow, and she could feel moisture in the seat of her pants since she wasn't wearing any panties. It was obvious he still had that affect on her. The fight started to leave her body slowly as she kissed him back and wrapped her legs around his waist.

"We can't do this." Her mouth was saying one thing, but her body was doing another. She didn't try to stop it.

"Yes, we can. I know you miss this dick and calling me daddy."

"Mm," she moaned. "This is so wrong, Quamae."

"But it feels so right. We were meant to be." He grinded against her center, and she could feel his erection. "We both fucked up."

"Please," she begged.

Quamae kept going and unbuckled her jeans. Easing his hand inside, he didn't stop until his fingers were on her clit. He rubbed it in a circular motion and sucked on her neck.

Sasha turned her head, because the last thing she needed were passion marks on her going back home to Blue. "Please, stop."

"You don't want me to stop, 'cause that pussy real wet right now."

She couldn't deny it feel good, but she didn't want to cheat on Blue. It just didn't feel right, especially since they were working on their relationship and getting it back to where it used to be. The last thing she wanted to do was go backward.

Quamae was licking and sucking on her breasts while tugging on her jeans. He was horny and ready to go knee-deep in it. As soon as he got them off, he removed his shorts and boxers and climbed back on top of her. Apparently she wanted the same thing, because her legs were wide open. Using his right hand, he rubbed his dick up and down her slit and kissed her again.

He was just about to put it in when they were interrupted by Bryson Tiller's *Exchange* ringtone. Sasha froze and grabbed his waist before she jumped up. It was Blue calling. Her heart was about to jump out of her chest, as if he was standing at the room door knocking and she was caught. She grabbed her cellphone, but before she answered she looked at Quamae, walked into the bathroom, and closed the door behind her.

"Hey, bae, what's up?" she answered, sounding a little winded.

"What you doing?" Blue asked.

"Nothing. What's up with you?"

"Why you sound like that? Are you home?"

"No. I was trying to hurry up and grab the phone, but I stepped out for a few to go to the store. I'll be home soon."

"A'ight I'm on my way there. Where is my baby?"

"She sleep."

"Okay. I'll see you soon."

"Okay."

"I love you."

"I love you, too."

After hanging up the phone, she grabbed one of the rags to clean herself off. When she opened the door, Quamae was standing right there. Sasha didn't know what to say, being that she didn't know how long he was standing there. However, she was willing to bet he heard the entire conversation. He licked his lips in a sexy way, but his words didn't match his expression.

"So, you love that nigga now?"

"Quamae, just stop, please." She walked past him and went to the bed to retrieve her pants.

"I asked you a question. Do you love that nigga?"

"Why does that matter?"

"I need to know what I'm facing."

Sasha didn't say anything, but he watched as she slid back into her tight-fitted pants.

"Where are you going?"

"I have to go." She strapped the baby back in her seat and grabbed her bag. "I told you I wasn't sleeping with you."

"Yeah, that's why you let me get that far, huh?"

"I'm sorry, but I have to go."

"You choosing that nigga over me?" He was pissed, to say the least. Quamae had her exactly where he wanted her and he blew it. Now he regretted not skipping foreplay and going straight for the pound game. Blue balls were not what he had in mind. The plan was to catch a nut or two and leave her with something to think about when she was laying next to her youngin'.

"You mean the way you chose that bitch over me?" she spat. His days of playing the victim were over, and she had enough. "We could've still been together if you were willing to work it out with me when I begged you for forgiveness. But no, you wouldn't forgive me or hear me out, and now since she turned out to be a psychotic bitch, you want me back. Your timing is really fucked up!"

Quame grabbed her around the waist and pulled her close. "I admit that I fucked up, I do. And I'm only human."

"That's the same thing I was trying to tell you when I fucked up, but I couldn't get another chance. You blew me off, remember?"

Of course he remembered. He was suffering right now behind it. He grabbed his clothing from the floor and put it back on. Sasha grabbed the baby seat and headed for the door.

"Wait, Sasha. At least let me walk you out." He took the baby seat from her hand and escorted her out.

They took the elevator down to the first floor, but no words were spoken. In the public eye, they looked like an average boyfriend and girlfriend strolling through with their bundle of joy, but they were far from that. Quamae peeped the smile of a familiar face in the lobby, gazing in his direction. He kept it pushing as they made their way to the parking lot and then her car. Sasha secured Dream in the backseat and closed the door. Once she faced Quamae, he pushed her against the car and shoved his tongue down her throat once more for good measure. Then he backed up.

"Remember everything I said to you. I'll be seeing you soon."

Sasha got into her car and pulled off without saying a word. He knew he had just affected her judgment, and he would be on her mind all night.

Back inside the hotel, Quamae walked through the lobby, but he didn't see the female who was smiling at him a little while ago. She was a chick from around the way who had been trying to get with him, but he never pursued it. They talked on the phone a few times, but it never went any further than that.

Quamae's mind was back on Sasha and Dream. Deep down inside he felt like he was her father, but there was still a chance he wasn't. The frown on his face displayed the unhappiness when he thought back to her last name. To him it was fucked up that she was still married and named the baby after the next man. Something had to be done about the little mishap that was going on. A plan needed to be put into motion, and it needed to be done expeditiously. All he had to do was sit down and figure out how he was going to make the plan work.

Stepping from the elevator, he saw the same female from the lobby bending over, looking through her bag. She was wearing a pair of pink joggers that gripped her ass just right. It was like she had been waiting on him, because as soon as he got closer, she looked over her shoulder and smiled. Quamae licked his lips sexily.

"You like what you see?" she giggled.

"That depends."

"On what?"

"You."

"How?"

"It depends on if you coming in or not."

Pink sweats grabbed her bag and sashayed her way to his room door. His eyes were glued to her pussy print. That thang looked like a balled-up fist. Since Sasha left Quamae with a hard-on, it was necessary he released some of his tension on somebody, and his old text buddy was down for the cause. He opened up the room door and watched her ass jiggle when she walked past. Closing the room door behind him, he knew it was about to be a very long night.

Chapter 22

"Where were you?" Blue asked as soon as Sasha walked through the door. He was sitting on the floor, counting his money.

"I told you, I went to the store." She sat Dream's seat on the floor and tossed the bag on the bed.

"Where ya bags at?"

"Huh?" The guilt was fresh on her breath and clothing, and she was certain he saw through the bullshit.

Blue paused and looked up at her. "Bags? What did you buy?" He held his arm out.

"Oh, they didn't have what I was looking for."

"Yeah, okay." He went back to his task at hand. "Don't play with me, Sasha. I'm telling you now."

"What are you talking about?"

"Keep playing dumb."

Sasha picked the baby up and got her ready for bed, then placed her in the bassinet. Blue had just finished counting the money and stacking it on the floor next to him when she walked up on him. She straddled his lap and kissed his neck.

"Stop tripping for nothing. I haven't done anything to warrant this interrogation."

"Interrogation, my ass."

Quamae had her hot and horny, and she couldn't wait to feel Blue inside of her. His neck was Blue's weak spot, along with his stomach, and she was aiming to take his mind off the thoughts he was having about her. She licked the side of his neck and grinded in his lap. He let his head fall back against the bed and closed his eyes. They had foreplay often, and he enjoyed every minute of it.

Sasha kissed all over his neck until she made her way to his mouth. Their kiss was intoxicating, and Blue reached for her buckle on her pants and loosened it. When he made his way to her treasure, he paused abruptly.

"Why the fuck your pants wet?"

"Because I'm horny, that's why." Trying to rush out of the hotel room, she forgot to check them.

Blue grabbed her by the throat, but he didn't squeeze it. He gripped her just enough to let her know he was serious about his. "I just told you don't play with me."

"I'm not."

"You must think I'm slow or some shit." Blue wasn't about to play with her ass because she was definitely capable of cheating. Where she just came from couldn't be proven, but he would be watching closely from now on. The wet spot in her pants wasn't hot at all. To be honest, it was sorta cold. The only thing that saved her was the fact her pussy was still intact. Meaning it didn't slide right in, as if she had just finished fucking.

"No."

"Gotta be if you think I believe these bitches just got wet."

She had to lighten the mood, since he wasn't trying to choke the life out of her. "Bae, come on. I wanna fuck, not fight."

He let her go and unbuckled his pants, freeing his semi-stiff dick. "Get it up." That was all he had to say, and she knew he wanted some head.

Sasha stood up and removed her pants before getting down on her knees and fulfilling his need. She didn't suck him up for his cum, but only enough to get him in the mood and rock hard. When she was done, she straddled his lap and eased down on him. The carpet on the floor was the cushion she needed for her knees, but she hoped it didn't result in a rug burn later.

Seconds into riding him, she closed her eyes and thoughts of Quamae surfaced. That was the last person she needed to see while having sex with her man, but it was inevitable since she was two seconds away from fucking him. Had he not called in the nick of time, she would still be in that room, getting tossed up. She shook her head, thinking the image of his face would go away, but boy was she wrong. Then she opened her eyes so she could focus on the man facing her. It didn't help whatsoever, 'cause she still saw his face. Going with the flow, she ignored it and rode him until she released her juices on him. After sitting for a few minutes to catch her breath, she eased up off of him slowly.

"I'm going to take a shower."

"I'm right behind you," he added.

***

The next day Quamae went to IHOP to meet up with Jon for breakfast. They sat off to the side in a booth all the way in the back of the restaurant to converse in private.

"So, what's going on, man?" Jon asked genuinely. Quamae was his boy, so when he said he needed to talk to him, he dropped everything he was doing and came to see what was up.

"Man, the craziest shit happened to me." He took a sip of his orange juice and sat it back on the table. Jon was tuned in. "This ho crazy as fuck, man. I fucked up this time, for real."

Quamae went play-by-play explaining what happened the day before with Gigi. Judging by the many faces Jon was making, he knew he had a lot to say once he finished. One thing he could count on was some sound advice from the realist white boy he had ever met in life.

After he finished talking, he nodded his head toward Jon to let him know he had the floor.

"Bruh, what the fuck you done got yo'self into?"

"Man, I don't fuckin' know. That's why I called you."

"I'm a financial counselor, not a mental health counselor." He laughed even though it was far from comical.

"I need help with that, too?"

"What you mean?"

Quamae knew Jon was about to flip out on his ass when he found out about the money. Despite that fact, he had to tell him if he wanted to get it back. "Remember the $25K I had you write a check for?"

"What'chu did with it?"

"I gave it to Gigi for the babies."

Jon closed his eyes and rolled his neck in a circle. He couldn't believe the bullshit he just heard. "Why the fuck would you do that?" He spoke through clenched teeth.

"I was trying to make sure my kids are straight when they get older."

"First of all, you need to find out if those kids are yours. I don't trust that ho. If she'll go that far to get you, ain't no telling what she done rigged up."

"They are."

"Did DNA tell you that?"

"Who?"

"DNA. Did you have a damn test done on those kids?"

"Nah."

Jon shook his head. This was so unlike his friend of over twenty years. He was disgusted by his behavior. "How can you take her word for it over your wife?"

"Come on, bruh, I feel bad enough already."

"Good, muthafucka, you should feel bad. Did you forget what Sasha did for you? She's the reason you still here." He leaned in closely to make sure no one heard what he was about to say next. "How many bitches you think will bust they gun behind a nigga and catch a body?" Quamae sat in silence and took in everything he was saying. "My point exactly, bruh. None."

"I know."

"You need to fix this shit, like right now."

"I'm trying to get her back, but I think I lost her for good." He glanced out the window. "She slid up on me last night, and brought the baby with her."

Jon smiled. "Oh yeah. Who she look like?"

Quamae pulled out his iPhone and showed him the picture he took of her when Sasha went into the bathroom. "I think she look like me."

"Oh yeah, bruh, this yo' li'l girl, man. She look just like you."

"You think so?"

"Hell yeah. So what you gon' do?"

"I'm working on a plan as we speak."

"Well, this what you need to do." He leaned back in his seat. "First, you need to get those kids tested, all of 'em. At least this way you got the shit in black and white, and there won't be any doubts."

Quamae agreed.

"I don't trust that snake-ass bitch Gigi. She think she got all the fuckin' sense, and you need to handle her ASAP! I will hack into her bank account and take that money back, 'cause I don't know what the fuck you was thinking."

"The property, too."

"Damn, nigga, you gave her that, too?"

"Yeah."

"Damn, she must've sucked the wisdom from your brain when she sucked yo' dick."

"Nah, her head game ain't better than the wife's."

"Well, shit, that's who gets the property. She deserves that, and so much more. Don't worry, we gon' fix this shit together, and you gon' get my sister back." Jon shook his head. "I can't believe you let this triflin'-ass bitch snake you like that, and you left my sister 'cause she cheated."

"She ain't have no fuckin' business cheating."

"Aye, I'm not defending her on that tip, because she was wrong, but I rather see y'all together. It's not too late, and it can be fixed, but I think you should go and see a therapist to address your own issues first. Then the two of you can work on your marriage."

"I filed for divorce already," he mumbled.

"You bullshittin'?"

"Nah."

"Did they file the papers yet?"

"I don't know. I ain't heard nothing from the lawyer, but it should be finalized any day now."

"No wonder why you said you lost her for good. You probably did, stupid! Why would you do some dumb shit like that?"

"I don' know." Quamae thought back to what Jon said earlier. "Hold on, who you said needed a therapist?"

"You."

"For what?"

"Everything that made you who you are today. You should've spoken to someone when you were younger, but black people don't believe in therapy."

Quamae laughed because Jon was right. He didn't believe in therapy. "That's true, 'cause we don't need it. Y'all do."

"Bullshit!" he laughed. "We ain't the only crazy muthafuckas out there. Y'all crazy, too."

"Don't I know it!"

"I'ma give you the number to my girl Christine, and she'll help you get in touch with your inner feelings and shit." Jon chuckled, and so did Quamae.

"Thanks, I guess it won't hurt to check her out."

"Hell nah, it won't hurt. Just remember they help black and white people, okay?" He laughed once more.

Quamae slid out of the booth. "I gotta piss. I'll be right back."

"Take ya' time."

Jon looked back to make sure Quamae was gone before he made a call.

"Hello."

"Carlos?"

"'Sup, Jon?"

"Aye, are you at the office?"

"Yeah. What do you need?"

"I need you to dig up something on Quamae for me."

"Well, swing by the office. I'll be here for another hour."

"I'll be right there."

Just as he hung up the phone, Quamae was walking up to the table. "Who was that?"

Jon looked down at his phone. "My lady. She ready for me to pick her up. I promised to take her shopping for a bag today."

"Oh, that's what's up. Tell sis I said hey."

"A'ight, well, I'ma get out of here, and I'll keep you updated on what's up.

"Thanks, bruh."

"It's all love."

They stood up and G-hugged before going their separate ways.

Chapter 23

The past 48 hours had been the longest hours in history for Quamae. He had finally received the phone call he was waiting on, and in his hands were the answers to his question. Gripping the envelope tightly, he sat in his truck and took a deep breath before finally ripping the envelope open. Quamae declined the counselor's offer to read them inside. This required alone time when he read the results, just in case he lost his marbels.

The beating of his heart was at a fast pace. Deep down inside he was afraid Jon might be right about Gigi. His hands were trembling out of fear, unaware if there was a possibility they were not his. He ripped open the envelope, and he couldn't believe his eyes. Staring at him in black and white was the answer he felt in his heart. Quamae was *99.98% not the father* of Gigi's twins!

He was shocked and angry at the same time. He hopped onto I-95 and floored it to his house. That trifling-ass bitch had some explaining to do.

Gigi's conversation was cut short when the door to their bedroom swung open and an angry Quamae barged in, giving her the evil eye.

"We need to talk, now. Hang up that muthafuckin' phone."

Gigi's heart was beating in her stomach. The last time she saw him he beat her ass, so she didn't know what to expect at that point. She ended the call quickly and sat the phone down.

Quamae was pacing the floor. "Who you was fuckin' besides me?"

"Huh?" she replied, knowing damn well she heard his ass.

"Bitch, don't play with me. Who was you fuckin'?" When he asked her again, he walked over to the bedroom door and locked it. Today was the day the nanny couldn't save her ass.

"Nobody," she lied quickly, but his fist to her mouth was quicker.

"Stop fuckin' lying to me."

Gigi cried and held her mouth, certain her tooth was loose. One thing she hadn't learned was how to duck from his powerful punches. "Quamae, what are you talking about?"

"This," he yelled as he pulled the results from his pocket and slapped her in the face with them. "Explain this shit to me."

Gigi was confused. "Explain what?"

"Read the fuckin' papers."

She picked up the papers and skimmed through them. At that very moment she wished she could escape the lethal wrath coming her way. Tears started to stream down her face like Niagra Falls, but those tears meant nothing. The results slipped from her shaky fingertips and scattered on the floor.

"Shut the fuck up. I don't give a fuck about your tears, 'cause that ain't gon' save you from this ass-whoopin' you 'bout to get."

"That's not right. Those are your kids."

Quamae backhanded her, causing her to fall back on the bed. "Who the fuck do I look like to you? Those ain't my muthafuckin' kids." He straddled her and wrapped his left hand around her throat, slapping her repeatedly with his right hand.

"That test is wrong, I swear," she gasped.

He grabbed a fistful of her hair and wrapped it around his hand. "Lie to me again and I'll snatch yo' ass bald."

"Quamae, stop!" she screamed.

"Nah, you wanted Sasha's life so bad, now you got it!" He dragged her from the bed to the floor. With his free hand unbuckled his belt. Gigi never saw it coming. Quamae swung the belt and lit her ass up when it smacked against her bare legs.

"Ah!" she screamed and kicked her feet. "No!"

Whap! Whap!

"Shut up!" he screamed back.

Gigi continued to kick and holler for what seemed like forever. After five long minutes, he stopped and sat down on the bed. For one, he was tired, and two he wanted answers, and he wanted them now. It was about to be a long day for her.

He pointed in her direction. "Now, you better tell me what I need to know. Who the fuck do these kids belong too?"

"I–I."

He chomped her off quickly. "Don't you fuckin' lie to me." Quamae pulled his pistol from his waistband and sat it beside him on the bed. "Now, let's try this again. Who the fuck do these kids belong to? 'Cause it ain't me."

Gigi's eyes stretched out of her head when he pulled out his gun. She swallowed the saliva that dripped in her mouth. "It could only be one other person," she confessed.

"I don't give a fuck how many, I said who!"

"This guy that I work with named James."

When he busted out laughing, she thought he was on lunatic mode. "You know, this shit is hilarious. I remember when you told me you was pregnant, I asked if you was sure it was mine." He rubbed his chin. "I didn't give a fuck because I had a wife, and I didn't want no baby from you. We were just fucking, so I figured it couldn't be just me laying the dick."

"How could you say that to me?" She paused. "I thought it was you because me and him only slept together once, and that was only because I was upset with you."

"I don' believe shit you saying."

"It's the truth."

Quamae picked the gun up from the bed and sat it in his lap. Gigi scooted back across the floor.

"This is what I call bad karma. I sat at your fuckin' house and told you what I was going through with her, and you were doing the same thing all along."

"I didn't mean to, you gotta believe me."

"Fuck you! I don't believe you loved me this time around. All you wanted was for a nigga to take care of you. You 'round here braggin' and boastin' about your job and being independent when all you wanted was Sasha's spot this whole time." He shook his head. "I should've never left my wife, but that's alright. I'm bringing her back home."

"What about us?"

"Ho, ain't no us." He stood up, walked over to where she was sitting, and hovered over her. "You need to call that nigga James and let him know he has two kids over here and y'all need somewhere to stay. Tomorrow I want you out of here, because my wife is coming back home."

"Quamae, please don't do this," she begged. "I love you, not Sasha."

He reached down and struck her repeatedly wherever he could land a puch. It didn't matter if it was her face, legs, stomach, or side. Gigi screamed at the top of her lungs, begging him to stop.

"Shut the fuck up!" he yelled. All of the noise she was making drove him insane. He pressed the gun against her temple. "Why did you do it?"

Her voice trembled. "Do what?"

Quamae cocked the gun back. "You knew I wanted kids with my wife, and you took advantage of the fact I didn't have any."

Gigi was afraid to answer. This was certainly not the man she fell in love with years ago. The man standing over her with a gun to her head was a savage, a killer, and someone she wished she would've left in her past. Now she wished like hell she would've stayed out of their marriage and just moved on. Sasha's face flashed in her mind. *How in the hell did she put up with him under these circumstances. How many times was she on the same floor, begging him to stop hitting her and begging for her life?*

"Answer me," he demanded.

"Quamae, please put the gun down. I wanted us to be together. I just wanted you back by any means, and I wasn't gonna stop until that happened. Am I so wrong for wanting that?"

In her mind she felt like she could talk him out of anything, no matter how he was feeling, and that would be her only way out of the mess she created. What Quamae didn't know was Gigi had an emotional break down and tried to commit suicide when he left her. She spent three months in a mental health hospital before she was released. With the help of her godfather, the pastor, he was able to have her record disappear without a trace and get her a job in the hospital. Death was staring her in the face, and all she could think of was convincing him to stay with her.

"Baby, we can work this out. I love you, and I know you still love me. You're just upset. The twins still belong to you. You've been there since day one. They have your name."

Just hearing her lie to him over and over again triggered his insanity button, and he lost it. Quamae savagely attacked her while she lay on the floor. While punching her repeatedly, he paused for a brief second and began to kick her in the ribs. Gigi balled up and screamed, hoping the pain would somehow go away. When the kicking came to an end, she remained sprawled out on the floor, squirming.

"Open your eyes," Quamae shouted. When Gigi opened them, the barrel of his gun was directly in her face.

"Quamae, please don't," she cried. Her body was sore, eyes swollen, lip busted, and she just knew a few of her ribs were broken.

"Ho, choke on these bullets." Quamae pulled the trigger.

Click!

The gun jammed. Gigi was relieved, but not Quamae. He was pissed. "Ain't that a bitch? Somebody praying for yo' ass."

Rising up from his position, he examined his weapon to see what the hell just happened. As soon as he took his eyes off of her, she bolted across the room like lightening, and he chased her.

Gigi's destination was the nursery. Locking the door behind her, she sat on the floor and cried her eyes out. There was a powerful kick on the opposite side of the door. *Boom!*

"Open this muthafuckin' door."

"No!" she screamed. "You're crazy!"

"You ain't seen crazy yet. I'm about to show you how bad shit can get." He kicked it again.

"Stop it." Gigi ran to get her phone. "I'ma call the police."

"Go 'head. You'll be dead before they get here." He kicked the door again. *Boom!*

Quamae was just about to shoot the knob off the door when he was interrupted by the front door unlocking. He already knew it was Ms. Mildred, coming to start her shift.

"Somebody just spared your life, so you better get on your knees and thank the man upstairs."

In the meantime, he walked away. She was gon' get hers, and that was a promise. Right now he had a very important meeting to prepare for.

Chapter 24

A few hours later, Quamae sat in the truck anxiously awaiting Dirty's arrival. There were so many things going on he needed to address. He was due to arrive within the next ten minutes, but rarely was he on time for anything. While he sat trying to be patient, there was a newer model car with limo tints coming toward him. It was strange because he was sitting in an alley. He picked up the gun from his lap, adjusted his seat backward, and aimed the pistol toward the passenger side. If anyone stopped and tried to act badly, was gon' wear a wet t-shirt from fucking around with him.

The car pulled up, the window came down slowly, and he could see a head looking to see if anyone was in the truck. Once he recognized it was an older white man, he knew there was no threat on his life. The older gentleman politely rolled his window back up and drove off. Watching from the rearview mirror, Quamae waited until the car was off the backstreet and got out. There was no way he was about to continue sitting out there.

Fifteen minutes later, Dirty walked inside the warehouse wearing a hoodie with his hands in his pockets. Quamae stood up to greet him.

"What's up, patna?"

"Just coolin', what it do?" Dirty asked, slapping hands with him.

"Shit, just need to talk a li'l business wit' cha."

"A'ight."

"Have a seat." Quamae sat down after Dirty. "So, it's like this," he paused. "I've been thinking about the whole ordeal with the driveby shooting at the traphouse.'

"What about it?" Dirty asked.

"I find it strange that those bullets were only coming toward me and Chauncey and not you. I mean, we were all on the porch, and when the shots rang out, they came only in our direction."

"What'chu saying, bruh?"

"That shit was a set up."

"Damn, you think so?" Dirty tried to remain as calm as possible to keep from looking suspicious.

"I know so." He leaned back in his seat and folded his arms. "But here's where it gets interesting. You called us over there so we can make up, right?"

"Yeah."

"Why?"

"'Cause with all the heat when you took Dred out, we couldn't afford to have any division in our squad. That's when them niggas think they can try something. It wasn't a good look, so I was trying to fix it."

"Okay." Quamae nodded his head, thinking that was a good come-back answer. "That's a valid reason, but then here's where it gets tricky and a little strange for me. The day I got shot in the plaza, no one knew where I would be that day, at that very moment."

"Bruh, what'chu saying?"

"I'm getting there." Quamae sat up and looked him dead in the eyes. "I told you where I was going, so you knew my exact location. This happened right after I talked to you."

"You think I had something to do with that?"

"I know you did. I also know that you workin' with Blue to take me out."

"Nah, bruh, that ain't true. You know me."

"I thought I knew you, but you have already proved you have no loyalty and can't be trusted."

"How can you accuse me of some shit like that? I'm yo' A1 from day one. You need to be worried about Chauncey. He the one that betrayed you, and I bet he the reason you blaming me for this."

"Yeah, he fucked my wife. I know all of that, but he ain't never set me up, though."

"Can you prove I set you up? Tell him to show you." His defensiveness was off the charts, and the more he spoke the gultier he made himself sound.

Quamae laughed. "I'm glad you said that." He pulled the recorder from his pocket and placed it on the table. "I want you to listen to this and tell me how I should take this."

Dirty didn't know what the hell he was talking about, but he was ready to hear whatever proof Quame thought he had. There was some crackling noises before the voices started.

"Hello." It was Dirty's voice.

"When you gon' handle ya' boy? I've been patient with you, but I'm starting to think you done jumped ship," Blue asked.

"Nah, I ain't jump ship. I'm waiting on the nigga to get comfortable. This nigga is smart, and he pays attention to detail, so it ain't that easy. I have a feeling he don't trust me right now."

"Ain't you staying with him right now? How much more comfort do you need?"

"It's not that simple. One night he went to bed, I waited for a few hours to make sure he was asleep, but his door was locked. I couldn't do shit 'cause if he would've heard me coming in, he would've blasted my ass."

"Listen to me, and listen good, if you want me to stay out of Hollywood, away from the ones you love, you better make that shit happen. I'm talking ASAP. You have a choice. It's either gon' be you or him."

"A'ight," Dirty answered.

"Who it's gon' be?"

"Him. I got it."

When the recording stopped, Quamae looked over at Dirty to read his body language. What he observed was he was scared and there was nothing he could say to justify what was on that tape. Sweat beads were evident on his forehead.

"So, who you not working for again?" Quamae asked with a sinister laugh.

Dirty didn't part his lips to say a word. He knew he needed to be quick on his feet and was certain he couldn't talk his way out of this one. The only thing left to do was pull the gun from his waistband and take Quamae out before he took him out.

"If you wanna kill me, go 'head." He was steadfast on his feet. "I'll even turn my back toward you since you don't have the heart to shoot me while I'm looking."

Quamae stood in place for thirty seconds before he heard a gun cock. Dirty had his piece trained on his comrad as he spoke.

"I swear, bruh, it was never supposed to go down like this. I was only communicating with the nigga to keep him away from my family. I was gon' take him out myself. The nigga came to my babymama house and held my git in his arms while he threatened me. He said I was gon' help him take you out or he was gon' kill the both of them."

Quamae turned to face him. "So you couldn't come to me, nigga, and tell me what was up? We got a army full of niggas that's ready to catch a few bodies."

"I didn't know what to do. This man had his hittas on my trail everywhere I went."

"So you rather go against the grain like that?"

"I—" he hesitated when he felt someone behind him.

"Gimme yo' muthafuckin' piece, nigga."

Dirty's eyes popped out of the sockets when he felt a cold piece of steel on the back of his head. Chauncey snatched the gun from his hand and stepped to the side so he could see him.

"Tellin' those muthafuckin' lies. Throwin' salt on a nigga name and shit. Nigga, you set us up from the jump wit'cho bitch-ass."

Quamae pulled the banger he was toting from his waist and trained it on Dirty. "So, you was really gon' shoot me in the back, huh?" He stepped from around the table. "You ungrateful, bitch-ass nigga. I helped you come up so you can take care of yo' kids. If it wasn't for me, nigga, you wouldn't be eating, watching cable, chillin' in the AC or none of that shit. You'd be a bummy-ass nigga right now."

"Let's smoke this nigga and bounce, bruh."

"What else this nigga got you doing?"

Dirty ran his mouth at the drop of a dime. "He wanted us to kidnap yo' girl if we couldn't get to you. He was gon' hold her hostage and make you pay a ransom so he could kill you when you show up." His hopes were high, assuming that snitching would spare his life.

Quamae nodded his head because it was sho'nuff a dirty world. First Sasha cheated on him with the enemy, Chauncey fucked his girl, Dirty switched out for the enemy, and then Gigi lied about him being the father. That was too much drama for one man to consume. "It's all good, 'cause I always keep my enemies close, nigga, and you should've known that by now."

Simultaneously Quamae and Chauncey pulled their triggers, and bullets went to flying. One bullet went straight through his forehead and out the back of his head. The other entered his temple and exited the right side. Blood squirted everywhere. His body jerked and went crashing to the floor.

Quamae walked over to check his pockets. The only things in his pockets were his cellphone and his identification card. He put the phone in his pocket and they left the building.

A few hours later he found himself inside another hotel room. There was no way he could go back there and not catch a case, 'cause that's exactly what would've happened if he saw Gigi's deceiving-ass face. To take the edge off, he rolled a blunt and poured himself a shot of cognac. If he was gonna execute his next plan to perfection, he needed that yak in his system to level the playing field. There were two more people on his payback list, and he wasn't sleeping until his plan was complete.

Suddenly, an idea popped into his head. He picked up the phone he took from Dirty and texted Blue. The only thing to do next was wait on a text back.

***

Gigi was just returning to her now-temporary home from the twins' first check-up. Quamae hadn't been home since their fight and the nanny wasn't due to come in for another hour. He texted her earlier and indicated she needed to be gone before he returned to his residence. The text also stated there were no hard feelings toward her, but they could no longer be in a relationship together. It also said he loved her and to have a nice life. That messaged rubbed her the wrong way, because she could've sworn he hated her guts. Regardless of how he felt, she was definitely getting out of that house. All she had to do was go inside and pack up her things and she would be out of his life for good.

The sun was scorching outside, and she couldn't wait to get her babies indoors. She pulled both of the carriers out at the same time because she refused to leave them in that hot-ass car to suffocate. Too much of that went on in south Florida as is, and her babies were not about to be another statistic.

Once she sat them down in the middle of the floor, she jogged back to the car to get the baby bag. As soon as she backed up from the front seat, she was greeted by a young man. He scared her, causing her to jump.

"Sorry, I didn't mean to frighten you," he said politely. She had never seen him a day in her natural life.

"That's okay. How can I help you?"

He pulled a gun out and stuck it to her stomach. "Don't scream, or I'll pump yo' ass with some lead babies."

Gigi's heart was beating like a drum. "My newborn babies are in the house. Please, don't shoot me," she begged. "If you want money, you can have it. Just don't hurt me."

"Nah, you ain't got the kind of money I want."

Gigi was confused. She knew Quamae was into the drug game, but she didn't know how deep. "I don't understand."

"Don't worry, I will help you understand. In the meantime, you coming with me. I'm sure your babydaddy will be home soon."

She did as she was told, and he forced her into the backseat of an all-black Chevy Tahoe where she was blindfolded, gagged, and tied up.

Gigi was scared to death, and all she could think about was her babies. She prayed they weren't crying and Quamae or the nanny would indeed return home quickly. She silently prayed he would find her before it was too late.

The truck came to a complete stop after traveling for what seemed like forever, and she was carried out over the stranger's shoulder. She could hear another guy talking, the door unlock, open, close, and then lock again. He took a few steps, and then sat her down on a cold, hard floor, removed the gag, and uncovered her eyes.

"Why are you doing this?" she cried while checking out her surroundings. It was obvious they were in a house.

"Shut up before I cover your mouth back up."

Gigi sat back and zipped her lips.

"What's ya babydaddy number?" he asked.

As soon as she provided Quamae's number, one of the men walked over to her with a rag in his hand. She had watched enough lifetime movies to know what it was: chloroform. That was the last thing she remembered before she passed out.

Chapter 25

Nate and NJ had just moved into the Somerset apartment complex, complimentary of Slim's girlfriend, who happened to be the manager. She helped them with the paperwork and got them into a two-bedroom. His foster mother was sad to see him leave, but happy he had a father figure in his life to help guide him. NJ promised he wouldn't forget about her and would continue to check on her from time to time.

They sat at the kitchen table, bagging up weed and coke to sell, when there was a knock on the door.

Nate scrunched up his face. "Who the fuck is that?"

"Probably Jazz." He leaned back in his seat and glanced out the window. "Yeah, that's her." NJ got up to open the door for her.

Jazz walked in with a smile on her face. "What's up, baby?" she tiptoed to give him a peck on the lips, but he didn't kiss her back.

"You're early."

"I know. I got tired of sitting in the house, so here I am. And besides, you've been ignoring me for two months now. You must be seeing somebody else now."

"Go in the room. We need to talk." He wasn't in the mood for all that lovey-dovey shit.

"Alright," she giggled. She glanced over in the kitchen and saw his father sitting at the table. "Hey, Nate."

"What's up?" he nodded his head.

"Nothing much."

NJ followed behind her. "I'll be right back, Pops."

Nate shook his head. "Boy, we don't have time for that right now. Money before pussy, keep that in mind."

"Get cho mind out the gutter. I need to holla at her real quick."

NJ walked into the room and closed the door behind them. Jazz sat on the bed and took off her shoes, shorts, and then her shirt, getting prepared for a quickie. She lay back on the bed and he straddled her, gripping her hands tightly and pinning them above her head.

"What are you doing?"

"Why the fuck did you tell your cousin that I hit you?"

"I didn't tell him shit." A look of panic was plastered on her face because she didn't know what to expect. The last time she made him angry, he slapped her up.

"Quit lying, 'cause the nigga confronted me about it. The nigga said, and I quote, *why did you put your hands on my cousin?"*

"He saw the bruise on my face and he asked me what happened. I told him I got into it with some girl from school, but he didn't believe me. Then he asked me why was I covering up for you, but I didn't say anything else after that. I swear."

"Yeah, your silence was a dead giveaway." The tears in her eyes were visible, but he ignored them. NJ squeezed her jaw with his hand. "I'm telling you now, keep your cousin out of our business or you can get out of here right now."

She wanted to scream badly, but she just nodded her head up and down, letting him know she understood. The last thing she wanted to do was upset him more than she already had. When he let her go and climbed off her, she sat up in the bed and picked her shorts up off the floor. NJ was headed to the door, but he stopped and turned around to see what she was doing.

"Stay just like that. I'll be back soon to drop this dick off in you." He grabbed the remote and threw it on the bed. "Watch TV or something." Then he left her alone in the room.

Nate was in the same place he was moments ago. He looked up, and the expression on NJ's face let him know they wasn't fucking, despite the fact the room was silent with the exception of some talking.

"Fuck wrong with you?"

"Shit." He sat down and continued to bag up the work.

"Bullshit. Try again, muthafucka," he joked. His son was an open book, and he knew something was wrong. "I know when you mad."

"That bitch talk too much. She always gotta put a bitch in our business. That bitch two seconds from getting her permanent walking papers."

Nate let out a hearty laugh from deep down in his soul, as if he had just heard the funniest joke in his life. "She really pissed you off."

"Hell yeah. I hate people in my business, and she know that. I started to hit that ho in the mouth, but then I gotta worry about her fuck-ass cousin."

"A nigga?"

"Yeah."

"Listen here, you ain't gotta worry about no nigga coming for you as long as I'm here. You got that?" Nate looked him up and down. "But you shouldn't be hitting on no female, anyway." NJ looked straight ahead at nothing in particular with no response. "Do you hear what I'm telling you?"

"I hear you. Do you work tonight?"

"Yeah, why?"

He thought long about his question before saying anything. "I thought you were supposed to be on a good path when you got out here. What happened? Why you back selling dope?"

"I'm doing this for you."

NJ placed his hand over his chest. "For me?"

"It's like this: I know I can't stop you from selling dope because you've been doing it all this time. I'm just getting in the picture, and I'll do whatever it takes for us to have that father-son relationship we both crave. Selling dope is not something I want to do, but I'm doing it so I can teach you how to do it without getting caught or robbed. At least this way I will always know what you're doing and I can protect you from the streets."

"If you feel that way about it, why not just ask me to stop instead of telling me that you want me to stop."

Nate tilted his head to the side and looked him dead in the eyes. "Would you have listened to me?"

"Not right away, but eventually I would have," he said, returning the same stare.

"Okay, let's do this." Nate leaned forward, clasping his hands together. "How about we stack this paper for the next six months and start up our own business?"

He liked the sound of that. "What type of business?"

"I don't know yet, but it needs to be something lucrative."

"And what does that mean?"

"Profitable." He stood up and walked to the fridge to get himself a beer. "We need to figure out something together. It has to be something we will both enjoy doing."

NJ smiled. He always wanted to be his own boss, but didn't know where to start. Having a father around wasn't so bad after all.

A few hours later Nate was headed out to go to work at some warehouse gig. He knocked on NJ's bedroom door. "I'm gone to work, so I'll see you in the morning. But if you need me, call me."

"A'ight, Pops. I'll check you later," he shouted while gripping Jazz's ass. She was riding him slowly.

As soon as he heard the door close, he flipped her off of him. "Get on your knees," he demanded, and she obeyed.

NJ couldn't wait for Nate Sr. to leave so he could punish her. It ain't like he was sneaking, but he wanted an empty house when he put it down. Once he positioned himself behind her, he entered her roughly, causing her to screech. Jazz couldn't handle him when he was rough, so he was using that to his advantage. Plunging in and out of her slit, he gripped her waist and pulled her close to him with every thrust. All she did was moan loudly, but he tuned her out, pretending not to hear a sound. With every stroke he dug deeper and deeper, as if he was trying to break something. She was wet, really wet, and he was so turned on.

He could feel the nut building up inside of him, but he pulled out and shook his dick to calm it down since he wasn't ready to bust yet. NJ gripped her hips again and slid in quickly, ramming his stiff member into her ass on accident.

Jazz screamed and begged him to stop. "No, that hurts," she cried.

They had never tried anal sex before, but the tightness of it felt good when he stroked her. "I'll do it slow, be quiet."

"I don't like it."

"Just relax," he coached her.

Jazz just knew she would pass out at any moment or make a bowel movement, because that's just what it felt like. Burying her head in the pillow, she closed her eyes and went to a place that would make her forget about the pain she was feeling.

After NJ thrashed her for hours, she was too sore and sick to move.

"What's wrong with you?" NJ asked. It was obvious something was on her mind.

"I'm. I'm." She struggled with the words to say.

"What?" his eyebrows slanted downward. "Just say it."

"I'm pregnant."

Chapter 26

Quamae sat comfortably on the leather sofa across from Christine, without a care in the world. The news about not being the father of the twins was devastating at first, but he got over that news rather quickly.

"You're glowing today. What changed?" she asked with a smile.

"I broke off my engagement and I'm ready too move on with my life."

"How did she take the news?"

He thumbed the hair on his chin. "You know how females are. She wasn't happy with my decision to end things, but hey, what could she do? She betrayed me and played up under me, and I never saw it coming."

"And how does that make you feel?"

"Like I ruined the best thing that happened to me for nothing." He looked away, breaking their eye contact. Thinking about the nasty things he did to Sasha, broke his heart all over again. "No matter what I did, she was always there for a nigga, and I chose another bitch over her."

"Do you feel like you abandoned her when she needed you the most?"

"Yeah." He paused for second to get his thoughts together. "I let her mama come into our home and tell me things about her. I never gave her a chance to defend herself before I cut her off." He turned back to face her and sat up. "You know, when she came home to tell me her side of the story, I shut her down."

"Why?"

"Just the thought of other niggas touching on her made it hard for me to look at her, yet alone talk to her. She let them explore places that were meant for me and me only."

Christine could see the tears well up in his eyes, and she knew he was finally having his breakthrough. "Go ahead, Quamae. Continue."

"I made a promise to God that I would love and cherish her through the good and the bad, but I didn't do that. I left as soon as I heard the bad, and I should've stayed, whether we worked it out or not. I let my pride get in the way of how I feel for her, and I was wrong. She deserved better treatment than what I gave her."

He shook his head and continued. "I wasn't even there for her during her pregnancy, but I was there for a bitch whose kids don't belong to me. I guess that's my karma for being so nasty to her."

"I noticed that you said *feel*, which means you still love her?"

He looked up with the saddest puppy-dog eyes. "I never stopped."

"So why did you chose Gianni over her?"

"Gigi would do anything I told her to. If i told her to jump, her only concern would be how high. There would be no back-talk. When I found out Sasha was cheating, I went out and did the same thing, and that's how I got caught up in that pregnancy shit. That ho knew I wanted kids, so she used that to her advantage."

"Is there a chance the two of you could reconcile before it's too late?"

He dropped his head. "I don't know. I served her with divorce papers, and she's still messing with the young nigga I caught her with."

"Have you tried to call her?" Christine wrote down a few notes.

"No. And when she had the baby she texted me, but I didn't respond." He lied, not wanting her to know he tried and failed.

"Why?"

"I was afraid of finding out if the baby was mine or not."

"And why is that?"

"I didn't want to be connected to her after what she did to me."

"So, are you going to call her? By law, you're still married."

He sat up and looked at her. "You think I should call?"

"If you love her like you say you do, then yes."

Quamae folded his hands. "So, after hearing everything about me, what do you think I should do?" He grinned. "I mean, I'm paying you a buck fifty an hour to talk, discuss my problems. I need you to give me some feedback or a plan or something."

Christine laughed. "Fair enough. I can do that." She adjusted herself in her seat. "Okay, so here's what I think. I think you should try to get her back. I believe true love conquers all. I agree that she messed up, I really do, but she needs help." She paused. "When dealing with a person like Sasha, and no counseling was ever a factor in her life, she is prone to mess up. It doesn't excuse what she did because she's an adult and she knows better, but if you don't know better, then you won't do better. Many rape victims act out in different ways. Some turn to men, and some turn away. I believe that you are remorseful for what you did because you've owned up to your bad judgement and mistakes."

"So, what are my next steps?"

"You need to get a paternity test to see if you are the father, because right now you are giving the next man a chance to raise your child. If the child is yours, then you have a shot at becoming a family."

"What if she doesn't want to hear what I have to say?"

"You make her listen, but you need to address her issues first. An apology is mandatory, a genuine apology. If the love is real, then she still feels the same way, because you don't fall out of love overnight."

"So you saying I shouldn't give up?"

"I believe any marriage worth having is worth saving. The problem nowadays is young people give up too easily. Love is not what it used to be like back in the day with your grandparents." She sat back in her seat. "Do you know how many times my grandfather cheated on my grandmother?" She waited for him to answer.

"I'm guessing a lot."

"Yes, but she didn't give up on their marriage, and eventually he changed. You have the potential to be the perfect man."

He rubbed his head. "She probably hates my ass right now."

"Are you afraid of rejection, Quamae?"

"There is nothing I ever wanted that I didn't get, including her."

"Well, keep that mentality and you'll get her back."

"Getting her back 'bouta dent the pockets."

Christine removed her glasses, revealing her pretty brown eyes. "To be honest, it doesn't have to. I want you to understand that money will never buy you love, and you should know that from dealing with Gigi. All she wanted from you was the lifestyle you provided to Sasha. This time around, put your money to the side and use your heart and mind instead. Sasha knows that you have money, and she knows that taking you back will give her access to your funds." She exhaled slowly. "Give her something that you have never given her.

Quamae was a little confused. "I've given her everything."

Christine shook her head. "No, you haven't. I can name two," she held up two fingers, "things you haven't done."

He was confident he was on the right track. "Name 'em."

"Understanding and forgiveness."

Quamae's eyes moved around in his sockets, but he didn't respond, and she peeped that.

"If you have to think on it, then you didn't do it."

"You're right," he admitted.

"You have to get an understanding about the things she went through as a child." She pointed her finger at him. "Then you have to forgive her. You think you can do that?"

"I would have to hear her out first."

"About the cheating?"

He nodded his head yes. "I need to know why she slept with Chauncey. That shit hurt me to the core more than the affair with Blue. I can forgive her for that because he told her everything she wanted to hear. She crossed the line with Chauncey. I considered him a brother to me."

"So why fight so hard to get her back if you feel that way?" She grabbed her pen and jotted down some notes.

"I blame him more than I blame her due to her past. She was vulnerable and weak when I got shot. He knew our marriage was on thin ice, and I feel as if he took advantage of that fact. He knew how I felt about her because I confided in him about everything."

"Sometimes we confide in the wrong people. Everyone in your corner does not care about you or your feelings. They pretend to be loyal just so they can tear you down in the end. Loyalty is so hard to come by these days."

"Shit, who you telling?" he replied.

"Once you find out her mindframe on love and sex, you'll understand why she acts the way she does." Christine jotted down a few notes. "Remember when you said she shared an emotional connection with him?"

"Yeah."

"You admitted you were absent quite often and distant in that department. With the traumatics she went through, no one taught her how to love, when to love, or who to love, so she will take it any way she can get it. Sasha needs attention and validation in order to feel loved. She never had it as a child, so she's seeking it as an adult."

"So, it's my fault?" he asked, placing a hand on his chest.

"No, but you contributed to it. Listen, Quamae, if you want this marriage to work, you have to accept your part in this. I'll give you props because you are doing what a lot of men wouldn't do, and that's forgiving your cheating wife."

"Is that right?"

"Most definitely. A man could cheat on his woman on several different occasions, with multiple sex partners, and expect forgiveness. Let a woman cheat once, she will be outta there quicker than she could say *I'm sorry*, and I guarantee he gon' act like she killed his mother."

Quamae couldn't do anything except laugh at her joke because she was telling nothing but the truth. "I ain't got nothing to say on that note."

"Am I lying, though?"

"Nah, you right."

Christine cleared her throat. "Well, I must say I'm pretty impressed on the progress we've made in our sessions. I think everything will work out in your favor if you keep your word and your hands to yourself."

Quamae laughed once again. "My hands, huh?"

"Yes, and anger management will do you some good, too."

He smiled just a little. "I wasn't always like this. She provoked me a lot."

"Quamae, remember the first step to recovery is to admit that you have a problem and take responsibility for your actions. I'll see you next week."

"I'll be here." He stood and headed for the door when Christine stopped him.

"Hey, do you think she would come to one of our sessions? I think having the both of you here will open up a line of communication. There are some things you need to share with her from your past as well."

"I'll let you know. Have a good day."

Quamae walked away feeling like the weight of the world had been lifted from his shoulders. For the first time in a long time, he was at peace with the decisions he made. The progress he made with his therapist put him in a good place, and he had Jon to thank for that. At first he was skeptical about sitting on a couch, expressing his feelings and shit, but at the end of the day he had nothing to lose, only something to gain. Those sessions were well worth the money spent, especially if that meant getting his wife back. True enough, she partook in hoish activity, but Christine came to her defense and recommended he give her one last chance. He had to think long and hard, but in all honesty he figured how many women would actually pull the trigger and blast for their nigga when shit got hot? Sasha was his backbone, and definitely his ride-or-die chick, so he decided to make it his mission to bring her back home where she belonged. With Gigi out of the picture for good, Sasha would never have to worry about ever seeing or hearing from her again. That was his promise.

Finally inside the truck, Quamae revved up the engine and rode out to Tupac's classic *Hit 'Em Up*. Bopping to the beat, he rapped along with the biggest smile on his face. *"Grab your glocks when you see Tupac. Call the cops when you see Tupac, who shot me, but you punks didn't finish, now you 'bout to see the wrath of a menace. Nigga, I hit 'em up."*

The sudden ring from his Bluetooth cut the music. He looked down at the screen and saw it was an unknown caller, so he picked up with no hesitation.

"Who the fuck playing on my phone?"

"How much do you love your babymama, nigga?"

Quamae smiled. "It depends on which one you talking 'bout."

"Gigi, nigga! I gotcho bitch right here," the private caller responded.

He remained calm, and that same smile was plastered on his face. "Is that right?"

"Yeah, you wanna hear the bitch?" The gunman stepped to her and slapped the taste from her mouth, causing her to yelp. "You heard that, nigga?"

"That could be any bitch, nigga."

"Say something so he know it's you," he instructed his prisoner.

"Quamae, please do what they say or they're going to kill me. I'm so scared," she cried. That voice definitely belonged to Gigi.

Her kidnapper moved the phone away from her, but he kept it on speaker. "Here's what I need from you. You need to bring me $500K if you want to see your bitch alive, and you better not call the cops, because I will blow this ho brains out."

Quamae laughed as if he was just told some sort of joke. "You must be on fleek if you think I'm giving you that kind of money."

"Nah, but yo' bitch 'bout to be choking on gun smoke in a minute."

"Man, listen, I don't give a fuck about that bitch. You can kill her while I'm on the phone. Shit, let me listen."

Gigi couldn't believe what she was hearing. "Quamae, don't let them kill me, please."

"Fuck you, ho," he spat.

"You think this a game, nigga?"

"Yeah, it is if you think you gettin' a half a mill for that ho."

"A'ight, I'ma show you."

"I'm listening."

Quamae heard a single gunshot. *Pow!* A smile spread across his lips as he ended the call, then he rolled down his window and threw his cellphone out into traffic.

***

Sasha and Blue were enjoying a day of relaxation in the hotel suite on South Beach. They started their day off with alcoholic beverages for breakfast, and they were going strong. Since they returned from their trip, Blue promised they would spend a weekend in the hotel of her choice every two weeks to keep that flame going.

"Bae, what are we doing today?" she asked.

"Drinking and fucking," he laughed while taking a sip of his drink.

She smirked. "Really?"

"Why not? You had me out for 15 hours yesterday in the hot-ass sun. I was tired, I couldn't get no ass, so today we're making up for lost time."

"Yeah, you were snoring, too. And it was fun, so be quiet."

"We about to have some fun right now."

Sasha didn't respond. Instead she downed her drink in one gulp. Then she stood in front of him, unbuttoned her shirt, and let it fall to the floor. His eyes widened in excitement. She got down on her knees and unbuckled his pants, freeing his soft dick. With one swift move of her tongue, she made him stand tall as the Eiffel Tower. Compliments went to the peppermint she held in her mouth.

Sasha took the whole pipe into her mouth and down her throat. Blue grunted, closed his eyes, and rested his head on the back of the chair. He grabbed her by the hair and guided her pace. Sasha chewed him up like an animal. He enjoyed every minute of it.

Not wanting to cum so early in the game, he pulled the meat out of her mouth, causing it to make a popping sound. Still on her knees, he stood up and she was face-to-face with his one-eyed monster. He pulled his polo shirt over his head and dropped it to the floor. The rest of his clothing followed. He pulled Sasha up by her shoulders and guided her to the bed. She lay down and opened up with no hesitation, anticipating the moment when he eased himself into her slippery tunnel. He liked her to wrap her legs around his waist, giving him full access to her honey pot. The sound of the headboard and Blue were in accord.

"Ah," she moaned. "It feels so good."

He knew exactly what she needed and how to give it to her. He put his weight down on her, placed both hands on the top of her head, giving her no chance to wiggle at all. "You like the way I fuck you?" he breathed heavily in her ear. Whenever he was on that liquor, he turned into this untamed gorilla.

"Yes," she moaned, hissing like a snake.

"Say you like it."

"I like it."

With every stroke he went a little deeper. "Now say you love me."

Sasha didn't hesitate. "I love you."

"I love you, too." He was sweating profusely, but that didn't stop his show. She hated when he put her feet over her head and pinned them to the headboard, applying all his weight, but that was exactly what he did.

"No," she cried.

"Shut up and take it," he grunted aggressively.

Sasha tried to relax her body, but she couldn't. He was applying too much pressure, making it hard for her to even think of moving a muscle. The deeper he stroked her, the louder she got. That was music to his ears. Sasha was helpless, and he loved it. When she was in control, she could make him tap out, but he wasn't having that today. A buildup of pleasurable pressure he had been working toward finally showed up. The tingling sensation is his scrotum was almost too much to bear. The intensity was so severe it felt like bolts of lightning shooting through his body.

"Ahh," he yelled out, unable to contain himself. His dick began to have contractions, and a gush of semen came spilling out heavily into her womb.

Blue dropped her legs and fell face down into the pillows. "Damn, that just sucked the life out a nigga."

Sasha lay on her side and placed her leg on his. "Which one, the head or the kitty?"

He turned his head to face her. "Shit, both of 'em."

"Well, turn over, because we not finished."

"Gimme a few minutes."

"Nah, nigga, you said all day, and I'm ready."

"I didn't say non-stop, though. My nigga need to rest for a few."

Sasha moved her leg and rolled him over. "I'm giving you what you asked for, so participate. Besides, I know how to wake him up."

"Hold on."

Ten minutes later Sasha was on top, riding him like a pony when his Android started to blow up. They ignored it the first couple of times. By the fourth time Blue remembered he told his boys to call him in the event of an emergency.

"Bae get up for a minute. This might be important."

Sasha eased up off him and sat up in the bed while he answered the phone. Many thoughts were running through her mind, and she wondered if the emergency was about Dream.

Blue picked the phone up. "Hello."

Sasha listened closely to his responses and quickly learned the call wasn't about their baby afterall. She was relieved. Blue stayed on the phone for a quick 60 seconds, speaking in code, and she was confused as hell. There was no way she could decipher what was going on, even if she tried.

Once he ended the call, he had the strangest look on his face.

"Is everything okay?" she asked.

"Yeah." He hesitated. "Just some issues with the package." He walked back to the bed.

"Oh."

"I need to make a private call, so give me a minute, okay?"

"Alright."

Kissing her on the forehead, Blue picked up his phone and went outside on the patio, closing the sliding door behind him. He quickly dialed his boy.

"So, what happened? I just got a call saying I needed to call you."

"They found Dirty dead in a warehouse. But peep this: we got the nigga Quamae bitch right now, but he told me he ain't coming up off that cash and to off that ho."

"What?"

"That's the same shit I said."

"I think the nigga bluffing."

"I don' know, bruh. The nigga told me to shoot her so he can hear it."

"Did you do it?"

"Yeah, but I ain't shoot her, though."

"Where she at?" Blue was thrown with everything going on.

"Right here, tied up. What I'm supposed to do with this bitch if he don't pay?"

"Don't do shit until I call you. I'ma hit you right back."

Something wasn't sitting right with him, and he needed to get to the bottom of it. He dialed Dirty's number immediately to see if it would go straight to voicemail. The phone rang and rang, and right before the voicemail picked up, someone answered.

"Damn, I was starting to think you wasn't gon' call at all."

"Who the fuck is this?" Blue asked.

"Well, you know it ain't Dirty," he laughed. "And now you don't know me, but you got my wife and baby living in the house with you."

Blue scrunched up his face. "Quamae?" he questioned.

"The one and only."

"Nigga, don't play with me about my lady or my baby. Yo' only concern should be saving yo' bitch life and coming up off that cash."

Quamae found it comical they actually thought he was gon' pay that ransom. "Nigga, I ain't saving shit but my marriage. So get ready for me."

"I see I have to show you I'm not fuckin' 'round. I'll send you yo' bitch in a box." Before Quamae could respond, Blue had bammed it in his face and placed a call back to his boy.

"What's up, bruh? What we doing?"

"Gift wrap that ho and send her back to her nigga."

"Say no mo'. It's done," his goon replied and hung up the phone. "A'ight."

Everything that was said to him wasn't registering at all, and nothing made sense to him. He sat back in the patio chair and allowed the wheels to turn in his head until he could put it together. Blue pulled his phone out to see when he received the text message from Dirty. It was close to midnight, and Dirty was already dead by then.

Dirty: Aye, get them boys in place to kidnap his bitch

Blue: A'ight. Have yo' ass in place too

Dirty: Got it Boss!! ☺

Blue read that text message over and over again, and then it dawned on him what had just happened.

Chapter 27

Gigi jumped up from the most horrific dream, but when she looked around she realized it was actually reality. All she could remember from that dream was talking to Quamae, and he wasn't coming to find her. Then she figured she was probably just trippin'. The hot-ass basement wasn't a joke, either, and for the life of her she couldn't figure out how in the hell she ended up there. Looking down, she realized she was tied up to a chair with duct tape over her mouth. Blinking her eyes rapidly, the scenery never changed, and she couldn't wiggle herself free. Whomever did this wanted to make sure she didn't move a muscle.

Squirming around in the seat, she tried to at least get one of her arms loose so she cold break away. This was a real workout. It was already hot in there, so moving around made it worst. It felt like the sun was shining directly on her. Suddenly, there were voices. Gigi was praying for help. Too bad she couldn't scream. The door to the basement opened, so she stopped moving. One figure appeared before her, so there was no telling who he was talking to.

The guy who forced her into the car at gunpoint walked up on her and rubbed her hair. "You a bad bitch, and I wouldn't mind having you on my arm, but it's too bad I have to kill you. Yo' babydaddy ain't coming up off that cash for your ransom, so I gotta do you in."

Gigi's breathing increased, and the tears began to flow. Her chest was moving up and down rapidly, and the tape on her mouth began to move up and down from the saliva.

"Relax, baby. I'ma make this as painless as possible," he assured her while rubbing on her legs.

His hands continued to roam up her thighs, and it made her squirm since she was wearing a dress. The very touch of his rough, yet ashy hands made her want to throw up, but she couldn't risk choking on her own vomit. The pervert was slowly making his way to her vagina, but she wanted him to stop. She jerked her body so he would know she wanted him to stop. Too bad that didn't stop him. She could feel his index finger penetrating her pussy before he added a second one.

Gigi felt violated by the monster in front of her, and hurt Quamae wouldn't pay her ransom. The only thing she kept thinking about was her twins and how they would have to grow up without a mother. Deep down inside, she knew they were going to take her life after they raped her. The way he was grunting and licking his lips let her know sex would be next.

"Damn, this pussy wet. You like this?" She shook her head no. "Yes, you do. You enjoying this just as much as me. You a freak, too, ain't it?"

God as her witness, if she made it out alive, she was gon' kill his nasty, perverted ass.

The door to the basement shook her thoughts. In came another dude, and he was wielding a gun in his hand.

"What the fuck you doing down here, Scooter?" he asked the pervert.

At that very moment, she knew it was about to be lights-out, because he addressed him by name. If they were going to let her go, he would've never said that. Gigi began to say a prayer in head, asking God to forgive her for every hurtful thing she had ever done.

Scooter jumped. "Nothing, and why the fuck would you say my name?"

"This bitch finna die, so it don't matter," Joker replied.

"Who 'bout to kill her?"

"The muthafucka with the tooley. Who you think, nigga?" He aimed his gun at her.

"Wait!" Scooter interrupted. "She said she wanna give me some pussy before she dies. One last nut," he smiled.

"Shut the fuck up wit'cho nasty-ass. I knew you was down here doing some freaky shit to this bitch."

"I ain't lying, she said it."

Joker looked at Gigi. "Did you tell him that? 'Cause I'll come back in ten minutes."

She shook her head no. If she was about to go see Jesus, it wouldn't be with a wet pussy.

"You a lying-ass nigga."

Without any further words, Joker shot her five times in the chest and kicked the chair she was bound to. Gigi's corpse went crashing backward.

"Damn, Joker, I ain't think you had it in you." He looked down at Gigi and smiled as she bled out, admiring her tear-stained face and thighs.

"She's dead. Stop looking at her like that. Damn!" Joker was disgusted by Scooter's sick and twisted ways. He swore the man watched that show *Criminal Minds* entirely too much.

"Shawty was fine."

"Whatever man, go untie the bitch so we can get her outta here."

Just as he was about to walk away, he got a call from Blue.

"What's up, B?"

"Aye! Hold off on what I said earlier about the bitch," Blue instructed his shooter.

"Too late, bruh. Lights out."

"Damn! For real?"

"You said gift-wrap the bitch. What happened?"

"I'll holla at'chu when I get back."

"So, finish the job?"

"Yeah."

"A'ight."

Joker sat his phone down and removed his shirt. "Aye, go upstairs and get me some black trash bags."

"What'chu 'bout to do?"

"What the fuck you think? Gettin' rid of this fuckin' body."

***

Blue walked into the basement during the middle of a capital punishment. Joker was dressed like a butcher with his coat, face mask and rubber boots, going to work with the chainsaw. There was blood and body parts scattered in the middle of the floor. The smell of death was thick in the air and it was enough to make a grown man throw up. However, Blue had a cast iron stomach and that wasn't the first time he witnessed such a gruesome scene, so it didn't faze him one bit. Growing up around Dred, he was accustomed to seeing things that a boy his age should've never seen. That was how he picked up on his killer traits.

He turned the machine off and removed his mask, when he saw his boss standing there. "I see you made it just in time." Joker smiled, looking over his shoulder at Blue.

"I see." He smiled and took a seat on the metal chair. "'Cause you ain't fuckin' off."

"Hell nah! I came down here and this nigga," he pointed his head in the direction of Scooter, "was trying to fuck somethin'."

Scooter frowned due to the embarrassment. "Why you gotta tell my business? That shit ain't cool."

"That nigga was down here getting a stank finger when I came in. He thought I ain't see his ass, but I did."

"You a nasty muthafucka, Scooter." Blue laughed, but Scooter didn't find it funny. He just sat back and watched him cut up their prettiest victim. Everyone they've ever dismembered were normally men. The women were generally spared, unless they were in a situation like this.

Joker re-covered his face and turned the chainsaw back on. The sound of the machine hitting the bone was music to his ears. There was nothing on earth that could gross him out. From as far as he could remember, he always had a thing for killing. Back when he was in elementary school, he used to kill the cats and dogs in his hood. The neighbors would ask if he saw them and he would say no, but would help them look for their family pet. Seeing the life leave a body was therapeutic for Joker and there wasn't a better feeling. Not even an orgasm could bring him to that much satisfaction.

When he was in middle school, the seventh grade to be exact, he lost his virginity to an eigth grader. She didn't know he was a virgin because he didn't tell her and he seemed experienced. But that came from watching porn and jacking off. During sex he choked her a lot with his hands and even with his forearm on some occasions. To this day, any chick he slept with was getting choked and they had no clue as to why he had such a fettish. They would never know.

"So what's up witih the cash?" Joker asked.

Blue was confused. "What cash?"

"For kidnapping this bitch."

"Didn't he say he wasn't paying?"

"Yeah, but shit I figured that you would pay since the nigga ain't."

"Nah, ain't no bread." Blue had to think about what he was saying. "Hold up! You think I'm supposed to pay out the ransom for this bitch? 'Cause if you do, you crazy as fuck."

"It's like that, huh?" Joker nodded, pissed off that his boss had just tried him like one of his flunkies.

"I can hit you with a few bands, but that's it. A half a mill, nah."

"It's cool."

Blue didn't like where their conversation was going and he knew what type of nigga Joker was, so he pulled out his cellphone. Pressing record, he propped the phone on his lap to make it less obvious.

After he was finished with chopping up all of Gigi's body parts, he placed them into the black trash bags.

"Are you disposing that body tonight?" Blue asked, trying to see where his boy's head was at.

"Hell yeah!" he was just a little too excited.

"Well, make sure no one can find it."

"Shit." He removed the gloves from his hands. "I was gone dump this bitch all over his front yard and fertilize the nigga grass."

"Bruh, you have no chill, man." Blue knew that he would really do it to, but that was too risky. "Nah, man, take that bitch to alligator alley and let the wildlife handle that."

"Damn, bruh, you take the fun out of everythang."

"I'm trying to make sure you don't get caught, Mr. Chainsaw Massacre."

"I never get caught. I'm too smooth." He then removed his apron. "You see how you never got caught selling dope?"

Blue nodded his head. "Yeah."

"That's because that's your craft and you know how to maneuver and stay out the way. Slaying bodies is my craft and I know how to maneuver without being messy. I've been doing this shit for years." Once he finished bagging up the body, Blue stopped the recording.

Chapter 28

Sasha was chilling in the hotel when she kept receiving calls and text messages from Carmen. Since the day she found out about what went down between her man and best friend, she had been ignoring her. There was nothing she could say, or do, to make her understand. She had been contemplating for the longest time about how to approach her. Then it finally hit her.

Picking up her cellphone, she placed the call to Carmen.

"Well damn, bitch, I've been calling you for weeks. What the fuck is up with you?" Carmen said upon answering.

"I've been dealing with a lot lately and I didn't feel like talking."

"Yeah right, you letting Blue come between our fucking friendship and I don't like it. Everything was fine until he popped up into the picture and you stupid enough to let him run you. "

It took everthing in her power to keep from checking her ass over the phone. What she wanted was a face to face visit. This way she could look in her eyes when she explained herself and slapped that bitch if she got out of line again.

"I need to talk to you about something important."

"What's up, girl?" Carmen was just happy to hear her sister's voice once again. She didn't care what the conversation was about. It was bad enough she lost India. She couldn't afford to lose Sasha, too.

"No!" After realizing her tone was a tad bit too harsh, she brought it down a notch. "I need to come over and talk to you in private."

"Okay well come on. You know the way."

It took no time for Sasha to get to Carmen's house. During the entire drive over she tried to calm herself down, but she couldn't. All she felt was hate in her heart and it had to be erased. Living day to day with those types of emotions in her system wasn't gonna fly.

Sasha slammed on brakes in front of her house and got out, taking quick calculated steps to the front door.

Boom! Boom! Boom!

She damn near beat the door down. Carmen snatched the door open with an attitude.

"Why the fuck you banging on the door like that crazy ass girl?" she put her hands on her hips. "Somebody better be chasing yo' ass."

The gloves were off and it was time to set the record straight. The scowl on Sasha's face should've been a dead giveaway, but Carmen wasn't focused enough.

"Did you try to fuck Blue?"

"What?" Carmen frowned, as if she didn't know what the hell she was talking about.

"Carmen, don't play stupid with me. I'm trying to give you a chance to explain yourself. Did you try and fuck Blue when I was in the hospital?"

Carmen stood there in shock. Blue had finally come clean about what happened and it all made sense as to why she'd been avoiding all communication with her.

"It didn't happen the way you think it did." That was the best response she could come up with in order to kill time and create a solid lie.

"I don't give a fuck about that. All I wanna know is, did you try to fuck him?"

"Sasha, I'm sorry. We were drinking and I just…"

Before Carmen could finish her sentence Sasha snatched her up by the shirt and pulled her outside onto the porch. "Ho, you got me fucked up 'bout that one." Grabbing her hair, she punched her repeatedly in the face. "You s'posed to be my sister bitch."

Carmen turned her head to the side in an effort to stop the blows to her face, while swinging wild punches. "Let go of my hair." She screamed, as Sasha slung her, causing her to lose her balance.

"Get up ho! I'ma give you a head up fade." Sasha planted her feet firmly on the ground and went into a fighting stance. Out of the people on Earth to betray her, she never thought that it would be her sister from another mother.

"Run it ho, don't catch me off guard." Carmen didn't want to fight her, but she didn't have a choice. There was no way in hell she was about to let anyone come to her house and beat her ass without a fight. True enough she was wrong, but Sasha had just taken things to a new level.

They had been friends long enough to sit down for a heart to heart, instead of a cat fight.

Carmen took her stance directly in front of her and all hell broke loose, when Sasha threw the first punch. They were pulling hair, ripping shirts and trying to claw each others eyes out.

The fight seemed like it was going on forever until they heard a voice from the loud speaker.

"Stop the fighting right now before I haul both of your asses down to the station." The officer in the patrol car realized he had to get out and break it up and just for that he had something for the both of them. As he made his way over, he pulled his billy club from his holster. "I said break this shit up right now."

Sasha let go of Carmen when she felt someone grab her arm. "What the fuck?" she looked up to see that it was a police officer.

"Who lives here?" he asked.

Carmen raised her right hand. "I do." She was damn near out of breath. It had been a long time since her last fight and she was tired as hell.

Officer rudeness looked at Sasha. "I guess that makes you the transpasser huh?" she rolled her eyes. "I'll take that as a yes and for that nasty attitude, I'll take your little pretty ass down to the station."

Sasha waved him off. "Whatever!"

"Yeah I know." He pulled his handcuffs out. "Put your hands behind your back."

Carmen was pissed off, but she couldn't see her girl going down like that. "It's okay, you don't have to arrest her."

He smirked. "Yeah I actually do. If her attitude wasn't so bad she could've got a warning for trespassing and starting a fight. Your neighbor made the call about a disturbance."

Sasha wasn't up for the bullshit, so she snapped. "Can you hurry up and take me in, so I can post my fuckin' bail?"

"Sasha just be quiet and he might let you go." Carmen pleaded.

"Fuck you!" she screamed. "Don't you ever talk to me again you backstabbing bitch."

"I understand that you mad, but you need to calm down. I'll come post your bail, so we can talk about it."

"I don't need you do shit for me. The only thing I want from you, is for you to leave me the fuck alone for good." And she meant that with every fiber in her body. Their friendship was over for good.

***

Down at the station, Sasha was placed in the holding cell with another female. She was rocking designer gear, so she figured that maybe she was in for fraud and not prostitution, or maybe she had just took a drug charge for her boyfriend. She walked over to the phone mounted to the wall and frowned before picking up the receiver.

"That phone don't work you gotta use the other one."

"Oh thanks." She went to the other phone and picked it up. The smell coming from the mouthpiece smelled like ass and sweat. "Eww." She scrunched up her face, rubbed the receiver against her pants leg and called Blue. The first time she dialed his number, he didn't pick up, so she called back.

"Hello." He answered with a little hesitation in his voice.

"Bae come get me."

He recognized her voice immediately. "Where you at? And who phone you calling me from?"

"I'm calling from the free phone at the jail."

"What?" he shouted.

"I'm in the Broward County Jail."

"For what?" he was lost because he left her in the hotel room on the beach.

"Fighting Carmen."

"How the fuck did you end up in Broward?"

"I went to her house and we fought."

"What the fuck you went to her house for? I left you in Miami and that's where you s'posed to be."

Sasha was not in the mood for the lecture or 21 questions. "Blue!" she shouted. "Can you please just post my bail and pick me up. We can fuss about this later."

"I'm coming damn!" he didn't wait for a response, he simply ended the call without another word.

In her mind she already knew that it was about to be a very long and noisey night. He was gone preach to her and say how wrong she was for going there in the first place. Sitting down on the cold, steel bench, she leaned up against the wall and pulled her knees to her chest in order to rest her head. Assoon as she closed her eyes she was being interrupted.

"Excuse me."

When she looked up, it was the girl sitting on the opposite side of the cell. "What?"

"I don't mean to get all in your business, but-" Sasha cut her off quick.

"Well don't."

"All I was gone ask you was," she paused and smirked. "If that was Darian on the phone?"

Sasha heard his name and looked up. Now she had her attention and she needed to know how she knew her man. Clearly she knew him because she addressed him by his government. "Yes it was and who are you?"

The chick smiled. "I'm not important, so don't worry about me. I just want to give you a warning."

"About?"

"You having energy when he pick you up cause he gone whoop yo' ass when you get home." She smiled and pointed in her direction. "You Sasha right?"

"You asking a lot of questions for someone that don't know me." Sasha sat up in her seat just in case she needed to beat this bitch ass.

"I know your man tho and that's all that matters."

"And how the fuck do you know him?"

"I used to be in your shoes once upon a time and he has a very bad temper. When he was that mad with me, he would come home and fight me all the time."

"Well guess what, you and me are not one in the same and he has never put his hands on me."

"Well tonight is your lucky night cause he gone beat that ass, whether you believe me or not."

"Bitch please, you got me fucked up 'cause he ain't gone do shit to me."

She ignored the fact that Sasha had just called her out her name. "I would've been his babymama, but he beat me so bad that I lost the baby. And you know he never apologized for taking my child's life."

Sasha tried ignoring her, but she wouldn't shut up to save her life. The only thing she could do was hope and pray that Blue had posted her bail already.

A few hours later the door buzzed and in walked a female officer. "Banks, lets go. You just made bail."

"Damn he got you out quick. Good luck girl and remember what I said." Sasha ignored the irrelevant comments and kept it moving.

"Tell our man Red said he can come through tonight and punish this pussy again, when he drop you off." Sasha stopped in her tracks and gave her a homicidal stare. That was the bitch Blue cheated with. Red smiled and blew her a kiss.

To Be Continued...
Bride of a Hustla 3
Coming Soon

<u>Coming Soon from Lock Down Publications/Ca$h Presents</u>

TORN BETWEEN TWO

By **Coffee**

LAY IT DOWN **III**

By **Jamaica**

GANGSTA SHYT **III**

By **CATO**

BLOOD OF A BOSS **IV**

By **Askari**

BRIDE OF A HUSTLA **II**

By **Destiny Skai**

WHEN A GOOD GIRL GOES BAD **II**

By **Adrienne**

LOVE & CHASIN' PAPER

By **Qay Crockett**

I RIDE FOR MY HITTA **II**

By **Misty Holt**

THE HEART OF A GANGSTA **II**

By **Jerry Jackson**

<u>Available Now</u>

RESTRAING ORDER **I & II**

By **CA$H & Coffee**

LOVE KNOWS NO BOUNDARIES **I II & III**

By **Coffee**

LAY IT DOWN **I & II**

By **Jamaica**

PUSH IT TO THE LIMIT

By **Bre' Hayes**

BLOOD OF A BOSS **I II & III**

By **Askari**

THE STREETS BLEED MURDER **I, II & III**

By **Jerry Jackson**

CUM FOR ME

An **LDP Erotica Collaboration**

BRIDE OF A HUSTLA

By **Destiny Skai**

WHEN A GOOD GIRL GOES BAD

By **Adrienne**

A GANGSTER'S REVENGE **I II III & IV**

A SAVAGE LOVE 1

By **Aryanna**

WHAT ABOUT US **I & II**

NEVER LOVE AGAIN

THUG ADDICTION

By **Kim Kaye**

THE KING CARTEL **I, II & III**

By **Frank Gresham**

THESE NIGGAS AIN'T LOYAL **I, II & III**

By **Nikki Tee**

GANGSTA SHYT **I &II**

By **CATO**

THE ULTIMATE BETRAYAL

By **Phoenix**

DON'T FU#K WITH MY HEART **I & II**

By **Linnea**

BOSS'N UP **I & II**

By **Royal Nicole**

I LOVE YOU TO DEATH

By Destiny J

I RIDE FOR MY HITTA

By **Misty Holt**

Stay Connected with Us!

Text **LOCKDOWN** to 22828 to stay up-to-date with new releases, sneak peaks, contests and more...